~ PRAISE FOR CHILD OF EARTH ~

"Like some perfect fusion of Clifford Simak's *Ring Around the Sun* and Robert Heinlein's *Tunnel in the Sky*, David Gerrold's *Child of Earth* depicts a vivid, alluring future of limitless possibilities, where world upon world awaits human exploration and colonization. His adolescent narrator, Kaer, offers a charming and wise-beyond-her-years perspective on the thrilling events of what I predict will be a landmark trilogy."

   —PAUL DI FILIPPO, author of *Neutrino Drag*

"*Child of Earth* provides further evidence that David Gerrold has to be a clone: his genome clearly includes genetic material from Robert A. Heinlein, Theodore Sturgeon, Ursula K. LeGuin, Anne McCaffrey, Roger Zelazny, Edgar Pangborn, Frederik Pohl, and James Tiptree, Jr., at a minimum. For newcomers to sf, that means he is *better than* as good as it gets, and this is one of his very best novels."

   —SPIDER ROBINSON, author of *The Crazy Years*

~ PRAISE FOR DAVID GERROLD ~

"David Gerrold is one of the most original thinkers and fluent writers in contemporary science fiction."

   —BEN BOVA

"Gerrold bores easily—that's why you'll never see him using the same idea or angle of attack twice. Hold on for the ride!"

   —GREGORY BENFORD, author of *Timescape*

"Without question, David Gerrold is one of the most talented and creative writers of this generation and always fun to read."

   —JOHN C. DVORAK, columnist, *PC Magazine* and *CBS Marketwatch*

CHILD
OF EARTH

CHILD
~OF~
EARTH

DAVID GERROLD

BENBELLA BOOKS
Dallas, Texas

Copyright © 2005 by David Gerrold

BenBella Books
6440 N. Central Expressway, Suite 617
Dallas, TX 75206

PUBLISHER: Glenn Yeffeth
EDITOR: Shanna Caughey
ASSOCIATE EDITOR: Leah Wilson
PR DIRECTOR: Laura Watkins

Send feedback to feedback@benbellabooks.com
www.benbellabooks.com
Printed in the United States of America

10 9 8 7 6 5 4 3 2 1

Library of Congress Cataloging-in-Publication data

Gerrold, David, 1944–
    Child of earth / by David Gerrold.—Benbella Books ed.
        p. cm.
    ISBN 1-932100-47-4
    1. Life on other planets—Fiction. 2. Moving, Household—Fiction. 3. Space colonies—Fiction. I. Title.

    PS3557.E69C48 2005
    813'.54—dc22

                                                    2004024648

Cover illustration by J.P. Targete
Cover design by Melody Cadungog
Interior designed and composed by John Reinhardt Book Design

Distributed by Independent Publishers Group
To order call (800) 888-4741
www.ipgbook.com

For special sales contact Laura Watkins at laura@benbellabooks.com.

for Brad Frank,
with love

THE OLD WOMAN
WHO LIVED IN THE GRASS

A VERY LONG TIME AGO, in the time before time, an old woman left her village and went out into the fields. Why she left, no one knows. She took nothing with her but a knife and a song.

As she walked, she sang of the sun and the rain and the good dark earth. And the sun shone, and the rain fell, and the shoots of grass came up fresh in the ground. She walked for a very long time, and wherever she walked the grass came up at her feet, happy to grow in the sun and drink in the rain.

The old woman walked across the whole world, singing, and soon the grass grew everywhere, so tall and so thick that she couldn't walk anymore. At last she came to a place where the grass reached up to twice her height. She stopped and sang to the grass, "I will live here. I will sing of the sun and the rain and the good dark earth. I will sing every day." This made the grass very happy and the tallest and the strongest plants around her responded by bending low over her head to form an arch. Still singing, she reached up and wove the ends of the stalks together. When she had finished, she had the frame of a little round house. It looked like an upside-down basket.

Then, still singing of the sun and the rain and the good dark earth, she asked the grass to help her furnish her house. So the grass reached up and caught a great wind; it lay down as a carpet for her. The old woman walked out into the field and cut the grass gently. She laid it out in the sun to dry, all the time singing her thanks. Every day she went out into the fields and cut down only as much grass as she needed, always laying it out to dry with reverence and care.

1

When the grass had dried, she began to weave it. She used every part of the grass, the stiff stems and the soft leaves. She began by weaving a roof and walls onto the frame of her house, careful to leave herself a door and three round windows. She put one window on the east side of the house so she could watch the sun rise in the morning, and she put one window on the west side of the house so she could watch the sun set in the evening—but she put the third window high up in the roof, so she could look up and see the stars at night. She made the door wide enough so she could always look out and see the endless sea of grass.

She wove an awning for each of the windows and another for the entrance as well, so she would have shade. She wove herself shutters and a door, so that in the winter she could close the house against the cold and wind. She dug a hole in the middle of the floor and lined it with rocks. She built a bed of dried grass and started a fire to keep herself warm and to cook over as well.

But even after she had finished her house, she still had not finished her work. So she kept on singing of the sun and the rain and the good dark earth. And the grass, happy to help, lay down in the fields again so she could cut what she needed. She needed so very much—much more than you would think just to look at the little grass house. But the grass didn't mind. As long as she sang of the sun and the rain and the good dark earth, the new green shoots came up happily.

The old woman took the thick strong stems of the grass and tied them into bundles to make a chair and a table and a bed. She used the softer parts of the grass, the shoots and leaves, to make cushions and blankets and baskets and curtains and mats. She even wove herself a hat and a skirt and a jacket of grass.

And finally, at the end of the day, as the very last thing she did, she made herself dinner. She ate the roots of the grass, the fresh young shoots, and the tender stems. She ate every part of it that her old teeth could chew, and when she was done with the grass and had passed it through her bowel, she returned it as night soil to enrich the good dark earth.

Every evening, as the day turned orange in the west, she went out into the fields and thanked the grass for its bounty. She sang of the sun and the rain and the good dark earth.

And the sun shone, and the rain fell, and the shoots came up fresh in the good dark earth.

A FAMILY MEETING

WHEN I WAS EIGHT, Da showed up for a visit with pictures of a world where they had horses so big a whole family could all ride at the same time. They were bigger than elephants. Da said the world was called Linnea, but we kids called it Horse World. He also showed us pictures of some of the other worlds that you could get to through the gates, but none of them had horses and some of them looked pretty awful.

Horse World had a sea of grass all the way out to the end of the world. Da said it was called razor grass and it covered half the continent, all the way from the Rainbow Ridges in the east to the Desolation Mountains in the west, which were like a big wall that stretched from the far north almost all the way down to the equator. On the other side of the mountains were the broken lands and the long deserts, full of wild howlers and swarms of biting things, and then another mountain range that fell into the Ugly Sea.

But I didn't care about any of that, I liked the horses and I asked if we could go there. Da-Lorrin grinned at me—that big grin of his that made me want to marry him when I grew up; except we were already married, sort of, because of the family-contract; but I meant the old-fashioned kind of marriage, two people only—and said, "Maybe we could. But only if everybody else in the family agrees. Because if we go there, we'd have to stay."

I said that was okay with me, and he rumpled my hair affectionately and told me to go set the table for dinner.

So I asked Mom-Lu, "Da-Lorrin says we might go to Horse World. Will we really?"

She said, "It's not decided yet, honey. And if we do go, it won't be for a long time. First, we have to see how everyone in the family feels about it."

That meant a family meeting. Uh-oh. Most of the time, family meetings were just an excuse for a big party, and folks would phone in from all over, wherever they were. But sometimes there were important things to decide, like whether or not to start a new baby or offer someone a contract. And once even, before I was born, whether or not to divorce someone. Mom-Lu said she'd tell me about that when I was older. I didn't pay attention to a lot of the discussions, partly because most of them weren't very interesting, and partly because nobody listened to the kidlets anyway. Not until after you're thirteen do you get a real vote. But this time, because it was about the great-horses, I made sure to do all my chores and extra too, so I'd at least have merit points to spend.

The meeting didn't happen for two weeks. It took that long for everyone to arrange their separate schedules. There were more than twenty voting adults, and everyone had to attend, even though we were scattered across four continents. Mom-Lu had to coordinate all the time zones, and she spent a lot of time sending messages back and forth, because Cindy was in Paris and Parra was in Sydney. Cindy and Parra were clone-twins, except Cindy was a boy now. All the little-uns lived in New Paso with the moms, so most of them were put to bed at their normal times, but I cashed in my merit points and Mom-Lu agreed I could stay up past midnight for the conference, but only if I took a long nap in the afternoon.

According to Da, a contract family is a corporate entity, with every member holding an equal share of common stock but unequal shares of voting stock determined by age and seniority, parentage and reproductive status. Which meant that Mom-Trey, who came into the family after Mom-Lu, actually had more voting shares, because she'd borne three babies and Mom-Lu had only borne one. And Cindy and Parra, because they were purchased babies from before my time, had different shares because that was part of the terms of the adoption. So even though it's supposed to be equal, it isn't. Not in voting, and not in distribution of resources. And that always makes for arguments. Mom-Woo used to say, "That's why you should never marry a lawyer," which was her own little joke, because she was a lawyer and she was the one who negotiated the various member-contracts every time we married someone new.

Tonight's conference started out pleasant enough. Da-Lorrin had mailed out the prospectus way ahead of time so everybody could review it. I watched it every day, over and over, especially the parts with the horses, but after two or three days of that, Mom-Lu had had enough. Instead of shutting it off, though, she plugged into the Gate Authority Library and put the big display on a random-shuffle recycle of scenery, but keyed to the time of day, so we could have a 24/7 window on Linnea. By the time of the meeting, the New Paso branch of the family were the experts on the great-horses. Especially me.

Horse World was the most interesting of all the parallel planets, because it was the most Earthlike of all the worlds. And it was the only one with real human beings on it, although that had happened by accident. But it also had a lot of its own native life too, a lot of different plants and animals that looked like they could have come from Earth. But that was because of the way the world-gate had been calculated; they designed all the gates to open up to worlds as Earthlike as possible, but it didn't always work. Sometimes one little digit at the far end of one little equation was enough to throw the whole thing out of kilter. Even the same set of equations could open up on to two vastly different worlds; it was because of something called time-congruency, but it meant that nobody was really sure yet how to predict what any gate would open up onto, it was still a big gamble. But with Linnea, they got a nearly perfect planet.

Well, I thought it was perfect. But not everybody else did. The more the family talked, the more it became clear that not everybody wanted to go to Horse World and pretty soon, it turned into a big fight. Aunt Morra got very upset, arguing that she had invested ten-ten years into this contract and if the family moved out now, her investment would be thirty-devalued. "I'll have to start over. I'll never earn senior in another cluster. I'll lose my representation. And who's going to take care of me when I get old?"

On the wall display, Lorrin shook his head. He was in Denver this week. "You knew when you signed your contract that we had a long-term plan."

"But I thought we would be staying here! No one ever said—"

"Yes, we did," said Mom-Trey. "We said it over and over. And every time, you kept saying, 'No, no, we can't go. I don't want to go.' You've been saying it for ten-ten years. What did you think, Morra? That the decision was yours alone to make? That if you said no every time the subject was raised that the rest of us would change our minds? If you didn't want to go, you should have opted out before this."

"But I didn't think you were serious—" she wailed. She left the room in tears, leaving her place in the wall display blank.

Then Auncle Irm got angry at Mom-Trey, shouting over the channel. "Now look what you've done!"

"I told the truth," said Mom-Trey in that voice she always used when she was annoyed. "Perhaps if more of us had told the truth before this, we wouldn't have this problem now."

Mom-Woo sighed then. A dangerous sign. She said, "I feared this would happen. I hoped it wouldn't. So many families break up over this issue." But from where I was sitting I could see her laptop screen; she was already reviewing contracts.

"Well then, don't break up the family!" Irm snapped. "If we're really a family corporation founded on representative process, then let's respect the wishes of those who don't want to go."

"Why do we have to respect *your* wishes," said Cindy, interrupting. "Why can't you respect *ours?*"

"Hush, son," said Mom-Woo.

"You're *splitting* the family," accused Irm.

"The family is already split," Mom-Lu said quietly. And that seemed to end that part of the argument very uncomfortably. Then there was a long silence that ended only when Gampa Joan declared a recess to conference on a private channel.

That's when Mom-Woo and Mom-Lu abruptly decided it was time for all the kids to go to bed, meaning *me*, even though they'd promised I could stay up till the end of the meeting. But I didn't mind. This part was mosty boring. And listening to all the parents hollering at each other made my stomach hurt. Even though we turned the sound down on Irm.

The next day all three Moms gathered all the kids together and explained it to us. Part of the family might be going to another world, and part of the family didn't want to go. And the part of the family that didn't want to go was very angry at the part of the family that did.

"Are we divorcing?" Rinky asked. I remember it was Rinky because I was sitting on her lap. Rinky was old enough to be a parent, but had deferred puberty for a while. Probably because of the move-out.

Mom-Trey looked sad. "I don't know, honey. Irm and Bhetto have filed for temporary partition of resources. If our application to emigrate is accepted, then the partition will be finalized. Except, if our resources are partitioned, then we might not have enough to pay for our training, so we wouldn't be able to go after all." She looked very sad; I think she was more unhappy about the bitterness of the argument than the disruption of the plan to go to the new world. "But it might not happen anyway. Our application could be turned down again. That's part of what the meeting was supposed to be about. To make a new long-range plan if we can't move out."

Mom-Lu explained that Da-Lorrin had filed new papers with a contracting agency with a forty shared-placement rate. I didn't understand a lot of it, but the parents thought that this time it might really happen. "We passed both the first and second reviews," said Mom-Lu, "and the next step will be the interviews. That's why Gampa thought it was time for the family to think about what we should do if the application goes forward—or if it's turned down again."

The reason I remember all this is because of the question I asked while I was sitting on Rinky's lap. "But if the family divorces, what's gonna happen to us?"

"That's what we're trying to figure out, sweetheart. I promise you, nothing bad will happen to the little-uns." Mom-Woo patted me on the knee, but that still didn't make it a satisfying answer.

THE TALL AND THE SMALL

NOTHING HAPPENED FOR A LONG WHILE after that. There were more meetings about stuff I didn't understand. But except for the meetings, everything went on just like before. Mosty. Except the arguments were meaner. Us kids weren't supposed to know about the arguments, but we did anyway. Mom-Woo said not to worry, there were negotiations underway and maybe it would all work out. There might be a way to take care of everyone.

And then it all started to change. First, some people came from the bureau and talked to the parents about stuff. They did that a lot. And there were a lot of papers to sign. And then we all had to fly to Houston so the doctors could take pictures of our insides. The trip was fun, but the doctor part was boring. But we stayed over an extra day and visited Mars Dome where people practice living before they go off to Mars. Gamma said we'd have to live in a dome too before we went through a gate, not like Mars or Luna Dome, but like whatever world we were going to.

One day, some people in suits came out to our farm to visit. We didn't grow much on our farm, mosty what we ate ourselves; but we made a lot of electricity to sell west. And a little water too. The people in suits looked at our evaporators, our windmills and our solar panels like they were inspectors from the buyers' co-op or something. But they were really just looking to see how well we managed everything. Big Jes, who managed all of the machinery and who always let me ride on his shoulders, said that you had to know how to take care of all kinds of stuff by yourself before they'd let you move out, because on Horse World you couldn't just pick up the phone and call for a service truck, because there weren't any. That was why it was so important for the visitors to see that our farm was well run and that we were self-sufficient.

One of the visitors talked with the parents for a bit and then came out to play with us kids. Her name was Birdie and she had a puppet with her, a floppy blue wabbit that hopped around on the porch. It tried to climb up onto a chair, but it couldn't; it fell down on its butt and laughed and said, "Oh, dear. Faw down, go boom!" Then it ran around and asked all the kids to kiss its boo-boo, pointing to its waggling butt. Nobody wanted to do it. Everybody said ick and pointed to everybody else. "Ask Mikey. Mikey will do anything. Go see Shona. Go to Nona." But nobody would kiss it, so the wabbit sat down and began weeping into its paws. That made everybody sad, so sad we almost started crying ourselves. But then the wabbit sat up and announced it was ready to play again, and began doing clumsy somersaults until it tumbled itself into Birdie's purse, hiding itself and refusing to come out again, no matter how much we begged.

Later, Birdie sat and talked to each of the kids, one at a time. When it was my turn, she asked me what I knew about moving out. I explained how we would go through a world-gate to another place just like Earth, only different. Did I understand about parallel development, Birdie asked. I thought I did. I said that the two worlds started out mosty the same, but then turned out different. Like Cindy and Parra were cloned from the same egg, only Cindy decided to be a boy when he grew up and Parra didn't. Moving out would be like going to another Earth, but one with different animals and maybe even different people, if we went to Horse World.

Birdie told me that was exactly right. She said that there were a lot of different ways to explain how the worlds on the other side of the gates worked, but her favorite description was that they're not really *different* worlds at all; they're just different possibilities of the same reality, places where Schrödinger's cat had kittens. (Whatever that meant.)*

Then she showed me pictures of some of the worlds that were open for settlement and asked which ones I liked. I didn't even have to look. I told her I liked the one with the big horses best. She smiled and said

---

*According to researchers Connolly and Wolf, Schrödinger's cat has eighteen Planck's Constant lives, or none at all. Quantum cat uncertainty: You either know where your cat is or you know how fast it's going, but never both at the same time. It is, however, very possible to know *neither* of these things at the same time.

she liked that one too, but there were a lot of other parts to any decision and we might not get to go to that world, if we got to go anywhere at all. We might have to go somewhere else, so I should find something on each world to like. That was good advice.

She also asked me if I was good at keeping secrets. I had to think about that. I wasn't sure if I should say yes, because I was the one who accidentally sorta blurted out the surprise before Mom-Trey's birthday. But I'd never told anybody about sneaking into Rinky's room and trying on her bra either. That was something only I knew. So after a minute, I just said, "I think so."

Birdie said, "Keeping secrets is very important, especially if you go to a world like Linnea, the one with the horses. See, Kaer, the people on that world, they don't know about Earth, not yet. And we're not ready to tell them, because—well, because they're not ready yet. So you can't tell them where you're from, because they won't believe you, they might think you're crazy. So you have to pretend you're one of them, born on their world. On Linnea, they still believe in witches, so if you start talking about coming from Earth, they might lock you up. Or worse. I'm not saying this to scare you. I just want you to know how important the secret is. This isn't a secret for sharing. This is a secret for keeping."

I nodded and pretended to understand. I'd already figured out that if you nodded and pretended it made sense, grown-ups would drop the subject. But if you argued about it, whatever it was, they'd just keep talking until they won the argument. So mosty I nodded and pretended to understand. Except not this time. "If we don't like it, can we come back?"

Birdie looked as if I'd said one of those words that embarrass grown-ups. "You can, but the whole point is to stay and build a life on the new world. It's not a vacation, Kaer. We don't know enough about the people living over there and we want to learn. The best way to learn is to have families live with them and report back."

"But it's dangerous, isn't it?"

"Yes, it could be. And everyone in your family will have to be very careful, Kaer. But we're going to train you very well, all of you, so you won't make any mistakes. The training will take at least two or three years. And you won't go to the new world until everybody is sure you're ready. And this is the important thing: if at any time you decide you don't want to go, you don't have to."

I thought about it. "I'll be ten or eleven when we go."

"That's about right."

"Will there be other families there?"

Birdie nodded. "Absolutely. You won't be alone. We have scouts on Linnea now. Their job isn't just to plant cameras; they're also learning how to mingle with the people, so they can learn the language and the history and how to behave. And from time to time, they come back to teach us. We have a whole dome just for training, and only when we think it's safe will we start sending families over. We'll only send a few families at first to see how they manage; and then later, if they do okay, we'll send more after them. But we'll spread them out so they can see things all over the world.

"If we sent your family to Linnea, you would be in the third wave of immigrants. We already have a few families over there, working as scouts, and more are already in training. Our very best rangers will help you and your family learn the language. When it's time for you to move out, you and your family will have had the best training possible."

"When do we find out what world we're going to?"

"That takes a while to decide, sometimes as long as a year. Your family will have to keep looking at pictures from all the worlds for a while longer. You don't mind, do you?"

"Nuh-uh. But I still want to go to the world with the big horses."

"Would you like to see some of those horses in real life?"

"Really—?"

"We have them at a special place in New Mexico. We brought some over and we've been learning how to breed them at the big ranch. We're going to arrange a visit for your family. When you come, I'll take you to see them. Maybe we can even go riding. Would you like that?"

"Oh, yes!" I was ready to leave, right then. "When can we go?"

"How does next month sound?"

"I have school—!"

"It's all right. You can miss it," Birdie said.

"Really? Mom-Woo never lets me miss school."

"This time, I think she will."

NEW MEXICO

—WAS HOT AND BRIGHT. Too bright. The sky looked so high it was scary. We had to wear sunglasses and hats and smear ourselves with lotion. But inside it was too cold. Gamma Joe complained that the air-conditioning made her bones hurt.

Almost everybody was there. It was like Celebration Day, only without presents. Cindy and Parra both flew in. Da-Lorrin came down from Montreal. Even Morra and Irm and Bhetto showed up, so I guess they'd patched up their quarrel somehow. I stayed close to Rinky and held her hand everywhere. Shona and Nona hugged Mom-Lu's side. Jerre and Klin and Marle also took time off from school. And there were three relatives I didn't recognize and whose names I forgot as soon Mom-Woo told me.

There were other families visiting too, so there were lots of kids and it was pretty noisy for a while. The Kelly family came in from Florida; the second-eldest child was Patta. She was here to see the horses too. Patta still dressed like a boy, but she'd already become a girl. When I asked her about it, she said it felt better than she expected, and she was glad she did it.

Finally, after everybody was registered and badged, we all got on air-conditioned buses and went for a tour around the whole campus. They called it a campus, but it was really a town, with domes and towers and tube-clusters everywhere. Our guide was Birdie; she was our caseworker now, and she said that every building was connected

12

to every other building by underground tunnels, because the winter storms were as bad as the summer heat. She said there was an enormous amount of work to do and not enough people to do it, and they couldn't just go out and hire more people because everybody had to be trained and the training took a long time, so they had to train people just to do the training. Except the only people who could train other people were also needed to do their own work, so everybody was always working two jobs at a time, which was sort of good news if you were applying for work, because it meant that there were a lot of placements available.

Birdie told us that there were sixteen active world-gates: three in New Mexico, with two more coming online next year; plus two in Canada, six in Australia, two in China, three in Russia—she didn't count any of the gates that weren't open for traffic—and there were seven more under construction in India and Africa, plus four more scheduled for Brazil, Chile and Argentina. Plus a whole bunch more proposed, but not yet funded. She didn't count the gates that opened onto uninhabitable worlds, even though some of them were open for mining. I already knew most of this from shows on the net, but Birdie told us a lot of stuff that hadn't been posted yet.

Not all the world-gates went to viable worlds, she said. Despite all the very best calculations of what kind of a world they were targeting for, there were too many time and energy variables that couldn't be controlled beyond the initial parameters, so it was always a surprise what they'd find on the other side when the gate was opened. The world might not be very good for our kind of life. Some worlds were too hot. Some were too cold. Most had the wrong kind of atmosphere. Some worlds had life, but it was the wrong kind, things that we definitely could not share a planet with. And then there were some worlds that no one talked about. I couldn't imagine how bad a world like that would have to be.

"When they find a bad world, do they shut the gate down and try again?" Mom-Lu asked.

"It's not that easy," said Birdie. "Once a world-gate is calculated, they have to build the gate specifically to that world. It's not like television where you can change the channel. Every gate is unique to its own destination. You can only build one gate to a world. The physics are very rigid. And as carefully as we plan, as carefully as we target, every time we power up, it's still a Heisenberg event."

"What's that?"

"A surprise." She smiled. She told us about a gate they'd just opened in Canada. That world was in the middle of an ice age so bad that even the carbon dioxide had frozen out of the air.

"So what do you do if you don't like what's on the other side? Just turn it off and forget that gate?"

"Sometimes, yes. We tear down the operative part of a nonviable gate and build a new one in the same frame. But it always depends on what's on the other side. We have a checklist of over a hundred different standards that a world has to meet before we consider it viable. Gravity is first on the list, then atmosphere. Length of day, length of year, what kind of light the star puts out. The angle of inclination of the planet's axis. Whether it has a moon or not—if it doesn't have a moon, it wobbles on its axis; it can end up with one pole pointing directly toward the sun. Magnetic field. Heavy metals in its mantle. Radiation levels. Meteor and asteroid bombardment. Those are the obvious ones. The not-so-obvious things are where the planet is in its geologic cycle. Are tectonic plates active or settled? How much volcanic activity is there? Is it in an ice age or a temperate period? And so on. If a planet passes all these tests, then we send through robots and science teams. It's never routine. Every world is different. Even if we start out with the same criteria, we can get wildly divergent results; and when we try to compensate in advance for those results, things get even more chaotic.

"I know that this isn't very exciting to some of you," Birdie interrupted herself. "But this is what the tech teams live for. It's all about probability theory. The more gates we open, the more information we have. So each time, we should be getting better and better, right? But so far it hasn't worked that way—and that's because, at least some folks think this, that our attempts to predict what we're going to get affect the prediction in ways we can't predict. So that no matter what we do, every new world will be a surprise.

"Most of the worlds, they're not very livable, but they've got a lot of easily accessible heavy metals, nickel, iron, copper, silver, gold, so we've got mining and smelting operations. A few places, we've sealed the access, but we haven't turned off the gates, because even though we might not want to go to those places right now, maybe later we might change our minds. We're still considering those possibilities." And then she added, "Of course, you do know about the one gate that self-destructed, because it opened into a star. That was very bad news. But that was a long time ago when the gates were first invented and we don't make mistakes like that anymore."

Patta Kelly raised her hand. "I heard you have to keep the gates open for a million years before you can use them."

Birdie laughed. "Sometimes even longer than that." She looked around to the rest of us. "Every world exists in its own set of reality-rules. We have to compensate for all the different space-time energy levels; sometimes it takes years to stabilize a gate. Sometimes we get flickers of discontinuity. And that produces time-slips. On this side, normal time continues; but on the other side, sometimes thousands or even tens of thousands of years slip by in a single flicker."

"Does that happen a lot?"

"No. Not after a gate is stabilized. But sometimes we trigger a deliberate time-slip. Sometimes we find a world that's almost, but not quite, right. So we terraform it. Rather than wait ten thousand years, we just slip it a little. It's kind of like cooking. You add a few ingredients, you simmer for a while, you take a taste and add a few more things. We start out with anaerobic bacteria, then aerobic, then plankton and lichens and fungi; eventually kelp and grass. The great thing is that terraforming also gives us a marvelous evolutionary laboratory. We get to see how life-forms adapt and change. That's what we did with Linnea. We worked on that planet at least a million years." She stopped to smile at Patta and me. "Yes, those are Earth horses, only three hundred and fifty thousand years later."

"But how come they're so big?"

"Everything on Linnea is bigger. It's because the gravity on Linnea is a little bit less than Earth. So that changes the physics of growth." She frowned. "Let's see. How do I explain this in simple terms? Try it this way. Do you know what the angle of repose is? No. All right, I'll explain. I apologize for the science lesson, but it's necessary. The angle of repose is the maximum angle at which a pile of material remains stable. Like a sand dune. You can only pile up so much sand before it starts sliding. Well, that's a function of gravity. On Linnea, there's less gravity, so the angle of repose is steeper. The sand dunes are taller and sharper. Now imagine that every plant and every animal also has a physiological angle of repose. It's the way that all the different parts of the body fit together and interact.

"On Linnea, plants grow taller—but not too much taller or they're more susceptible to wind, so they have to grow thicker stems and trunks as well, but that affects how much water they have to pump out to their leaves—see how everything has to fit together? It's the same for animals. Bones can grow longer, but then they have to grow thicker to be strong enough to support the length. Then the heart and lungs have to get larger because they're pumping oxygenated blood farther than before. But because gravity is different, the rhythm of walking is different and that means that the stress falls differently on all the joints, and that means that the skeleton has to adapt to compensate. Everything is connected to everything else.

"Linnea's sun is harsher, a lot more radiation than Sol, so we see a lot more mutation. That plus the ecological pressure to adapt to a profoundly different environment produced some very rapid changes. Rapid on an evolutionary scale, that is. Everything we introduced over there expanded to fill every available ecological niche. On this side, we worked on it for ten years. On the other side, three hundred and fifty thousand years of evolution reshaped wolves, buffalo, horses, ostriches, cats, mice, rats, rabbits, birds, ants, bees, beetles, worms, grass, wheat, bamboo, potatoes, trees of all kinds, you name it—everything. It's been a remarkable laboratory. Even human beings have been affected."

"Is that how long people have been on Linnea? Three hundred and fifty thousand years—?"

"Oh, dear, no. Humans have only been on Linnea for three thousand years, Linnea time. And that was an accident. It wasn't supposed to happen." Before anyone could ask how, Birdie said, "We had a time-flicker, an unscheduled discontinuity. The gate was restabilizing. We had several exploration teams on the other side. In that brief instant of disconnect, more than three thousand years passed. We could tell that by the difference in the recorded star positions. When we felt it was safe to send teams back in, we found that there were settlements on Linnea—the umpty-umpty-great-grandchildren of the lost explorers."

"Weren't they glad to see you?"

"That's the bad news. They'd forgotten all about us. They must have had a rough time those first few generations, and somewhere along the line, Earth stopped being history and became myth."

"Didn't you just tell them the truth?"

"It wasn't that easy. They didn't believe us. They killed the contact teams."

"Huh—?"

"Would you believe it if someone came up suddenly and said you were really the great-grandchild of alien explorers?"

"Oh," I said. "I guess not."

"That's the problem. They don't want to hear it. It sounds too outlandish to them. That's the problem with a lot of us—we don't want to hear anything that will unsettle us."

"Are we going to see a gate today?" That was Parra, changing the subject.

"Not today. There's a lot of other stuff that you need to see first."

Birdie was right; there was so much to see I couldn't remember it all. A lot of it was pretty boring. There were these big buildings where hundreds of intelligence engines worked night and day. The intelligence engines monitored all the hours and hours of video coming back from the different worlds, looking for interesting stuff. If they found anything really important, they posted it for people to review, only there weren't enough people to look at all the things they found.

Birdie said that the primary goal is to develop new Earths, places where people can just drive through the gate and go right to work, planting farms and building cities. Lots of farms and lots of cities. But opening a gate is a very expensive proposition; it costs three billion dollars to build the nexus itself, and at least a hundred million a year to maintain. And that's just for the physical plant. It costs three times that much to pay for all the people necessary to run the operation. See, the first thing they do when they open a gate is send over probes to bring back samples. Hundreds of thousands of samples. So opening up a new world also means building a whole city to service the gate traffic, and that means training thousands and thousands of people for all the different kinds of access and analysis and follow-through.

The most important thing to find out is whether or not the world can support human life; but if it can, it probably already has life of its own, so then the gate scientists have to see what kind of life it is; and eventually, what they really want to know is how hard will it be for humans to live in such an environment.

On one world, they found creatures like dinosaurs, only different; mosty what the dinosaurs might have turned into if a comet hadn't smacked into the Earth. That was interesting, but it was also an ethical dilemma, because if we moved over there, we'd have to wipe out a lot of local life.

On a second world, all they found was mosty barren rock and some kind of yucky green slime that only grew on the shady side of boulders near the acid shores. There wasn't the right kind of air to breathe, so the big problem there would be introducing the right kind of bacteria and plankton and lichens to create a breathable atmosphere, one with enough oxygen. But that was a heavy-gravity world. Nearly thirty percent heavier. So they decided not to terraform it and were using it mosty for mining operations.

On a third world there were giant hairy red worms and an ecology so aggressive and dangerous that only robots were allowed to go across. And most of those were dismantled by the local life-forms in a matter of hours. They weren't sure what to do with that world—they couldn't afford to study it forever, they didn't dare send people over, and they didn't dare risk any of its life-forms escaping to Earth. Eventually it would have to be closed, unless somebody could think of a compelling reason for keeping it open.

One of the places we toured was the robot factory. There was a whole unit dedicated to building probes to go into new worlds and explore them, making maps and charts of all the terrain. Every world had different conditions and so a new set of probes had to be designed and built for each world, depending on what conditions existed on the other side.

Birdie showed us all the different kinds of probes. My favorites were the ones that looked like transparent airplanes. They were sort of like city monitors, only better. These were built to stay up in the air for years if they had to, high enough so that you couldn't see them from the ground, but with cameras that were so good they could read license plates from a mile up—that is, if there were any license plates to read.

Birdie said that all the probes were set to self-destruct automatically at the first hint of danger or failure, vaporizing themselves so completely that there wouldn't be any pieces big enough to interfere with local life-forms; this was especially important on Linnea where the pieces might be found by people who weren't supposed to know they were being watched.

One of the factory guides explained that all the probes talk to each other. They're a stochastic network, reforming on the fly; they relay their signals back through the gate, back to New Mexico or Houston or Australia or wherever. There, the intelligence engines process everything, correlating and calculating and analyzing. "We know more about the weather on Linnea than the Linneans do," Birdie said.

That's when Rinky asked, "Do you ever find a planet with intelligent life already there? I mean *aliens*."

Birdie looked like she wished Rinky hadn't asked the question. "Well, yes and no. The Australians found a world once that looked promising, but it was filled with different species of—we don't even know what to call them. They're so different we have nothing to compare them to. They looked like two-legged termites. Or naked mole rats. About Kaer's size. They dig deep tunnels into the earth or they built giant mounds above the ground. We've studied them for years now, but nobody is willing to say if they're sentient or not. Their behavior is sophisticated, but so is the behavior of termites and ants. We've tried sending over contact robots—but every time, they immediately dismantled them. So we're definitely not going to risk human beings. We're not sure if they don't recognize other lives or what, we just don't know yet. It's an interesting world, but its very existence raises scientific and ethical questions that we're not prepared to address; there's even some talk about shutting down that gate."

Birdie went on to say that for every good gate that gets opened, there are at least five more that can't be used for one reason or another. In addition to the sixteen gates open to good worlds, there are fifty-seven more that are open but unusable, and nine gates that are permanently locked for security reasons—and these are the ones that they just don't talk about. Plus there are all the gates that were attempted, that were deemed unacceptable, and dismantled and rebuilt to new specifications. Gates are a big industry. We need them for the import of metals, water, fuels, electricity, gases and other necessary resources—even agriculture. Four of the worlds already have successful farming communities. According to Birdie, at the present rate of growth, gates will provide nine percent of all global mining resources within ten years, and within a hundred years, maybe 100 percent. She wouldn't say how much food, though; they hadn't yet decided if alien crops were safe.

After that, we saw a bunch of other buildings. Most of them looked like factories or schools. There were a lot of places where folks were studying the language of Linnea and watching videos of Linneans talking to each other. It all sounded like mish-mash to me. I didn't see how anyone could learn it, let alone speak it, but people did.

And then after that, we went over to the "macroscope" which was kind of like a multiplex theater, only instead of movies there were pictures coming in from the different probes so we could see what was happening in the three active worlds that the New Mexico campus serviced, and the two prospective sites. One was Linnea, of course. The second one was the dinosaur world, and mosty they were just studying it, trying to decide how safe it might be to have people go across. The third gate opened onto a world almost completely frozen over; but it was a good source for ice, which meant water for New Mexico, Arizona and Texas. Some people were arguing that they should shut that gate for a bit and then come back when the ice age was over; only nobody knew if this was a cold period or a warm period for this world, so they were still studying. And meanwhile, sucking out water and electricity for the southwest. The water made the gate cost-effective, so they might just leave it like it is.

Birdie explained, "*Every* world is useful in some way. If there's no life, we can still mine minerals and gases and chemicals. And if there is life, it's always different. That means new plants, new animals, new things that we can use. We're always discovering new foods, new spices, new flavors—and most important, new medicines. The thing about gate-worlds, you're always going to be surprised. More surprised than you can imagine—even when you know you're going to be surprised."

And then she got *very* serious. She looked at all of us when she said it. "Those of you who are planning to be scouts or emigrants, you need to start learning this now. If you go through a gate, you have to start with one single fact—you cannot assume *anything*. Remember that. Everything is *different* on the other side. Remind yourself of it every morning. And maybe you'll survive."

DINOSAURS

THE NEXT DAY WE VISITED the world-domes, each like a zoo, but not really. Each dome was at least a kilometer across, or more. And each one had a different environment in it, holding all the various plants and animals from whatever specific part of the gate-world it was simulating. There were twenty different domes. From a distance they looked like big pink pimples to me, but Rinky said they looked like tits. Mom-Woo gave her a look that said that kind of remark wasn't appropriate here and Rinky shut up. Mom-Lu whispered to Mom-Woo, "I think Rinky's getting ready for puberty. We're going to have to talk about that."

"I am not," said Rinky, and Mom-Woo gave her another look.

Most of the domes you couldn't go into. We had to look in through thick security windows. This was to protect the creatures inside from our bugs and vice versa.

Birdie said the most dangerous part of crossing over to any world with its own life was that the germs would almost certainly be different. Every world has its own microbe ecology. And germs go through so many generations in a week, a month, a year, that after a thousand or two thousand or ten thousand years, the bacteria and viruses and whatever else there was would have had the chance to evolve a million different ways. So one of the first things the scientists have to do to make it safe to visit any new world is develop vaccines and medicines for everything we find over there.

The other side of it, though, is even harder. When we cross over to a

21

new world, we risk infecting the things over there with *our* bugs. And they're no more likely to have any more immunity to our germs than we'll have to theirs. This is especially true for Linnea, which already has human beings—but with three thousand years of one-sided separation, so who knew what immunities they might have gained or lost? So we would have to be completely sterilized before we went. Everything inside and out—from the mites that lived in our eyelashes to the germs in our guts that help us digest our food. Birdie said it wouldn't hurt, but we might have queasy stomachs and diarrhea for a couple of days while we got used to their equivalents.

And it's not just the germs. It's all the plants and all the animals too. We can't risk accidentally introducing any of their species to our world, or our species to theirs. The Linnea we'd come back to when the gate was reopened was very different than the Linnea that had been there when the gate was closed. The scientists theorized that there had been some mass die-offs simply due to the consequences of exposure to terrestrial life.

Birdie said this was the most difficult part of the job, keeping the world-gates biologically secure—a lot harder than learning the language or teaching people how to behave on a new world or even figuring out a valid set of coordinates for a new gate—because there were so many different interrelationships in an ecology, we could never know them all.

That first day, we only visited two of the world-domes. The first one was the one with the dinosaurs. They weren't the same kinds of dinosaurs like we'd had on Earth 65 million years ago, but they looked like they could have been.

There weren't any people living on dinosaur world, except a few explorers who only went over there to study it. Birdie said we probably weren't going to colonize it. Maybe only a few little parts. Research stations, not real settlements. Because there was still so much that the scientists wanted to study that they didn't want to risk contamination.

We couldn't go down to the floor of the dinosaur dome. It was too dangerous. Instead, we rode above the simulated savanna on a kind of aerial-car hung from the roof of the dome. It was almost like flying. The pilot could drive the vehicle almost anywhere he wanted because the suspension carriage navigated on a set of overhead cables, kind of like those overhead cameras they use at football games. Plus, he could lower the car to give us closer looks or raise it quickly if any of the bigger creatures got too close.

There were a lot of different creatures in dino-dome. It was the biggest of all the domes, covering more than a hundred square kilometers. There were at least fifteen different kinds of herbivores there, all sizes, but they didn't have a lot of them, only a few small herds, but on dino-world some of the herds had thousands, even tens of thousands of individuals. There were birds too, of course, but not like Earth-birds. Some of them had long stringy feathers, some had fur; two of the birds looked more like big black bats.

We saw a large herd of herbivores that looked like small gazelles, only they had long lizardly tails that they held up in the air behind them, and birdlike faces with sharp beaks. They nipped at the grassy tufts like chickens pecking for bugs. Another family of creatures thundered through the grass like armored tanks with horns; they were the size of rhinos. They were big and leathery and had little piglike eyes that made them look distrustful and mean. Birdie said they *were* distrustful and mean.

And then we saw the biggest ones of all. They were the size of blimps, colored all shades of brown and gold, darker on top and brighter along their bellies; they had necks and tails longer than their bodies. They had to lift their tails every time they lifted their heads, something to do with equalizing blood pressure—but they could lift their heads high enough to peer into the monorail car. One of them did and all the little-uns screamed. Me too. But Birdie said there wasn't anything to be afraid of. Birdie called them Patty-saurs, after the woman who discovered them. She said they only ate people by accident and usually they spit them out after a few bites because they didn't like the taste. I didn't know if she was joking or not.

Birdie said that there were over a thousand species of smaller animals in this dome—a lot of little things that were sort of like lizards and squirrels and frogs and scorpions. It was tricky to balance a whole ecology, but they were doing pretty good with just this cross section. So far, anyway.

Part of the problem was balancing the herbivores against the carnivores. Birdie said that you need about 120 kilos of herbivore for every kilo of carnivore. And to support that many herbivores, you need at least 100 times that amount of edible foliage. The ratio varies depending on the diet, and because they weren't really sure what the right ratios were on dino-world, they'd brought in as much native foliage as they could, and were hoping that the animals would adjust their populations accordingly. So far, only a few species had gone into decline. And some of the others were thriving too well—so maybe there were some predators missing still.

But the predators they did have were impressive. We saw a family of things like allosaurs, only bigger. They were faster and meaner than the equivalent T. Rex would be. We stayed well above them, but they were snoozing lazily and paid us no attention.

We also saw a pack of red-brown raptor-beasts. They were striped with gold, and they had dark brown shading around their eyes, which gave them a kind of clownish appearance—but only until they started running. Then they held their tails high and their bodies low and forward, and with their necks outstretched, their heads waving back and forth, they bounded across the ground like giant roadrunners. Even though they were sort of funny looking, nobody laughed.

Birdie told us that this was a good day because we were getting to see so many different kinds of animals. The spookiest were the coyote-lizards, spidery-gaunt horrors that watched us warily as we flew past. They had the most intelligent faces. Birdie said they were mosty carrion-eaters, following the allosaurs like hyenas and jackals; but they'd occasionally been seen hunting their own prey in packs. She said that mosty they went after the gazelle-things, but they'd been known to worry some of the larger animals too, especially during calving season.

But the highlight of the afternoon was when the pilot checked his scanner-display and took us around to see King Rex, the one they show in all the videos. He wasn't as big as the allosaur-things, but he was impressive just the same, and someday he'd be a lot bigger. He had just killed one of the rhino-things the day before and he was still torpidly guarding the kill until he was hungry again. He made me think of a sleeping alligator and I didn't want to be around when he woke. Pilot must have felt the same way. We didn't approach too closely.

Later, three of the red-brown raptors chased underneath the monorail for awhile, hissing and screeching and leaping; but we were high enough off the ground that we knew they couldn't get to us. Mikey called them names, but Nona hid her eyes against Mom-Lu's side. The expression on Mom-Lu's face suggested that she didn't like the raptors either.

JINKER

It wasn't until after lunch that we got to Halfway Dome, one of only two domes that had great-horses. This one was a lot safer. You could actually go down to the floor. Birdie said that this dome was a "compromised" dome, where Linnean plants and animals could be safely exposed to Earth plants and animals. That's why we could actually enter.

There wasn't any danger of contamination. The Linnean creatures had all been sterilized of microbes and bacteria when they were brought over. This dome served as a halfway station where the Linnean plants and animals could be monitored for compatibility with Earth conditions. Eventually, some of these life-forms might be imported for Earth agriculture. But not for years yet. Not until they'd been fully tested in side-by-side conditions.

Inside, it was just like being outside—only outside on a different planet. We had to pass through six airlocks and a whole set of long corridors, but finally we came out on a balcony overlooking a giant bowl. From underneath, the dome looked just like sky. We walked down some wooden steps and we were *there*—on that other world.

The first thing you notice in the dome is the color of the light. Everything was yellower. It hurt my eyes. I thought that I'd get used to it after a while, and I did, sort of; but everything looked more orange, more red, more brown—not a whole lot, but enough to make everything more dusty-looking. It made my eyes water and I was rubbing them a lot more. Birdie said that was a normal reaction. Linnea's sun was just a few degrees redder than ours and they had accurately duplicated its spectral output. If we were actually living in the dome, she said, our eyes would adjust within a week or two. But for a while, I was wondering if I really wanted to live under such a yellow sky.

The rest of the landscape was different, too. There were rolling hills, and a lake, and that was normal; but there were scrubby little trees that didn't look like trees at all. They didn't have any real leaves, they were furry instead. And the grass was dry and brownish. It was end of summer here.

We followed a long dirt path that curved back and forth between some little hills without really getting anywhere. The little hills went all around the outside of the bowl. I guess that helped make it look more real from the center.

Then finally, we came around a curve and there they were. The great-horses. And I forgot everything else.

They were taller than trees. Bigger than elephants. They had huge, thick legs, thicker than tree trunks, all covered with shaggy white hair and great flat hooves that made the ground thump when they pawed at it. They were so big most of us stopped, afraid to approach the corral any closer.

"Come on, Kaer," Birdie said. "Let's go say hello." She nudged me forward. I let myself be pushed. In person, the great-horses didn't look so glamorous anymore. They looked *big*. And they smelled. Not a bad smell, but definitely a horsey smell.

"Are they, um...?"

"Friendly?" Birdie finished my question. "Yes. They're used to people. See that dappled one? That's Jinker. She's the mom-boss. You can't say hello to any of the horses until you make friends with Jinker first. She's very fussy about that. Here, Kaer—" Birdie reached into a big wooden crate just outside the corral. "Give her this apple. Go ahead, she likes apples. And she won't bite. Just hold it out on the flat of your hand, like this."

I took the apple. It was as big as a pumpkin, only heavier. I held it with both hands reaching over the wooden rail. Jinker raised her huge head and shook it ponderously. She looked directly across the corral at me. And then she snorted, a sound like an old steam locomotive warming up. Then, as if building up steam, she took a single step, then another, and finally three more and she was *here*.

She lowered her gigantic head toward me—I leaned back away as far as I could, I was afraid to look—but she never touched me. She just inhaled the apple up off my outstretched hands and it was gone in a single quick crunch.

"Attagirl," said Birdie, slapping Jinker's nose with her hand. Jinker took another step forward and lowered her great head so it was right in front of me. Her eyes were as large as spotlights. Her nostrils were deep caves. The flat of her nose was like a wall. "Go ahead, Kaer. You can't hurt her."

I reached out and touched her. She was *warm*.

"Harder than that," said Birdie. "Otherwise she can't feel you. You have to slap her. Don't be afraid."

Jinker snuffled impatiently, a sound like an earthquake clearing its throat. So I slapped her—gently.

"Harder."

I slapped again, this time as hard as I dared. Jinker bobbed her head once or twice in approval. She made an *mmph* noise in her throat.

"Good, she likes you," said Birdie. "Of course, she likes everybody who gives her apples."

"Can I give her another one?"

"She'll eat as many as you give her."

"Really?" I was already reaching into the barrel. Jinker watched me closely.

"Jinker's very considerate. She won't hurt your feelings by saying no to an apple."

I held out another apple. This time I watched as Jinker curled back her great lips, parted her teeth and vacuumed the apple into oblivion. I didn't think I would ever get used to the sight. But I reached for another apple.

"How much food does she have to eat a day?"

"You couldn't give her enough apples to keep her alive. She needs a dozen bales of hay per feeding. A half ton a day, just for maintenance. And a dozen barrels of oats on a heavy work day." Birdie slapped Jinker's head again. "And of course, all the carrots and apples she wants." Jinker snorfled in agreement.

"It sounds like a lot of work."

"No, feeding the horse is fun. It's cleaning up afterward that's a lot of work. All that hay comes out the other end. We've got half a dozen great-horses here. Each one leaves hundreds of kilos of droppings. That's quite a load. On the open prairie, dung-mice would take care of it. But here, we shovel it into a compost pit. On the world Jinker comes from, it gets plowed into the fields. It's very good fertilizer."

"Oh, ick!"

"Where do you think fertilizer comes from, Kaer? If it weren't for the great-horses, a lot of those folks on Linnea might starve to death."

I looked at Jinker with new respect. She nudged me with her nose and knocked me flat on my butt.

"She wants more apples," Birdie laughed, helping me up. "I think you've made a new friend."

SCOUTS

LATER, RINKY EXPLAINED TO ME that the great-horses were a test. Because if we were going to go to Horse World, we would probably have to go with horses and wagons, so they needed to see how everybody in the family felt about the horses. I didn't believe her, but she said, "If we passed the first test, they'll take us out riding. Then you'll see." Birdie had said we might get a chance to go riding, if the schedule allowed. So maybe she was right.

Dinner that night was in a big restaurant overlooking the interior of the dome. We could see the horses in their paddock as they pulled at the bales of hay, and I spent the whole meal talking about Jinker until Mom-Trey finally asked me to change the subject or be quiet.

They didn't serve normal food here. Everything was from Linnea. They had meat from a big bird, kind of like an ostrich, only scruffier looking. They called it an emmo. And there was boffili stew. The boffili was like a big hairy cow, even bigger than the great-horse. Birdie said there were vast herds of them on the western continent. I didn't like the boffili, but the emmo wasn't too bad. It tasted like hamburger.

After dinner, we met with some scouts—folks who had gone over to Linnea to explore and then come back to help train more families. They told us what it would be like if we went there. There wouldn't be any electricity, they said. The Linneans hadn't discovered it yet, so that meant none of us could have it either. And we weren't going to be allowed to "discover" it for them. So that meant no music or television or computers. And no lights after sunset except candles and lanterns.

"But what do you do—?" Aunt Morra asked.

"Mosty, we go to sleep. And get up at the first light of dawn. You'll get used to it. It can be a good life."

"I mean, what do you do for entertainment?"

"We make our own," said one of the mom-scouts. "We play instruments. We read books—usually one person reads aloud while others knit or do other work. We act out plays. We have our children recite their lessons. We do all the things that folks on that world do. Understand this," she said. "When you're over there, you have to fit in perfectly. You have to forget you ever lived on another world. We can't risk cultural contamination."

Auncle Irm said, "Morra and I won't be going, we'll be staying behind to manage the family affairs here. Will we have any contact at all? We're used to regular conferences, you know."

One of the da-scouts stepped forward then. "While we don't specifically discourage contact, we do try to limit it—for the protection of the families on the other side. It represents too great a risk. Someone might say or do something that's so bizarrely out of character for that culture that it would taint the local relationships."

He exchanged a glance with the mom-scout, then shrugged and added, "Look, it depends on the circumstances. Last year, the winter was so bad that some families were snowed in for months. We gave them an open line until spring. We fed them lots of their favorite entertainment. We're not out to punish anyone. But once the snow began to thaw, they had to work extra hard to get back into character. There's a price to be paid, no question. You're going to be isolated over there. Not everybody can handle it. Even the folks who think they can handle it sometimes crack and call for emergency pickup."

"You mean it's possible to quit?" Da-Lorrin asked.

The mom-scout nodded grimly. "If you're thinking that you can bail out the first time you hit turbulence, don't go. We don't want to waste the investment. And besides, we don't make those kind of pickups easily. There's too much risk. We have to send a chopper through, and that risks a UFO incident. We've already had one too many 'sightings.'"

The da-scout was even more direct. "Quitting is a disaster. If we have to pull you out, we have to fake your deaths. Usually by fire. We can't have you just go missing, and we can't leave bodies unless we find donors. If we have to go to that kind of effort, there's a mandatory board of inquiry. And if it's determined that it wasn't absolutely necessary, well...I don't like to say this, because it gives the wrong impression, but we've had people fined and imprisoned for putting the project at risk. You don't want to do it."

Lorrin held up his hands in defeat. "Okay, I got your point. I wasn't looking for a way out. I was just curious."

The da-scout had a hard expression. He didn't look like he laughed very often. Lorrin sat down again and the scouts went on to talk about other stuff, like crops and seasons and how to build houses and furniture and other stuff.

We wouldn't be totally cut off, he said. We would have some technology. Only it would all be disguised to look like things that were normal over there—a doll, a music box, a mirror, a book, ordinary-looking stuff like that. If you didn't know what it was and how to work it, you wouldn't know it was anything special, even if you broke it open. Everything would be nanotech. Even us. The scout said we'd each be implanted. And whatever tech we might have, it wouldn't work for anyone who wasn't implanted. There were all kinds of safeguards.

It was Mom-Woo who said what everybody was thinking. She usually did, that was why she was Mom-Woo. She said, "If it's that dangerous, why do you send families over there at all?"

"That's a good question," said the mom-scout. "I'll be honest with you. We've had that discussion ourselves—every time we meet a new family. We ask ourselves, is it a good idea to send *these* people over? But the truth is we *have* to send families. We can send singles or couples, but families work best. People trust families. And families can live in a community and observe its workings a lot easier than any other kind of observation team. And—" The mom-scout paused. "There's another consideration too. Our long-range planning.

"Eventually, at some point in the future, we hope to establish formal contact, leading to free and open passage through the gate, trade agreements and perhaps even colonization. Colonization was always the plan before the interruption, but now we have to figure out how to deal with the descendants without sending them into massive cultural shock. We don't want to risk a war or an inquisition. That means were going to need people over there who can act as intermediaries. People who have lived there and who know the culture will be the best representatives of all. So in the long run, we're training you to be part of the contact team."

"Spies," said Big Jes. "You're training us to be spies and propagandists. Right?"

"Well . . . yes, you can think of it that way. But we'd rather you think of yourself as guardian spirits. The people on Linnea aren't our enemies. They're our children. But we need them to be our partners."

WORLDS

AND I THOUGHT IT WAS just about horses. But we did get to ride Jinker two days later. So I guess we passed the test, whatever it was.

Just getting on the horse was hard enough. There was a huge wooden A-frame, taller than Jinker, with a giant saddle hanging from it, with baskets on each side. Two of the scouts led Jinker into the A-frame and lowered the saddle onto her back. Then they rolled some stairs on wheels up to her side and we climbed up to ride in the baskets. Jinker could carry four people on a side. The driver climbed up on a rope ladder and sat on a chair just behind her neck. He had a long rod which he used for tapping her neck to guide her.

At first it was scary, because we were so high off the ground. I thought we were higher than a double-decker bus, but the driver said not quite. But then he said there were some horses bigger than Jinker, so my guess wasn't all that wrong.

I sat in front on the left side. Rinky sat behind me. Then Mom-Lu and Lorrin. Aunt Morra and Auncle Irm were on the other side with Parra and Cindy behind them. Bhetto didn't want to ride. He didn't like the great-horses that much. Too bad. He missed a good time.

I was surprised that Jinker wasn't very fast. The driver said her natural gait was about ten miles per hour. She could hit thirty or forty at a gallop, especially because the gravity on Linnea was lighter than on Earth, but she couldn't sustain it for long. The great-horses were really too big and too heavy for speed; but they were strong, even stronger than elephants. A single great-horse was as strong as eight Percherons and could pull an enormous wagonload of goods. That's why the people on Linnea used great-horses where people of equivalent cultures would have already invented the steam engine.

Our driver was named Dando. He said he was scheduled to go to Linnea in a few months, just ahead of the first big group of settlers, to help select a target site.

"I thought there were settlers there already—?" Auncle Irm asked.

"Scouts and their families only. We're still in second-stage mapping. Third-stage is when we start a real immigration pipeline, and we expect that certification next month. The first group is in the last semester of training. Second group is halfway through. You folks will probably be in the third or fourth set, depending on how well you do in training. Of course, a lot depends on getting the support system in place too.

"Right now, we're working on getting the parts of a launch catapult over there so we can put up heavy satellites."

"Is that your specialty?" Irm asked.

"Uh-huh," Dando said. "It's tricky work. It turns out we need a lot more engineers and tech-specialists on-site than we thought."

"Really—?" said Irm, actually showing interest.

Dando went on. "We've found a number of sites on the equator where we can operate a catapult undetected, including several uninhabited islands. But the problem is getting the people and the equipment there undetected. It means shipping a small town. Do we look for secret harbors and build inflatable ships? Or do we try and move everything by air? We can't begin serious importation of families without reliable communications in place. Right now, we're still depending on the spy-birds—like the remote probes we showed you."

"You need engineers, eh?" Irm said thoughtfully.

"We need everything. But if you've got useful skills in that area, talk to your caseworker."

I wasn't really interested in that part. I wanted to talk about the horses again. "Mr. Dando?"

"Yes?" He glanced back at me.

"When you're over on Horse World—Linnea, I mean—are there any dangerous animals?"

He nodded. "Some."

"Dangerous to great-horses?" I was still thinking of the coyote-lizards from the other dome.

He hesitated before answering. Finally: "Yes, Kaer, there are things like wolves, only bigger. The Linneans call them kacks. They hunt in packs, and they'll track a single horse for days if they have to, worrying it to death, not letting it sleep, rushing in to nip at its legs, until it collapses from lack of sleep or lack of blood. It's not a pretty sight." Then he added, "The great-horse isn't defenseless, though. Mosty they keep to the plains, where they can see across great distances. And they travel in small herds, so they can share each other's protection. If a kack gets too close, a horse will rear up to stamp it flat. Mosty the kacks look for easier game than horses. They're much more dangerous to smaller animals. Especially people. But they prefer boffili."

"Oh," I said.

"You shouldn't have to worry, if you're careful. The people on Linnea have crossbows. Properly handled, a crossbow can be more efficient than a rifle—and you usually get the bolt back. But if you go over there, kiddo, you'll probably live in a town, safe behind a very tall fence." He said that to reassure me, but I had bad dreams about kacks for several weeks after that.

When we got back home, the parents had lots of grown-up talks about Linnea and the other worlds. We kids hadn't seen much of the other worlds. Apparently, the gate people thought we were best suited for Linnea, and the parents seemed to agree. The Linnean Scout Authority was ready to start training families now, and the other two worlds that New Mexico station was developing wouldn't be ready for years, and they were nowhere near as habitable.

Black-World was dry and hard. It looked a lot like Mars, only darker. There wasn't much life there either. So if anyone went over there at all, they'd have to start almost completely from scratch. The problem was that because there wasn't much life—just some lichens and little bugs—and there wasn't much breathable air either. There was atmosphere, but it was mosty carbon dioxide; not enough oxygen in it to live on. So you'd have to wear a respirator every time you went outside. Nobody in the family liked that. Black-World really was mosty an industrial place; there would be mines, and dirty factories, and maybe some observatories and science stations; but not a real colony.

And Blue-World was mosty water with a few scattered islands here and there. Some of the islands had life. The biggest island was in the north and it actually had real animal life, things that looked like big shaggy apes. They were cunning like baboons and just as vicious; not sentient, but enough of a hazard that the island was off-limits. Klin laughed and said it wouldn't be a problem because Jes could pass for one of those apes and Big Jes laughed too and offered to put Klin through a wall.

Anyway, it didn't need much discussion. Linnea was really the only world that the family would consider, and it looked like it was the only world we were eligible for in any case. If we'd wanted, we could have made application for one of the gates in Canada or Australia, but our chances of approval there weren't as good, and most of those worlds looked just as hard as Black-World. So that pretty much settled that. It was Linnea or nothing. The family talked about it for a long time at the airport while we waited for everybody to catch their different planes. Irm and Bhetto and Morra went off to talk by themselves, and Lorrin's face got all funny when they did.

I wasn't supposed to hear, but I did because Mom-Trey was wiping spilled chocolate soda off the baby's shirt and I was helping. Mom-Trey said to Da, "Let them be, Lorr."

He shook his head. "You know what we're up against. They won't take a split family. If those three won't go—"

"They don't want a divorce," said Mom-Lu. "Morra and I talked about it last night." I fussed with the baby; I started searching through the diaper bag, pretending to look for something important, hoping I would find something before they noticed me. I had my headphones on, so they must have thought I was listening to music; but the player was off, so I could hear everything they said. "Morra and Irm and Bhetto, all three know that if they keep the rest of us from going to Linnea, they might as well move out altogether. The family will never recover."

She lowered her voice, but I could still hear. "They're talking about splitting off into a separate partnership; they'll manage the family's affairs while we're in training and after we go to Linnea. It might work." She touched Da-Lorrin's arm. "They'll go through the training with us— as our support system—but they won't cross over with us. Morra thinks Irm and Bhetto will go along with it. But the rest of us have to give them time to see the logic of it. You know how Bhetto gets."

Da half-cocked his head as if weighing the idea on his tongue to see how it tasted. "There are a lot of details to talk over, but…it might work. Whose idea was it?"

"Morra thinks it's hers," said Mom-Lu in that harder voice of hers. She turned around and saw me, as if for the first time. She took the diaper bag away and pushed me toward the other children. "Go on now, Kaer. Thank you."

I pretended to turn off my music and looked blankly at her. "What?"

She wasn't fooled. "Don't tell anyone what you overheard. That's not for casual talk, you understand?"

I flushed and nodded, then hurried off to stand by the departure gate with Big Jes. At least she trusted me a little bit.

The grown-ups must have worked out everything by themselves, because I didn't hear any more about it. We went home and nothing happened for what felt like longest time, although it was only two or three months; but it was long enough. The memory of the horses faded and I began to think that we hadn't been accepted and we weren't going to Linnea after all.

Later on I found out that the family was taking care of all kinds of business, making arrangements about money and property and inheritance—all the stuff that had to be done if you were leaving a world behind. My tenth birthday came and went before we got the word that we were approved and we were going back to New Mexico to live in a training dome.

LINNEA DOME

LINNEA DOME II HAD ONLY BEEN open for three years; it was the newest and biggest world-dome ever built, even bigger than the dino-dome. It was over twenty kilometers in diameter and the sky was 800 meters up. It was thirty klicks away from the other domes and had been built right next to the gate.

The dome was built like a bunch of suspension bridges in a circle. Tall towers surrounded it; heavy cables were strung between opposing towers to support the weight of the dome's vast roof. It was the largest enclosed space on Earth. There were 320 square kilometers of usable terrain inside. Almost all of its services were located in the towers or underground. Next to the dome there was a rounded building with transport tunnels leading in and out of it. Supplies for the dome and for the world-gate came in through underground trains.

There was no way anyone could just drive up to the dome or get into the tunnels. Access was heavily restricted. And even if you could get past the guards, the dome was separated from the land around it by a wide moat. And even if you could get across the moat, there were no doors, only high concrete walls around the base. They looked thick too. There were helicopter decks on two of the towers, but those were for emergency traffic only.

We didn't go direct to the dome; we landed at Overlook Station instead. The station was built into the neighboring cliffside and it had a great view of the entire station; only we weren't given any time to enjoy it when we arrived. First, we all had to sign consent forms and insurance waivers and training agreements.

There were twenty-five of us—us and the Kellys—counting the little-uns, so everything took awhile, and it was boring. After the paperwork was finished, we were each given an implant to swallow; then we had to wait for calibration and confirmation, and that was even more boring.

After dinner, there was an orientation session, and then we were assigned to quarters that looked like hospital rooms. That was because we had to spend three days getting "transplanted." We had to have our Earth-bacteria "terminated" and the necessary ones replaced with Linnean counterparts. That was why the rooms were like a hospital—so the doctors could watch us for allergic reactions. By now they'd pretty well gotten the hang of "bio-transplanting," so the worst we had to deal with was upset stomachs and diarrhea and a little baby vomit. Just the same, it wasn't much fun.

But finally we traded our Earth clothes for Linnean costumes and took the cablecar down to the dome. Mom-Trey thought the clothes looked silly; Nona and Shona complained that they were itchy. One of the briefing videos said that the Linneans made silk from grass fibers, but when Klin and Rinky asked the trainers about it, they said that if we wanted silk underpants, we'd have to gather the grass, thread it, weave the cloth and sew the garments ourselves. Klin got *that* look on his face and I expected him to start harvesting grass before bedtime. Rinky put dibsies on the first pair.

Outside the dome, there was a receiving station. This was one of only three access points. Everything else was self-contained. This station was the largest; it included an external monitoring facility for scouts, administors and other support personnel. The cable car slid into the docking station and connected to an airlock. There was a soft whoosh as the air pressure equalized, and then we exited into a receiving chamber where we had to pass through another set of decontamination locks. They sprayed us again and scanned us to see if all of our pills and implants were working. Then, finally, we were escorted into a long circular tunnel, big enough to drive six lanes of heavy traffic through.

An Earth-Guide took us halfway through the tunnel, where we were met by a Linnea-Guide. She was dressed as a scout and spoke only in Linnean. We hadn't learned very much of the language yet, just the most basic words, like "come," and "stop," and she wouldn't answer any questions spoken in English, so we followed mosty in silence, only occasionally whispering among ourselves.

The far end of the tunnel opened into a receiving station, where several more guides looked us over. They took away Da-Kelly's pocket watch and some of the beads and jewelry that the children were wearing—and even Nona's teddy bear, which she carried everywhere. Da-Lorrin tried to argue, "Oh, for God's sake—it's only a teddy bear," but the scouts were adamant. Mom-Trey held Nona close and comforted her anguished sobs, but the rest of us put on our nasty-faces.

Finally, we entered Linnea.

As far as we were concerned, this was the *real* Linnea, not a simulation.

We walked outside into the yellow air and the first thing we noted was the dust and the stink. Everybody wrinkled their noses. The whole world smelled of shit and sweat. It wasn't pretty. My eyes started watering immediately. And Shona asked, "Mommy, what smells so bad?" Da grumpled, but said nothing. Big Jes and Little Klin exchanged a glance. "Linneans don't know much about sewage, do they?" One of the scouts heard that and gave them a disapproving glare.

We walked down the main avenue, gawking like Chinese tourists at Disneyland. It was hard to believe this was all real. It looked like false fronts, but the couple of buildings we peeked into were real all the way through to the outhouses in the back. That explained part of the smell.

The first night, we stayed at the Boffili Hotel, down at the far end of town; at least it was away from the stink. Mom-Woo had sort of been expecting it to be the kind of hotel with nice rooms and hot baths, but it wasn't. It was just a bunch of tents built against the outer walls of Callo City, which was kind of like an old-fashioned fort; all the walls were made out of sandbags. There was no electricity, so there were no lights or televisions or computers, and if you wanted hot water you had to boil it yourself. The bathtubs were brick washtubs and you had to fetch the water from a pump outside.

Lorrin and Big Jes both laughed at the moms' annoyance. Klin said it was a test. If we couldn't handle this, we certainly couldn't handle living on Linnea, and that pretty much ended that discussion. In short order, Klin organized all the kids into a bucket brigade to bring in water for the tub and start it boiling. Big Jes and Klin brought in firewood. Mom-Lu arranged a bath schedule, almost like home, and lined us up like a car wash. We went from station to station, and all of us kids were soaped, scrubbed, rinsed, toweled and tucked into bed in less than an hour. The beds were sort of soft and sort of lumpy. They were stuffed with feathers and a couple times I got stuck with the sharp end of a feather poking through the sheet. But I slept mosty okay.

The next morning, the sun came up earlier than it should have been legally allowed to and turned the whole world orange. That ugly light again. Almost all of us shielded our eyes against it when we marched across to the community hall for breakfast. It had sandbag walls, but a canvas roof. One whole end of it was an old-fashioned kitchen, with the canvas rolled back to let the smoke out, and cooks making *real* eggs and bacon! And fresh bread that they took out of the oven and sliced while I watched! And butter that came from a real boffili cow! I was afraid to eat food that hadn't been safely processed, but Mom-Woo said this was the only kind of food we could expect to find on Linnea. It smelled different, but not completely awful.

Most of the grown-ups said they liked it, but Klin and Rinky made faces as they tasted everything. I decided I sort of liked the food, even if it was weird. They told us we could eat as much as we wanted, so I went back for seconds and thirds—until I had tasted everything. Real sausage and real jelly and real syrup on real pancakes, so that sort of made up for the lumpy beds.

After that, we were supposed to go on a walking tour of Callo City with Birdie, but everybody had to wait until Nona and I threw up. Klin started to laugh at us, but he stopped when his stomach started to hurt. That was because Big Jes' elbow bumped into it a little.

The real Callo City on Linnea was a lot bigger than this, but there was only room in the training dome for a partial reconstruction. Most of the important places were recreated here, because we would need to be familiar with them. The Boffili Hotel was built along the northwest wall, which was called Immigrant's Corner. Southeast of that was Merchant's Circle. Long Avenue stretched diagonally between them, and most of the hotels and businesses along it were nearly-exact duplicates of their counterparts on Linnea. Any Linnean passing through Callo City would have traveled up "Immigration Alley." When we crossed over, we would have the same experience as the real Linneans.

The city was up on a hill because during winter, the snow sometimes got piled as high as ten meters. And during the spring thaw, the flood waters could be as tall as a great-horse. So settlements had to be on high ground. But also, the high vantage gave the people who lived there a good lookout for range fires, boffili stampedes, kacks, bandits, tornados, hurricane storms and other dangers.

All the buildings in Callo City were built on high foundations, and they had steep roofs slanting down into deep trenches. This was so that snow couldn't pile up too deep, and when it slid down, it wouldn't block the streets. Later, when it melted, it would fill the water tanks and canals under the buildings, or it would run off down the slope into the lake. Most of the buildings had covered arcades along their sides, again with steep slanted roofs. Lorrin explained that this was so that when the winter snows came, the people would still have clear walkways.

They hadn't simulated winter in Linnea Dome yet, because the dome was still too new, but they were talking about having one in the next year or so, certainly before we crossed over. And it wasn't just to test us. The Linnean ecology depended on regular freezing and flooding, so they had to schedule floods or the forests would suffer, and the animals that lived in them too.

There were already lots of boffili and bunny-deer and kacks living in Linnea Dome, except the kacks weren't running free yet. For now, the kacks were living in a long canyon with rocky walls too steep for them to climb. Birdie said there was a plan that someday the kacks would roam free in the northern ranges of the dome, so they could feed on the herds of bunny-deer when they started to get too big. Da asked if that might not be a problem for humans, but Birdie said that all the kacks were implanted; if they got too close to a great-horse or a human, they would be automatically stunned. The techs were sure that this would work, but nobody was in any great rush to test it yet. Linnea Dome was still too new. And the kacks were awfully big.

All of the people and all of the great-horses in Linnea Dome were also implanted, so everybody's health and location could be monitored constantly. Even though the dome was supposed to be a perfect duplicate of Linnea for training colonists, it was also a laboratory for studying how this part of that world worked, so they were always tinkering and measuring and monitoring.

There were spybirds overhead all the time; we couldn't see them, but we'd been told; and I was pretty sure there were wabbits in the underbrush as well, though we never really saw them either. Sometimes we'd see dog-things chasing wildly through the grass, but we never saw what they were hounding after. There were probably cameras in the rocks and trees as well. Lorrin told us that we should assume that everything we said and did was recorded, that the intelligence engines were always watching and listening, so this would be a good place for us to start practicing keeping secrets, so we'd be in the habit when we got to Linnea.

Over two thousand species of plant, animal and insect had been transplanted from Linnea and it looked like the ecology had been perfectly duplicated, but Birdie said there were probably at least ten thousand more species that they'd missed; no place is ever as simple as it looks. I couldn't figure out what other kinds of plants and animals there might be—maybe Birdie was talking about bugs and beetles and birds and different kinds of ground-rats and burrowing things. Critters you wouldn't see normally.

Mosty we were surrounded by rolling waves of razor grass. The grass was taller than a man, and on a windy day, you could see it rippling like green fire. Later in the year, it would turn brown and brittle. Here and there, the grass was spotted with those funny-looking short furry trees, and wherever there was a pond or a lake, there were also a couple of sleeping willows. Out on the prairie, travelers who needed to water their horses always looked for willows as evidence of water.

On the second day, we all piled onto a huge wagon pulled by two great-horses for a ride across the prairie to give us a sense of what we'd find across most of the continent. Once we were out of sight of Callo City, it was pretty spooky. There weren't any landmarks. And most trails were overgrown by razor grass in a matter of days. So cities had to put up markers for hundreds of klicks in every direction, pointing travelers the right way. We passed one of them, and an outpost tower too, with semaphore flags; but mosty, once we got away from Callo City, we were on our own. We didn't see any sign of people.

We headed toward the "mountains" first, so we could see what the limits of the world were. From a distance, the mountains looked white, but when we got closer, we saw the hillsides flashing with albino aspen, flickering like the noise on an old television screen. Here and there, up and down the slopes, were scattered groves of gnarly oaks, all twisted together so badly they were mosty one big wooden knot. Birdie said that some of the older cities had walls of gnarly oaks all around them, that's how hard it was to get through an old grove—unless you were a monkli and went up into the canopy. From the crest of one of the hills, we saw a herd of boffili. Later we saw some emmos and bunny-deer.

Later, we also saw farms. It didn't look like there were that many here, but Birdie said that every farm was at least a kilometer from the nearest neighbor, so we wouldn't see a lot of them. And no, not every farm had a great-horse. There were only a dozen great-horses in this dome and they all had to be shared. There were more on the way, but it was hard work buying a horse and transporting it. The problems were enormous—in more ways than one. Birdie said that every great-horse in the dome cost a million dollars or more; that's how hard they were to bring over. And they cost another half million a year to maintain.

Some of the farms were close to Callo City, because that's how the city got most of its food, but most were far away, so the colonists could learn how to be self-sufficient. "You'll have to learn how to grow your own food," Birdie said. "And you'll probably go hungry for a while, until you pick up the knack of harvesting and preserving."

"What if we don't grow enough...?" Rinky asked.

"We won't let you starve, if that's what you're worried about," said Birdie. "But don't plan on any pizza deliveries either. If you don't grow enough crops to make it through the winter, I promise you, your subsistence rations will be only marginally better than starvation. You will have to deal with the consequences of your mistakes here."

"Ick," said Klin. "I don't like the sound of that."

"We'll just have to make sure we grow more than enough. That's all," said Da-Lorrin, but even he didn't sound too sure of himself.

"Does everybody have to learn how to farm the land?" Rinky asked.

"Farming is the most important work in the world," Birdie said quietly. "If you don't farm, you don't eat."

"But here on Earth, we don't have to farm. We have machines to do it."

"On Linnea, you won't have machines. When we send you over, you'll know how to survive on your own. Or we won't send you." Birdie was quite insistent that all of the colonists had to learn self-sufficiency. Later, some could make their way to the cities; but so far, only scouts had been to the larger settlements. They'd come back with a lot of recordings and even a few artifacts, but they hadn't tried to live there yet. Birdie didn't say so, but I got the feeling there was something weird about the cities that she wasn't ready to tell us yet.

Apparently the society of Linnea—at least this part of it—was rigidly structured. Birdie said that not all the rules had been figured out yet. There were rules for marriage and kinship and inheritance and all kinds of conditions on contractual obligations. A lot of it had to do with their religion. Birdie said we'd start learning about that right away, because there was so much to learn. For instance, Linnean marriages were only one man and one woman, and they had to be approved by some kind of council and registered in each community. Families had to live in cooperative communities so all the children could be taught at the same school. If a family wasn't part of a community, they were denied important rights and privileges. There was no way around it—at least not yet.

This was one of the most serious problems Earth people faced when they crossed over. If there was no record of your family, you didn't exist in the eyes of God. That meant you were an outlaw, a "cast-out." And if God had cast you out, then God's Servants were obligated to cast you out too. If they didn't, it was a sin on their honor. An Obedient Community had to expel outsiders immediately—and then they'd have to have a ritual cleansing to purge themselves of any taint of sin. So communities were always skeptical of strangers.

If we went over now, we would have no way to prove we were part of a community. Our scouts sometimes used the identities of dead men, and sometimes they used forged family medallions, but it was risky. They could be executed. Birdie said we were trying to get a couple of acolytes into the church at Callo City; eventually, they would be able to forge family records for our immigrants, and if that worked we would probably be okay.

And if not, Authority had a couple of other plans to try.

Birdie told us about one of those plans. Some seventy years ago, a Linnea co-op had loaded up some big wagons and left Callo City heading west. They disappeared completely and no trace of them was ever found. Using the spybirds, Surveillance tracked the probable course of the missing caravan. They didn't find anything, but they think the missing families were swept away while trying to cross one of the great rivers. Authority's plan was to recreate the lost colony with our people. But first we had to get accurate records of who was on that caravan and who they were related to, so fictitious pasts could be created that matched the histories of the folks who'd died. Birdie said they were calling it the Pitcairn Project, and if it worked, that would probably be the way we'd cross over. We'd build a little town of our own, put up some outpost markers, and wait to be discovered.

Meanwhile, we were going to start out with three months of training in Callo City. We'd spend two hours in the morning learning the language and two more hours in the afternoon. The rest of the day would be spent learning skills like chopping wood, building fires, skinning wabbits, sewing clothes, making soap, canning fruit, milling flour and all the various rituals and prayers as well. And after we'd mastered as much of that as we could, then we'd get to build a farm.

IN TRAINING

AFTER A WEEK, they moved us to a cluster of sandbag cabins on one of the hills near the city. We had one big house where we did all the cooking and family meetings, and three little houses where everybody slept. All the kids and two of the moms were in one house, and the adults split themselves up in the others.

We forgot pretty fast that we were living in a dome. If you looked real hard, maybe you could see some lines in the sky where the cables attached, or maybe when you were up high enough, you could see that the mountains looked too close. But mosty, we felt like we were really on Linnea.

We weren't allowed to wear any clothes that we hadn't made ourselves. The clothes we had been given weren't new; they were hand-me-downs. Gamma sniffed and said they made us look like refugees. She and the moms started sewing almost immediately.

I didn't like Linnean clothes. They were itchy and scratchy, especially the underwear, but we had to live totally Linnean—we had to dress like Linneans, eat like Linneans, we had to speak like Linneans, and most important of all, we had to think like Linneans. So, it didn't matter if the underwear was itchy. We just had to get used to it.

We weren't even allowed to complain in English. If somebody used an English word, everybody would pretend they didn't understand for a while before telling us the Linnean word. But there were some words that didn't translate at all, so there were some things you just couldn't say.

We had classes two days on and one day off, children and adults all together in one room; the third day, we always had church. The trainers said that we would have to forget our seven-day week, that's not how time was marked on Linnea, but most of us kids felt it wasn't fair that we didn't get any days off at all.

At first, learning the Linnean language seemed impossible—then it got harder. For instance, the Linneans didn't have the verb *to be* in their language. Words like *am, are, is, was, were* and even *become* just didn't exist. You couldn't say, "I *am* hungry," or, "My name *is* Kaer." You had to say, "I feel hunger," or, "You may call me Kaer." At first, it was hard to say anything at all, because we all had to stop and think about how to say even the simplest things.

Our teacher told us one day—in English—that this actually represented an interesting philosophical problem. If you can't say something, you can't think it, because words are the bricks out of which we build thoughts. If the language didn't have the appropriate conceptual foundation, then whole domains of thought were impossible. You can't go somewhere that isn't on the map. So, it wasn't just a matter of learning how to speak like Linneans, we had to learn how to think like them—to live in their conceptual map, not ours. Some days, we'd suddenly get an *Aha!*—and we'd understand another piece of what we were struggling with, but most days it just felt like a lot of struggle without anything going klunk.

What made it even harder was that the language wasn't spoken as much as it was sung. Kind of like French, only worse. Everything had to have a specific rhythm, which conveyed emotional context. "I feel hunger" could mean six different things depending on how you sang it—hunger for food was only one kind of hunger. There was also hunger for news and hunger for friendship and hunger for courtesy and even hunger for something that was translated as "connection," but nobody was quite sure what kind of connection. Even the simplest sentence could be a trap. "You may call me Kaer" might be a pleasant invitation to friendship or a dreadfully arrogant and offensive dismissal—the context was even more important than the content. You can't grunt your way through life on Linnea like you can on Earth.

For the first two or three weeks, the language classes felt like torture. They were exercises in frustration. There wasn't one of us who didn't break down in tears or get angry at the difficulty of the language. Big Jes said it best: "I feel like my mouth has a big bite of something that I can't chew. I just turn it around and around in my head, trying to find a place to crunch, but all I get are corners, biting me back." But the instructors persisted. They wouldn't give up. And by the fourth week, we weren't allowed to speak in any language except Linnean. If we did, we got ten demerits.

This turned out to be a good idea. There were folks from all over the world there. At any given moment, there were fifty different families in training, and at least a thousand people were going through language classes. For the kids, learning Linnean gave us a chance to play together. We were able to play with the Africans and the Asians and the Europeans and make ourselves understood, so real quick, we felt like the language was opening up doors to new friendships.

None of the Asian families would be going to the same continent we were, because they looked so different from what we were now calling the native Linneans; but some of the Africans might. Apparently, some of the Linneans held slaves. And that was really horrifying, because if they were descended from Earth people, then how could they have backslid so badly? Nobody even wanted to try to answer that question. The only way to find out what was happening would be to insert some people who could pass as slaves.

The Asian families would be going over to the "Asian" continent, as soon as an appropriate scenario could be worked out. One plan was to set them up as a parallel civilization, but the eastern continent was difficult to get to from the Linnean side of the gate, so the scouts weren't completely sure what kind of conditions obtained there. Maybe after the satellites were up. We knew there weren't any people there, because we'd had flyovers, but the terrain was very different over there, almost all mountains. But it had to be done, and it had to be done quickly, because the Linnea gate had been cofinanced by a Japanese-Chinese consortium, and the terms of their investment entitled them to at least one continent, so the Linnean Gate Authority was working to provide that access as quickly as possible before the whole thing turned into an international incident and a hundred years of lawsuits.

Every so often, some family or other would quietly disappear from the dome, and then we'd hear later that they'd dropped out of the program. Sometimes a family would try to say good-bye before they left and explain to their friends why they were leaving, but usually Authority tried to get them out quickly.

Sometimes their reasons for leaving made sense, sometimes not. They'd say that it wasn't what they'd expected, or that it was too hard for them, or they were worried about the conditions on Linnea: the lack of electricity, communication, entertainment, supermarkets, hospitals and all the other stuff they missed. Living on Linnea was going to be very hard work.

And yes—we were starting to have our own doubts too. Nobody said it aloud, of course, but there was a lot of sighing about stuff that we missed. This wasn't a vacation anymore, this was forever.

One day, Shona fell down and broke her leg. And Mom-Woo burned her arm on the stove. And Big Jes and Da-Lorrin and Klin and Parra all got sprayed by a stink-badger while they were out learning how to plow a field, and that meant that their clothes had to be burned and they had to go and do penance in the stink-house for a week. And Rinky and I said a whole bunch of bad words where the trainers could hear us and they penalized the family twenty-five work points. And finally Mom-Trey just broke down and started crying and nobody could get her to stop. The other two moms had their hands filled with washing and cooking and dirty little-uns who needed baths, and everybody was all short-tempered and angry, and Mom-Lu started yelling at Mom-Trey, telling her to save her crying for some other time and get off her fat butt and help—so of course, Mom-Trey just bawled into her hands all the more. "I don't like it here, I'm not having any fun, I want to go home. Look at my hands, my face. I look like a hag. I feel like an old woman. I just want to go home again and take a hot bath and have my hair done, and feel like a real person again—"

And that's when Irm and Bhetto and Morra came in. They'd heard everything. I thought they were going to tell us (again) what a bad idea this was and that we should just call the trainers and tell them to pull us out of here. Everyone knew they didn't like it in the dome—but instead, Morra said something I couldn't hear and pushed Irm in one direction and Bhetto in the other. Irm grabbed the little-uns and hustled them off to the bath. And Bhetto went over and started chopping up meat and potatoes for the stew. And then Morra grabbed the three moms and made them all sit down at the table for a good bawling out. I got up to leave, but Morra said, "No, Kaer, you need to hear this too." She said, "All of us have worked too damn hard for this. I'm not going to let you quit. Not after all we've been through already."

Mom-Trey started to say, "Oh, shut up, Morra. You've been against this from the beginning," but Morra said a very bad word I'd never heard her use before, and before Mom-Trey could respond to that, Morra said, "Don't even think it, Trey. I'm not going to have you or anyone else blaming me for your failure. So I'm not going to let you fail." She took

Mom-Trey by the shoulders and looked deep into her eyes. In English, she said: "This is the biggest damn thing this family has ever tried. If we don't beat this, then this family is going to fall apart—and this family is all we have. And I'm not going to let it go. Not just because you're going through menopause or anything else. Yes, I know. So what? You'll get over it. I did. We all do. But don't you know how inspiring you all are to Irm and Bhetto and me? We made a commitment to you, Trey—*our* commitment is to see you succeed in yours. You might feel like quitting today, but tomorrow you'll regret it. So go ahead, have your cry; cry as much as you want, as long as you want, until you're through crying. But save it for later. Right now, we need you to get off your fat ass and help us get dinner on the table."

Mom-Trey sniffed and said, "My ass is not fat." But she got up anyway. And she grabbed Morra and hugged her tight. And so did all the other moms too. And that's when I knew everything was going to be all right. We were going to make it.

CHURCH

AFTER THE SIXTH OR SEVENTH WEEK, our skill with the language was good enough so that the classes began to include discussions of how things worked on Linnea and how they were different from Earth. That's when things got really interesting, because just like Birdie said, everything we knew was wrong. Nothing on Linnea was like we thought.

Our teacher was this old, rumpled, scruffy-looking guy with a pot-belly and a tendency to spit, so nobody sat in the front row. His name was Novotny; he'd been on the linguistics team studying the very first videos of the Linneans after the gate was opened. He was famous for figuring out large parts of the language; and later, he was one of the first people to cross over and visit a Linnean town.

Novotny had a funny way of teaching. He would say stuff about Linnea and let us react to it and then he'd say some other stuff and we'd start arguing about it, and then he'd grin at his assistant and sit down and listen to us for as long as we kept arguing—always in Linnean. Finally, when we'd exhausted ourselves, arguing about the way things should work, he'd get up and tell us the way things *really* worked over there. And then he'd tell us the annoying part, that we didn't get a vote on it. Deal with it, he said.

The biggest argument was about the Linnean Church. Linnea actually meant *mother* or *mother-world* or *mother-goddess*. The Linneans believed that the world was the living body of God, and that God had given birth out of her own flesh to everything that walked, crawled, slithered,

51

swam or flew. Therefore, they divided all life into two categories: life which honored the Mother, and life which despoiled the Mother—and life which honored the Mother had a sacred duty to wipe out life which despoiled the Mother; that meant outcasts, hostiles and nonbelievers.

The Linneans had a nasty word for things that despoiled the Mother; they called them *maizlish*. The word meant unclean or evil or hurtful—things that were infused with the dark spirit of a *maiz-likka*. The maiz-likka were demon-spirits. They didn't come from the Mother and they owed her no allegiance. They were the spirits of coldness and death; they came out of the dark between the stars, hungering for warmth and light, of which the Mother had plenty.

Like parasites, the maiz-likka burrowed deep into the Mother's flesh, drinking her blood, killing her eggs and poisoning her children. The maiz-likka thrived in dirt and corruption, they lived in cesspools, in rotting carrion, in pus and vomit and plagues. The maiz-likka hunted beyond the edge of the horizon or high in the mountains; they circled the world with the night, always fleeing the dawn. They dived out of the darkness to prey on warm-blooded life of all kinds. The maiz-likka caused illness and death in boffili and emmos, and even in kacks. Wherever the Mother's children died, it was caused by something maizlish—and if it was serious enough, it was the work of a maiz-likka. What the maiz-likka most liked to do was infect human beings and let them do maizlish things, so human beings constantly had to watch themselves for maizlish tendencies.

According to the Linneans, the maiz-likka hated the Mother and all her children and would not return to the dark between the stars until the Mother was dead and cold, a barren rock. Therefore, it was the responsibility of all human life to seek out anything maizlish and neutralize it. Maizlish things couldn't be killed—because killing was a maizlish act—but they could be neutralized. Although sometimes the way the Linneans did it, there wasn't a lot of difference between killing and neutralizing. Many Linneans believed that the maiz-likka were so powerful and so hard to stop that eventually they *would* succeed in destroying all life, and after that the Mother herself, so they tended to be a little fanatic about maizlish stuff.

But somewhere along the way, about a thousand years ago, somebody figured out, or realized in a vision—or maybe just made it up—that the Mother had some pretty powerful defenses of her own. Whenever the Mother felt uneasy or upset or threatened by dark demonic forces, parts of herself broke off and went out into the world to act like antibodies to neutralize the maiz-likka. The Linneans called these antibodies *eufora*. The word meant *mother-piece* or *mother-spirit*.

The same way the maiz-likka demons could infect human souls, so could the eufora. The Linneans believed that the eufora visited every human during his or her life, not just once but many times, and always during moments of great emotion or joy, like when you fell in love or when you got married or when you gave birth to new life. When the eufora visited you, you would feel overwhelming happiness and peace and clarity of vision—because in that moment, you would be at one with the Mother herself. Just as the maiz-likka lived in the darkness, so did the eufora live in the sky. Their job was to watch over Linnea and her children and invigorate all life with the spirit of the Mother's grace. The Linneans had a blessing which translated simply as, "Life celebrates life."

A lot of the Linnean scripture detailed the encounters of human beings with the eufora. Sometimes people sought out the eufora; sometimes the eufora selected you, whether you wanted to meet them or not.

Sometimes also, the maiz-likka took someone over and sent warnings to all humanity through his or her voice. And sometimes the eufora sent messages too, sometimes even direct from the Mother—not exactly commandments or laws, but parts of an ever-growing covenant between the Mother and her children. The Linneans didn't have commandments—they had *agreements.*

The way it worked, if a prophet went up onto a mountain and came back with a pair of stone tablets, he wouldn't say things like, "Thou shalt not kill," or, "Thou shalt not steal." He would say, "I will not kill," and, "I will not steal." If you accepted those agreements and made them part of yourself, then you accepted that part of the covenant with the Mother. And if you didn't, well then, maybe you were a parasite on the Mother. . . .

Apparently, not all Linneans accepted all the agreements. And that was the source of a lot of social unrest over there. But the Linneans had an agreement that they wouldn't force themselves on others, so if they disagreed, they moved on. They moved to communities that had agreements they could honor. Or they kept moving on. Settlements on Linnea weren't very big, and most of them were scattered.

We had a big argument about all that. Eventually, it came around to asking how did the Linneans know if a prophet told the truth or not? Anyone could say he was a prophet and come out of the wilderness with all kinds of outlandish stories. How could you know? Maybe all the prophets had been liars or delusionaries? And of course, that's when the discussion got really interesting because Big Jes said, "Well, maybe that's true about all the prophets in the Old Testament, too... even Moses." Oops.

The Dobersons didn't like hearing that at all. They'd been very uncomfortable during the entire discussion of Linnea the Mother-Goddess, asking lots of questions and arguing and just fussing in their chairs at having to listen to such heathen ideas. They said that all they needed to know about God was in the Bible; so when Big Jes said that about all the prophets being liars or madmen, Jim Doberson took it as a personal affront. He stood up and said, "Jes, you know that I won't tolerate blasphemy in my presence, or in the presence of my wives and children. I would appreciate it if you would keep a *God-fearing* tongue in your head."

Novotny clucked at that and held up a hand. There wasn't any way to say "God-fearing" in Linnean, and Jim Doberson's construction had been clumsy and grammatically incorrect. It was hard to explain without switching to English, but finally Novotny made it clear that some words weren't allowed to be used with some other words. Words that were negative—like *angry* or *frightened* or *crazy*—couldn't be used with the words for Mother or Linnea. If you tried to talk about someone being "afraid of the Mother" like Jim Doberson had just done, they would look at you as if you were crazy. Or worse, a parasite. Doberson scowled at that.

Novotny waved at Jes. "Go ahead, now. Continue with your discussion."

The interruption had only amused Big Jes. He just grinned at Jim Doberson and said something in Linnean, which really didn't translate well, but made everybody laugh anyway. "You can put a ribbon on it if you want, but that horse turd still stinks."

Novotny gave him two points for using a Linnean phrase, and took away three points for using it inappropriately, and we all laughed at that too. "Better you should have said, 'Why do you bring old turds into the barn when we have plenty of fresh ones?'"

And that's when Jim Doberson got really angry. I think he was angrier about being embarrassed in front of the whole class than he was at the blasphemy, but he made it sound like he was angry on behalf of God. He accused Big Jes and Novotny and everybody who laughed of disrespecting God. And he was ready to do some "God-fearing" of his own, if that's what it took to stop the swearing in here. He shook his fist in the air and glowered at anyone who dared to laugh at him again.

Novotny didn't back down and neither did he apologize. If the stories were true, he'd faced a lot more scary things than Jim Doberson. He waved everybody back down into their seats and waited until we'd all stopped talking at each other. By now, we knew the drill. He was going to tell us something important.

"Forget God, forget Jesus, forget Buddha, forget Muhammad, forget the angel Moroni, forget Confucius, forget Elron, forget Manson, forget all of them. Where you're going, they don't exist. The Linneans do not tolerate heresy against the Mother." He said this next part directly to Jim Doberson, stepping right up to him. "Are we asking you to abandon your religion? No, we are not. Are we asking you to keep it private? Yes, we are. Keep it as private as how often you masturbate, or which hand you wipe your ass with. Keep it even more private than that. Because if you don't, if you give the Linneans a reason to suspect you of treason to the Mother, you can be expelled and exiled. Or worse, tortured and burned."

"I'm not afraid to die for Jesus," said Doberson. "I would be proud to stand with the martyrs."

Novotny's face clouded. The rest of us didn't have to be told that was the wrong answer, and things had just gotten very serious in the room. "Perhaps then, you should rethink your goals, Citizen."

"How so?"

"What you profess is pure selfishness. If you die, that's your choice. I have no argument with that. But dying as a public martyr endangers others—especially your family."

"I speak for my family. We will be proud to die for Christ."

When he said that, I snuck a look at his wives and children, and while a couple of them were nodding in agreement, some of the rest looked scared. How could he say that without asking them what they thought?

"And how about Jes' family? Or Milla's? Or mine, for that matter? *Your* blasphemy—yes, I use that word deliberately—puts all the rest of us at risk too. Should we die for your faith too?"

"God accepts all sinners," said Doberson. That time, some of us had to work hard to stifle our laughter, because this was getting pretty silly now.

Novotny looked more sad than angry. "That kind of attitude will endanger the entire mission." He waved his hand as if to indicate the entire

Linnea Dome and everyone in it. "You would throw away ten years of preparation and ten years of work that casually? Is your faith so important that it gives you the right to discard all the hard work of others?"

"The word of God takes precedence over everything," said Doberson, and a lot more stuff in that same vein. "We do not have the right to set aside God's commandments." And a lot of people groaned and rolled their eyes upward.

But Novotny held up his hands for silence again. As silly as this had been a minute ago, the silliness was over. This was very serious business now. "Citizen,"—and he used that word deliberately—"the strength of your faith in your God is no less than the strength of the Linneans' faith in their Goddess. As willing as you are to die for your beliefs, that's how willing they are to kill you for them."

"What they believe is pagan superstition—"

"And they would say the same about what you believe. The Son of God, born to a virgin? He died and came back from the dead? Not exactly great theology when you compare it to some of the other great faiths. Kind of a slap-dash put-together-in-a-political-hurry thing, eh?"

Doberson was bristling. I thought he was going to punch Novotny, but he held his temper. "You try to goad me, sir. I refuse to turn angry."

"No, I do not goad you, Citizen. I challenge you to think about this." Without hesitation, he pushed on. "Do you understand the principles of the Contract?"

Doberson sniffed in annoyance. "Of course, I do. Everybody does. We start learning it in first grade."

"Tell me about the Contract."

"After the war—as part of the treaty—the leaders of all the great faiths signed the Contract of Human Rights, promising to respect everyone's right to his or her own faith." If he had stopped there, he would have been all right. But he didn't stop. "But not everybody signed the Contract, you know. A lot of people saw the perfidy in that document."

"The perfidy...?"

"The Contract requires a prohibition on evangelism. As such, it gives a tool to unbelievers for the suppression of the true faith."

"You may see it that way," said Novotny. "But the existence of the Contract protects your right to believe, free of the evangelism of others. Your faith is respected under the Contract, whether you accept the Contract or not."

Doberson shrugged and muttered something about one horse turd being like every other. Novotny gave him three points for that, then turned back to the issue at hand. "You will not have the protection of the Contract on Linnea. The Linneans have no Contract. They have only one faith—the Covenant with the Mother. The agreements may vary from place to place, but the Covenant is near-universal in every place we have explored. I tell you this in sorrow, not anger, because I respect the intensity of your belief; but you will have to set aside your commitment to Jesus and replace it with a commitment to the Covenant—or you will never cross over to Linnea. You choose, Citizen."

"Don't threaten me."

"I threaten no one. You make your own choice."

Doberson glowered and muttered darkly. "And so will you. You'll come before the judgment of the Lord soon enough. All of you who serve Satan's purposes...."

"What was that, Citizen?" Novotny had heard him well enough. We all had, but Novotny apparently believed in giving a person more than enough rope with which to bungee jump....

This time, Doberson thought better of it and sat down, smoldering.

That wasn't the end of it, of course. Doberson and his family fussed and complained for days, calling it religious prejudice and communism and everything else they could think of. It was weird, really, because the Doberson family was the best disciplined of all of us. They were always head of the curve, learning the language and all the other skills of farming and building. They were the best students of all. Da-Lorrin said it was because they were bringing a preexisting discipline to their Linnean lessons. So for Jim Doberson to become so abruptly resistant was like his brain had all suddenly seized up. Mom-Woo said only, "His head is full. It can't hold any more." And then she told us to drop the subject.

The Doberson argument lasted most of the month, and a few times people got so angry they leapt out of their chairs and almost started fighting. And not everybody was against the Dobersons either. The Kellys and the O'Hares stood up and defended Jim Doberson's right to believe in God as he saw fit. That wasn't surprising, because those three families stuck together on a lot of things anyway.

Novotny didn't say much during the arguments, except to correct someone's grammar or yell at him about his *nyet kulturny* accent. Sometimes someone would ask for help with a word; sometimes he told him, but more often he just shook his head because there wasn't such a word on Linnea.

Eventually the argument just died away with no resolution at all. Nobody had convinced anybody, and everybody was tired of fighting. A few people asked Novotny to settle it; but Novotny only said, "You've already agreed to the agreement. Why do you argue with it now?" And after a while, most of us got it. After you get on the boffili, don't complain about the smell. I got a point for saying that one in class. About a week after that, the Dobersons quit the program; the Kellys and the O'Hares stayed on, but they wouldn't talk about God anymore, at least not where anyone else could hear, so everyone figured they'd probably gotten the point about learning to think Linnean.

Not every discussion was that angry; most of them were sort of funny. One conversation, we all got angry about the clothes. How come the Linneans hadn't learned how to soften linen? How come they weren't cultivating cotton? We knew they had it. How come—?

That time, there was a scout named Zindre visiting the class. She was tall and had red hair and a great smile. She was beautiful; I couldn't take my eyes off of her. She said that the Linneans *wanted* to cultivate cotton, but the weevils were more ferocious on Linnea than on Earth. Science Division was working on a weevil-specific parasite to destroy the bugs, but Cultural Division said that if cotton became practical before industrialization, it would further the institution of slavery, and we weren't ready to give these folks the tools for industrialization, so we couldn't give them cotton either. So we couldn't have underwear that didn't itch. That's when three more families dropped out. I don't think it was the underwear; I think it was because they wouldn't be allowed to invent, not without permission. Besides, I knew that Rinky was already studying how to make grass-silk, because I was helping her in my free time.

I almost asked if we could quit too, that's how much the underwear itched, and that's how little progress Rinky was making, but that's when they started teaching all the kids how to groom and feed and care for the great-horses. We went out every afternoon—we had to groom them in teams of six, they were so big—and I didn't want to stop doing that, because I'd fallen in love with Mountain and Thunder and Jumbo. So I solved the problem my own way. I stopped wearing underwear.

But all that was only the beginning. The *real* argument was still to come, and that one did turn nasty.

MERDE

WE WERE WASHING THUNDER, six of us—more than that and we got in each other's way—and Tildie was acting like a skizzy, throwing wet sponges at the rest of us and laughing when we howled at the cold water. Jaxin, who was the young scout in charge, told him to stop, but he didn't. And finally Tildie hit Jaxin right in the back of the neck and Jaxin lost his temper. He turned around and said, "Tildie! If you don't stop fooling around, you'll have to leave! And it'll cost you and your family points!"

Tildie looked startled. Nobody in his family ever talked that sternly to him. Mosty they indulged him like he was some kind of little princess. He was always talking about all the things he had at home, and how his daddy was going to let him be a girl before they moved over, and how rich they were, with real servants instead of robots, and stuff like that. So when Jaxin threatened him with loss of points, he just stood there, with dripping sponges in his hands, and instead of saying, "I apologize, Jaxin. I did a stupid thing," he got real snotty-defiant and said, "You can't talk to me like that."

Jaxin didn't answer. He put down his grooming brushes and walked around to the corner of Thunder's stall where there was a big steaming mound of fresh manure. It looked like he'd forgotten all about Tildie. He scooped up as much of the manure as he could in both hands, came back to Tildie and *dropped* it on his head, rubbing it into his hair and all over his face and neck and shoulders. Tildie howled. Everybody

59

groaned at the yickiness of it, but we laughed too, because Tildie really deserved it.

Tildie didn't know whether to cry or get angry or what. He just stood there and spluttered. "You stupid doody-head!"

Jaxin said, "Actually, you're the doody-head." And then he turned around to the rest of us. "Anyone else want to be a doody-head? No? Well, the horses still have to be groomed, so get back to work."

"That's—that's *child abuse*," said Tildie, shouting at Jaxin's back. He had to pause long enough to make up the word before he could say it. "I'm going to tell."

"No, that's *not* 'child abuse,'" Jaxin answered quietly, repeating Tildie's awkward invention in the Linnean language. "It's horse shit. And I've got plenty more where that came from. Now get your butt up that ladder and help scrub this horse."

"No. I'm going to the showers!" Tildie said.

"You walk out of here before your work is done and you'll forfeit your points, Tildie. And you can't afford to lose any more."

"I don't care," Tildie said. And walked out. Jaxin shrugged and pulled his phone from his pocket.

About fifteen minutes later, two of Tildie's moms came screaming out to the stables. They were so angry, they were talking in their native French—which Jaxin pretended he didn't understand. I knew he did, but there was a rule: if you didn't talk in Linnean, nobody had to listen or reply. But that didn't stop them from talking. The only word I understood was *merde*.

Jaxin was still up on the ladder, brushing Thunder's mane. Great-horses tend to be shaggy anyway, but during winter months, their coats get thick and matted and they need to be brushed almost every day. It wasn't until one of Tildie's moms began shaking his ladder that he looked down and said, *"Speak in Linnean or I'll put you on report!"*

"To hell with Linnean! And to hell with you!" she said in perfect English. Apparently, she believed English was only good for swearing. Or maybe she thought Jaxin didn't speak French. "You're fired!" she said. "Do you hear me? You go pack your things! You're out of a job, you cretinous little weasel!"

She and the other one flapped off, like a couple of goblin-birds, shrieking all the way. They headed off in the general direction of the Administration offices. Jaxin just shook his head. "All right, everyone. Back to work. Thunder stamps her feet because she wants us to finish today."

Neither Tildie nor anybody from his family was at dinner that night. There were empty places all over the room. Gamma said that some of the families were *having a meeting*. The way she said it, it sounded very important. After dinner, mosty the kids went off to the theater to look at the latest news from Linnea, but tonight the regular evening Meeting promised to be more interesting, so I went there instead.

Tildie's moms were all there, looking like a row of gargoyles. They had their arms folded and their jaws stuck out and their eyes were blazing. Rinky whispered to me, "Medusa and her sisters are here," and we both giggled, which got us a dirty look from Mom-Lu.

Chief Administor Moffin came in to lead the Meeting. He didn't always do that, only when the subject was important. It was pretty obvious that whatever else had been planned, tonight's Meeting was going to be about horse manure.

Administor Moffin spoke in fluent Linnean, and several times he had to be reminded to speak slower so the rest of us could understand him. He said, "Some of you may have heard about the disobedience at the stables today. The Cretonne family has registered a protest with my office and I've asked the Scout Training Board to review the circumstances." I glanced over at Tildie's moms. They looked smug, as if they were about to be awarded some kind of a prize.

"The Board has reviewed the video and found that Scout Cadet Jaxin's actions were . . . entirely appropriate for the circumstance." This provoked yelps of surprise and outrage all over the room. Moffin rang his bell for silence. He had to ring it several times before the room quieted down. It was a big heavy thing and it had a very sharp clang.

He glanced around sternly. "First, let me remind you that we will speak only in Linnean here. Second, we will follow the customs of your intended Linnean subculture. *Acting as a Linnean horse trainer*, Cadet Jaxin responded entirely in character to the insubordination and defiance of trainee Tilden Cretonne. The Scout Board has put a commendation into his record."

"A commendation?" Marie Cretonne came shrieking to her feet. "For abusing my child?!"

"He did what any Linnean horse trainer would have done. He had not only the right, but the *responsibility* as well to punish the child according to Linnean law."

"But this isn't Linnea!" She spoke in English. "This is Earth, and Earth laws apply, and I demand an Earth court."

"*Speak in Linnean,*" he reminded her.

She looked flustered, then rephrased her comments. "We have not yet crossed over to Linnea. We still live on Earth. Therefore Earth laws apply."

Administor Moffin shook his head. "No. Please reread your contract. Perhaps you've forgotten that you agreed to abide by Linnean standards when you moved into this dome. Regardless of any other consideration, Linnean custom, law and tradition reign as the sole authority *in here*. Legally, you are already on Linnean soil. Now, sit down." Something about the way he said it—they sat.

Moffin looked back to his notes. "Additionally, the Scout Board recommends a loss of fifty work points for Tilden Cretonne as penalty for his refusal to accept the authority of Cadet Jaxin." More outraged yelps from the gargoyles, quickly stifled. "—And the loss of another hundred work points levied against Janine and Marie Cretonne for refusing to speak Linnean when ordered to by Cadet Jaxin." He peered over his glasses at the Cretonnes. "For the moment, I have ignored the outbursts of English in this room. I do not have to. If I hear any more English or French words, I will levy additional penalties." Marie Cretonne opened her mouth, thought better, and sat down again.

Administor Moffin saw that and nodded, then he glared around the room at everybody else. "Understand this," he said. "No matter what happens in this dome, no matter who does what to whom, *you will respond as Linneans!* You will think and act like Linneans at all times. Your lives depend on it. The lives of the people around you depend on it. The lives of countless people you have never met will depend on your ability to represent yourselves as native Linneans. If you cannot make and keep this commitment, my office will be open all night tonight and all day tomorrow for the acceptance of resignations. Any family choosing to resign may do so. We will levy appropriate financial penalties, of course. I will now adjourn this meeting." He rang his bell one more time and walked out of the room.

Tildie's parents were the first ones out the door after him. And several other families followed without saying a word. I looked over at our moms and they were shaking their heads sadly. Some of the other parents whispered together. Some just sat sternly by themselves.

The next day, Tildie's family was gone, and so were two other families, including Jik and Jin and their parents.

We talked about it at home for a long time too. The fact that we understood all the whats and the whys didn't reassure us. While it sort of meant that we were finally learning to think like Linneans a little bit, it also meant that we were leaving behind our Earth feelings too. And Big Jes, who usually made all of us laugh, was the saddest of all because up until now, he hadn't given much thought to how much we were leaving behind. So things were plenty grim for the next week or two while folks sorted out how they felt about that.

And meanwhile, three more families bailed out. They said, "They have too much money invested in us. They can't afford to have too many families quit. They need us. They'll call us back." That's what they believed anyway. We knew we wouldn't be seeing them again. Not here, and certainly not on Linnea. You either agreed to the agreements or you didn't.

A CHOICE

I DIDN'T MISS TILDIE ALL THAT MUCH, but Jik and Jin were fun, and I was sorry to see them go. I asked Mom-Woo if we were going to quit too. She said no. Morra and Irm and Bhetto wouldn't let us. And that made Mom-Lu and Mom-Trey laugh.

Mom-Woo explained, "When we move over to Linnea, they get all the money and property we leave behind. They can hardly wait to see us go. But they have to go through the training with us; that's part of the contract."

"In case they change their minds and decide to come with?"

"That's not likely, but yes, in case they change their minds."

"I'm still going to miss Jik and Jin."

"I'll miss them too, sweetheart. But they might not be out of the program yet. They might transfer to another dome and start training for one of the barren worlds. Or they might come back here. They have a three-month cooling off period to recommit to their agreements. The Authority doesn't lock people out; they either choose to be here or not."

"Does that mean Tildie and the gargoyles might come back too?"

"I don't think so. They were having a lot of other problems fitting in. Tildie's little adventure was a convenient excuse for them to quit and be righteous about it. But it wasn't any secret among the parents that the Administration was thinking of dropping them from the program. That's why they accused Jaxin of hurting Tildie. So they could quit and not be penalized. They forgot that the Administration has cameras everywhere.

That's why we don't speak English even here in our private quarters. We have to think like Linneans, just like Administor Moffin said. And that means we have to live like Linneans everywhere." Mom-Woo pulled the covers up to my chin. "Now get some sleep and tomorrow we'll talk about sewing you a new kilt."

But just because we said it, that didn't mean we could do it as easily. After Tildie's family and the others left, things felt different—like maybe the Gate Authority wasn't as much on our side as we'd thought. And I got the feeling that some of the parents resented the scouts now. Nobody said anything, but I saw people exchanging looks or lowering their eyes or just not raising their hands in Meeting anymore.

It bothered me, because Tildie's family had made its own choice. In fact, Administor Moffin made a big speech, saying the same things Mom-Woo had said, about how all of us would select ourselves in or out by our commitment. Nobody did it to us, we did it ourselves, so we had no one to blame for our mistakes. We had all agreed to the Covenant with the Mother Linnea when we entered the dome, so we had no right to complain when they asked us to keep our agreement. It made sense when Administor Moffin explained it that way, but it still annoyed a lot of folks, because so many of the agreements seemed so silly. But they only seemed silly if you looked at them with an Earth-mind. If you looked at them with a Linnean-mind, they didn't seem silly at all.

And Jaxin told us kids the same thing. We'd see the importance of our lessons once we got over to the other side—if we got over at all. The incident with Tildie's family had caused the Training Board to reevaluate large parts of the program. Originally the idea was to train us as rigorously as the scouts, but if families couldn't handle the training, then perhaps it was a mistake to send families over. But they didn't dare reduce the level of the training either.

Finally, about two weeks later, the Training Board held a special meeting about it. Administor Moffin presided. He didn't look any friendlier than before. I'd heard he had a lot on his mind. Some kind of incident had occurred on the other side, but nobody would tell us what had happened. Anyway, he rang his bell and started talking almost immediately.

"We cannot reduce the level of your training. We cannot. We will not risk your lives, nor will we risk the lives of any of our scouts. The Gate Authority has a contingency plan and they've authorized me to present it to you. You have a choice. Any family here can abandon participation in this program, *without penalty*, and we will transfer you to a different program, a different gate going to one of the uninhabited worlds—or you can recommit to a higher standard."

"What do you mean by a higher standard?" That was Da-Lorrin.

"For one thing, we may have to lengthen your time in training. For another, we may not let as many of you pass through Callo City on Linnea as we had planned. Some of you will have to head directly west instead. We intend to reevaluate everything for its appropriateness to the long-range plan. And no—" he added, "this has nothing to do with the Cretonne family. Some of you may have heard that they've filed a lawsuit. We expect the court will dismiss the suit, as it has done with similar suits in the past. In the meantime, we have to protect all of our people on Linnea, and all of you who want to cross over. So spend some time among yourselves, talking it over. Talk to our scouts, ask them what they think. We'll talk again next week."

Walking up the slope back to our cabins, Gampa said, "A cold splash of water really wakes you up, doesn't it?" Rinky and I started a fire and Gamma put up water for tea. The family settled around the big table and Mom-Lu started slicing bread and put out a plate of fresh-churned boffili butter. We hadn't earned enough points for jelly yet.

Morra and Bhetto and Irm sat quietly at their end of the table, not speaking, but looking very grim. So finally, Mom-Lu said, "For God's sake, Irm, spit it out before it poisons you."

"We can't quit," said Irm.

"Of course not," said Parra. "You've already made plans for our money."

"No. Uh—no—" said Irm, struggling hard to find the right words in Linnean. "We can't quit because…because—oh, *shit*." Irm couldn't find the right words and shifted to English. It sounded strange to hear English words again. "We can't quit because this is the best thing this family has ever done. Look at the children, they're happier than I've ever seen them. For God's sake, they have roses in their cheeks like real kids should! And look at yourselves, you all smile and laugh and joke like you're having the time of your lives! Yes, it's hard work—but so what? It's the kind of work that makes us happy to get up in the morning and get started. I don't want to quit because I'm having too much fun—a lot more fun than I ever had on Earth. And so are the rest of you!"

For a moment, everybody just stared at Irm. Even Morra and Bhetto looked shocked. And then Mom-Lu wiped her eyes with her hankie and Mom-Woo started laughing quietly. And Da-Lorrin walked over to Irm and offered his hand. And then everybody was hugging and crying all at the same time.

After a bit, Irm said, "When we got here, during those first few weeks at the beginning, I saw what you were all going through, the way you looked at Morra and Bhetto and me. How you all kept grimly pushing on, just so you wouldn't have to listen to us say, 'I told you so.' I'll tell you, that hurt. We felt like outsiders. We felt like...like you didn't believe our commitment to the success of this family. So we pushed ourselves harder than any of you. I don't think you noticed, but we didn't want you going over with any thoughts that Morra and Bhetto and I didn't fully support you, because we do. We've talked about this a lot, looking for ways to make up for our bad beginning. But I guess that was just something we had to do so we could get here." Auncle Irm said, "I know I won't fit in over there. Just look at me. That's why I was afraid of this. I didn't want to be abandoned. I didn't want to lose you. Because I love you all. I guess I need to say that more. But in the last two weeks, well...it feels like all the joy around here has died. And we've all had our noses rubbed in it, what it looks like when a dream is abandoned. And I don't like it any more than any of you do. I don't like seeing my family this way. I love you too much. We're not quitters. We're not failures. No thanks. As far as we're concerned—Morra and Bhetto and I—tomorrow, we all go back down the hill and sign this family up for whatever training it takes. This family doesn't quit."

And then there was a whole bunch more hugging and laughing. Gampa clapped Irm on the back and Rinky ran over to smother all of them with kisses, and Cindy and Parra apologized for everything they had thought. And for a while, it felt like the old times again. We knew it wouldn't last—the job had suddenly gotten a lot harder—but somehow in that moment, we all knew that we would handle whatever came our way.

MOUNTAIN

AFTER ADMINISTOR MOFFIN had made his speech, almost all the families came back and renewed their commitment, signing new contracts to continue the program, no matter how hard it got. A little while after that, Moffin transferred out and they promoted Jaxin's ma to take his place. Administor Rance seemed a lot quieter and a lot more thoughtful than Moffin, but nobody doubted her commitment. She had lived on Linnea almost since the day the gate first opened. She knew almost everything about Linnea. Shortly after she took over, Jaxin and several of the other scouts went back to Linnea, and some new scouts came in to replace them.

And after that, things got a lot stricter. But also a lot more fun. Both at the same time.

We took our language tests, which were both written and spoken and lasted two days. And even though some of the family stumbled over a lot of unfamiliar words, we still did well enough as a group to graduate to second grade. We were all pretty happy about that. And besides, it qualified us to start building our own house, just like we would do someday on Linnea.

But first we had to build a great-wagon, which was kind of like a covered wagon, only built to the same scale as a great-horse, so it was more like building a two-story house on wheels—*big* wheels, almost as high as the horse's rump. You could walk underneath the bottom of it without having to stoop down.

The wagon had ladders and stairs and compartments all over it. It was a lot more complicated than it looked. And inside, it was like a bus or a truck, both upstairs and downstairs. But it had to be big enough and sturdy enough to carry the belongings of a large family. And it also had to be strong enough to serve as a traveling fortress too. Most families our size built two or even three great-wagons for their cross-country trek, but for the purposes of the dome, we only needed to build the one. Just to show we could do it. On Linnea, though, we knew we'd have to build three.

When we were done, Aunt Morra had all the kids paint pink Linnean daisies on the sides of the wagon, and after that we all called it the daisy-wagon. Later, we found out that we'd actually reinvented a common Linnean tradition, so we all felt pretty good about that. We got twenty-five bonus points for that too.

Finally the day came that we loaded the wagon with all the supplies we'd earned, and we drove it out to our "farm"—the ten acres of prairie assigned to us. That was one of the best days of all. We didn't have a horse of our own—no one in the dome really did; all the horses had to be shared—but when we moved we were given a horse to use for the day, and we had to take care of it as if it were our own.

The day before we moved, the horse we were supposed to use, Lead-foot, threw a shoe; so instead we got Mountain. The Administration didn't usually lend Mountain out to families because she was supposed to be only for the use of the scouts. She was the biggest horse in the dome; but she was also one of the gentlest and best behaved. So because we'd done so well with our wagon and because they didn't want us to fall behind schedule and because they wanted to start winter soon, they made a special exception for us. I was thrilled.

Mountain was big and beautiful and probably the smartest great-horse in the dome as well. She was famous for poking her nose into second-story windows looking for her grooms whenever she got hungry. And there was a story that she'd scared the yell out of Molina's new bride on their wedding night. But that was a long time ago. Molina was head-groom now, and he warned us that we had to treat Mountain like a *lady* or she'd just ignore us. She'd head back to the stable, wagon and all. Molina said she could be pretty headstrong if she wanted to be, but I guessed anything that big would be. Mountain looked more like a force of nature to me than a lady; but she had such a sparkle of wisdom in her eyes that I fell in love with her at first sight.

I wished she could have been our horse all the time; Aunt Morra said I wished that about every horse I met, and she was right, I wished we could have a thousand great-horses. But Mountain was special. She pulled our wagon out to our site with barely a grunt, like she knew she was doing us a big favor. She shook her huge head proudly and stamped her feet impatiently while Lorrin staked out the boundaries of our house. I guess she thought he was taking too long. Then she plowed up the ground as good as any Earth-tractor could have done. All of us took turns riding the plow. We had to weigh it down; the ground was *hard*. Then we put a bulldozer-yoke on Mountain, and she began pushing the dirt back and forth into huge piles. She knew her job better than we did. Before midday we had a hole in the ground big enough and deep enough to bury a couple of buses, or a good-sized tube house.

After lunch, Rinky, Klin and I drove Mountain back to Callo City, even though that meant we'd have to walk the five kilometers back. But we didn't mind. We got back to the city while the sun was still high, so we decided to feed Mountain, then wash her and groom her, so Molina would feel good about having let us use her. When there are only three, it takes a *long* time to wash a great-horse, especially when you have to pump every liter of water yourself, but Mountain seemed to enjoy it and we had a lot of fun. And Molina was so impressed that he drove us home, saving us a long walk. That was the best day I ever had in the dome.

Now we started the hard part of the job—building a house. Well, actually a burrow. On Linnea, we wouldn't find much lumber on the prairie, so we would have to build our house out of dirt. The easiest way was to dig a hole and put a roof on it—a strong roof, because there might be boffili or emmo stampedes. Some of the herds were so large that even stampeding they could take two or three hours to pass overhead. We had to dig a burrow strong enough to withstand that. If we could do that, then we would prove we could live on Linnea. That was the test.

We already had the hole. Mountain had dug most of it, but there was still a lot of work to do, shaping the walls and hardening them. Lorrin and Big Jes and Klin were still designing, and we would have to make a lot of bricks, no matter what, so we expected to be living under the stars for several weeks. Sort of.

They weren't real stars. They were just the lights in the sky; and it wasn't a real sky, it was just the dome. But it looked real enough. Almost too real. That first night, I had a lot of trouble falling asleep. Even though we'd worked hard all day, it felt like someone had left the lights on. I'd never seen so many stars so bright and beautiful before, but Lorrin said that was how the stars really looked without a dirty atmosphere in the way. That was hard to believe, and I spent a long time on my back just staring up at the lights in the sky. Wondering.

After a few days, though, I stopped wondering how the Dome Authority had created such a convincing illusion and simply accepted it that we were already on Linnea. That was the easiest way.

THE DAY OF THE SEA

THE LINNEANS COUNTED TIME IN TRIADS. A week was nine days long, and there were three weeks to a month. On Threeday, you went to a morning service at church, on Sixday you went to an evening service, and Nineday was an all-day Sabbath. In this way, the people of Linnea reenacted the Nine Days of Creation when the Mother of the World created human beings.

The first few times we went, the Linnean services were very confusing, mosty because I didn't understand what was happening, but later, after I learned the words to the songs, I started to enjoy going. The Linneans celebrated the changing seasons, so every service was a little different from the last, because everything cycled with the calendar. There were ritual dances to mark each week of the calendar, and those were a lot of fun. The game was to get everybody in the room participating in each circle. And when we did get everybody circling, we cheered because that meant that the Mother would bless us for the completion of our intention.

As much fun as that was, I liked the singing the best. Those who wanted to play the part of the wind would sit on the upper balcony; it ran all the way around the whole building. And at key moments in the service, we would make whispering or shooshing or howling sounds. The little-uns loved that the most, so I spent a lot of time up there in the balcony with them. Gamma and Gampa usually sat up there with us too.

Down on the main floor, the adults sat in a circle around the center dais, a platform representing the house of the Mother. They would sing the songs of the sun and the rain and the good dark earth, and they would try to drown us out. But their songs had happy hand-clapping and exuberant words, melodies easy to sing and piquant harmony that made your feet dance—and our song had only sounds of shooshing and whispering. The adults always had stronger and louder voices, and the song would rise buoyantly to the rafters, drowning us out.

Sooner or later, we couldn't help it, some of us in the balcony would start singing along with the adults below. Their songs were more fun than just shooshing and giggling. And pretty soon, everybody in the whole church would be loudly singing the songs of the sun and the rain and the good dark earth—and the songs of the wind would be banished from the sea. At least for as long as we kept on singing.

Even people who couldn't sing had a good time, because if you couldn't sing you could bring an instrument—a drum or a crackler or a jubilator,which was kind of like a drum, but with six or twelve strings tight across its surface. You played it like a guitar or a banjo, either strumming or picking. There were a lot of other instruments too, mosty handmade. During the winter, families had time to invent different kinds of noisemakers and music boxes, and Jaxin told us there was quite a spirited competition every spring, when the new services began. All spring long, families would bring their new instruments to services, adding a new noisemaker to every service, each trying to outdo the other, building to a grand celebration of beautiful jangly enthusiasm on the third Nineday.

Three Ninedays completed a month, so the third and last Nineday was always the grandest day of the month. Kind of like a New Year celebration. The Nineday to celebrate the end of three months was the grandest day of the season. Then there was a period of three, six or nine more days—depending on the calendar—until the next season began.

During the times of no-season, there were different kinds of celebrations. One holiday was the celebration of the wind. It was celebrated twice yearly, once between winter and spring and once between summer and autumn. During the celebration of the wind, the people of the Mother honored and thanked the wind for bringing the rain to the great sea of grass. Of course, you couldn't properly thank the wind during the Mother's seasons, so you had to do it during a time of no-season. If the wind hadn't brought rain in the season past, the celebration became the cursing of the wind. In that way, the people reminded the wind of its responsibility to the Mother's green sea.

Another holiday, held in the no-season between autumn and winter, was the Day of the Sea, when the living were permitted to visit with the spirits of those who had gone to live in the sea. On the Day of the Sea, people dressed in brown clothes and built houses of grass for their loved ones in the sea to come and live in for the day. The celebrants would bring various carved and woven totems representing places or moments or things in the lives of the spirits for whom the houses had been built. They would bring baskets containing the favorite foods of the spirits, so they could nourish their memories of their lives.

Families would often start building their houses days before the celebration, and if they had many people to remember, they would carve or weave many totems as if they were inviting all the spirits they knew to a great grand party.

On the Day of the Sea, when the house was completed and furnished with baskets of food and an altar of totems, the people who built it would invite the spirits to enter. Then they would enter themselves. Inside, the oldest living person would pour a cup of tea for everyone present, including the spirit or spirits who had been invited to visit. Then the celebrants would share themselves with the spirits, thanking them for their gifts—their heritage, their traditions, their care and their love. They would tell the spirits why they had brought this item or that, what they were remembering and why it was important to them. They would tell the spirits what was happening in their own lives and what they planned next. And finally, they would ask the spirits to watch over them in the name and the service of the Mother for the coming year. In a large family, the Day of the Sea could take all day.

In the evening, all the grass houses would be taken down and gathered together in a huge pile, and a great bonfire would be held. Part of the preparation for the Day of the Sea meant clearing a great circle of grass, lest a spark from the bonfire find its way into the sea. This was usually considered an ill omen, and if the spark ignited a range fire, somebody's spirit had been really pissed off—maybe by not being remembered or by being remembered the wrong way. A fire was always seen as a punishment. But mosty, the spirits were joyous and grateful for another happy day with their loved ones. As the smoke rose into the air, it carried the jubilant spirits high into the sky. There, the impish wind would catch them and carry them off to the land beyond the horizon, where they would return to their lives in the sea. And finally nothing would be left but the twinkling stars and the dark rustling of the distant sea, whispering its thanks for another good year.

The next day, winter would begin.

THE OLD WOMAN AND THE WIND

A VERY LONG TIME AGO, in the time before time, an old woman lived in the grass. She lived in a house of grass, she slept on a bed of grass, and she wore a dress of grass. She sang of the sun and the rain and the good dark earth and the grass grew tall and strong around her.

One day, while she was singing, she began to hear a new song in the world. She didn't hear it every day, but she heard it often enough. Sometimes she heard it as a soft whisper, and sometimes she heard it as a distant howl, and sometimes she heard it not at all—but it always came back again. Sometimes it harmonized with her song, and sometimes it whistled and roared and drowned out her song altogether. And every day, the new song sounded just a little bit closer than the day before....

So one day, when the new song whispered so close it sounded as if it hid just below the near horizon, she sang back to it across the sea of grass. "Who sings there? And what do you sing of?"

And the answer came back on a breeze of air that lifted her hair away from her face. "I sing of me."

"What a beautiful song you sing," said the old woman.

"I sing of the sky and the clouds that sail in the sea of air," said the voice.

"Ahh," said the old woman. "I thought so. Only the wind can sing such a beautiful song."

"Would you like to sing with me? I will teach you my song," invited the wind.

"Thank you, but no. I sing of the sun, the rain and the good dark earth. And when I sing my song, the grass grows tall and strong."

"No, you cannot sing that," the wind replied in an angry burst. "Your song will clash with mine. Here the land belongs to me and I will not permit you to sing any song but mine."

But the old woman just shook her head. "Your song has a great and powerful beauty and it gives me great joy to hear it. But your song celebrates only the sky and the clouds that sail in the sea of air. My song celebrates the rest of the world, the sun and the rain and the good dark earth. Together our two songs make a joyous noise greater than either of us alone can sing. Let us celebrate each other's partnership in the greater glory of the world."

But the wind would have none of that. "No. I will not allow you to diminish my power. I rule this land, not you, and we will sing no song but mine."

The old woman bowed her head sadly, and for a moment, the wind thought it had won. But then the old woman raised her head and said, "I will sing my song and you will sing yours. We will sing together or we will sing apart. You can choose how you wish to sing. You can sing in harmony or discord. But I will not leave here, nor will I stop singing of the sun and the rain and the good dark earth."

At this, the wind howled in fury, whipping the old woman's hair about her shoulders and flattening her robe against her body. "Hear me, old crone. I will drive you from this land, and I will sing alone."

"Hear me, angry wind," the old woman shouted back. "Hear me well—" She wrapped her robe around her and turned her back to the furies of the wind. She began to sing as joyously as she could of the sun and the rain and the good dark earth. The wind howled around her, but she ignored its fury.

She sang her song both soft and loud, but always sweet, and her gentle notes soared generously above the deeper moaning of the angry wind—and somehow the two songs became as one. The grass grew tall and strong around her, twice as tall as a man. It waved in the wind, keeping time with both songs, rippling in joyous celebration of the sun and the sky, the clouds and the rain, and the sea of grass and the sea of air above it.

And to this very day, if you go out into the sea, you can still hear both of the songs, sometimes separate, and sometimes together, but always clear.

GOD'S THUMB

WE WENT TO CHURCH EVERY THIRD DAY, just like we would do when we crossed over to Linnea, only, because we were in training we also had classes *about* the church services, so we would understand the why as well as the what. On Threeday we had an afternoon class after services. On Sixday, we had a morning seminar. On Nineday, we had no training sessions at all, just a real Sabbath.

We attended the Threeday seminar as a family. Even though a lot of the discussions were held at the adult level, everybody was supposed to participate. The course leaders said that it was necessary. If the Agency was going to put children into a new world where they would have to take on the responsibilities of adults, then the Agency had a corresponding obligation to give the children the corresponding adult privilege of discussion. The course leaders said that a full understanding of the responsibilities meant that we would be able accept them as our own commitment instead of as an authoritarian restriction placed on us by someone else. All of which meant that we spent a lot of time sitting through stuff that made no sense at all—or if it did make sense, we couldn't understand why anyone would bother with it. Who cared? We wanted to get outside and feed the horses or make bricks or build our house.

But even though most of the discussions were boring, there were a few times when it was very exciting too—mosty when one family or another raised the issue of *why* we had to give up our old religions. That's when the arguments broke out. Sometimes the arguments were already raging even before we got to the seminar.

Some of the families, the Kellys in particular, always sat through the morning service as if they were determined not to enjoy it. They looked as if they'd been forced to suck sourberries. When it came time to sing the Mothersong, they'd just sort of mumble and mouth the words. Only the littlest Kellys, sitting up in the balcony with the rest of the kids, would get into the spirit of the moment. The grown-ups just looked pained and insincere.

No matter how much everyone else around them tried to get them to just relax and have a good time, the Kellys—and a couple other families who always sat with them—acted like they had been dragged to church against their will.

Afterward, everybody else might be feeling joyous and exuberant, with the Mothersong still bouncing in our hearts—and the Kellys would take their children aside and whisper to them. Once, while we were walking up the hill to the seminar building, I asked Patta what her da had said to her after church that morning. She didn't want to tell me, but I promised not to tell anyone, so finally she admitted that her da was worried about losing the true faith. So he reminded everyone in the family every day: "Remember, we go to do the work of the Lord. These heathen ways have no power over us. We only pretend to share them so we can go to the new land of Canaan."

At dinner that night, I shared that information with the rest of the family. There was a brief embarrassed silence, as if I'd brought up a subject we really shouldn't be talking about, but then Gamma said, "No wonder they all look so constipated."

And then Gampa said, "I suggest a simpler explanation for the way the Kellys look. They've fallen out of the ugly tree and hit every branch on the way down."

And then Mom-Woo said, "Kaer, you promised Patta you wouldn't tell. Now you've broken your promise. And the rest of us have to pretend we don't know. Please don't put us in that position again."

"Yes'm."

But the Linnean religion was a big issue for everyone. It meant giving up all our old holidays. Especially my favorites—Halloween, Thanksgiving and Christmas. And my birthday.

And we talked about that a lot at the Threeday seminar. The trainers were very patient. One of them was an old white-haired man in a wheelchair. His name was Whitlaw, and we only saw him once or twice a month, because he had to fly in special just for the seminar. He spoke in English, because he was a visiting lecturer.

The first time he came in, he talked about parallel worlds. "All these different worlds exist, each in its own timeline, each one a reflection of this one. We haven't even begun to discover a hint of what's possible. Think about it. There may be a million different versions of yourself out there. And very likely, there's a million different versions of me, teaching you or a million someones like you what they most need to know, all of us living a million different lives and dying a million different deaths. Do you ever wonder how many different ways you could die? I sometimes do. I hope I have died well." And then he grinned. "In this timeline, I intend to die in bed with a beautiful redhead. At the age of ninety-two. Shot in the back by a jealous husband."

But today, he spoke with a much more serious tone. "Don't think we don't understand what you're giving up. We do understand. To put aside your culture, your heritage, your traditions, your cherished memories—that's a terrible break in your identity. It's an enormous loss that can't be replaced. We know you'll never feel really comfortable with the worship of the Mother, because you'll always be aware of what's been taken away from you."

He wheeled his chair up and down the aisles, talking to each of us directly. "You think I haven't seen you in church? Some of you look like you have red-hot pokers up your butts—and I can't think of any better way to advertise that you're a maiz-likka than that. The celebration of the Mother is supposed to be a cleansing of sorrow, and an inspiration of new energy for the work still to come. It's supposed to be joyous and jubilant. If you look like you're in pain—well, only a maiz-likka would find the celebration of the Mother painful.

"Yes, we know it *hurts*. And we know why. We can probably tell you more about it than you know yourself. You're afraid of losing who you are, what you believe, what you stand for. Going to Linnea means giving up your whole world—and not everything the new world has to offer is big enough or intense enough or powerful enough to replace what you're giving up. Do you think you're the first ones to go through this? You're not. Everyone who goes through the training here experiences a profound sense of loss and abandonment. And it doesn't go away. You just learn to live with it. Some people can't deal with it and they have to drop out of the program—or they change their commitment and join the support service teams instead. But it's part of the job, part of the service, part of a much larger goal that will take decades or even centuries to accomplish.

"We know it isn't easy for most of you. That's why we work so closely with you. We want you to succeed. What's wanted and needed here is simple to say, but hard to achieve. Each of you, in your own head and in your own heart, has to find a way to make the Linnean faith work for you. You have to reinvent yourself, so you can create the same joy and strength for yourself out of the celebration of the Mother that you find in your respective Earth religions.

"Are we asking you to convert? Yes, in a sense we are. And no, in a larger sense, we are not. We are asking you to change the way you say your prayers—we are not asking you to pray to a different god."

When he said this, I turned around in my seat to look back at the Kellys. Gamma immediately tapped my leg and made me turn forward again, but not before I saw how red-faced Buzzard Kelly was. He looked like he had the worst case of I-Don't-Wanna-Be-Here I'd ever seen.

But Mr. Whitlaw wheeled himself right up to the Kellys, so then it was all right to turn around and look. Whitlaw said, "I'll give you this. You try it on and see if it works for you. It's like a new jacket. If it fits, it's yours. If it doesn't fit, put it back on the rack and try another one. All right? Here goes.

"Suppose, just suppose, that there's only one God for the entire universe. You can wrap your head around that idea, can't you? You probably already have. That's the core idea for almost every major religion on Earth. 'There is no God but Allah.' Everybody else says the same thing, too; they just plug in a different name.

"And the way we all get along together is that we pretend that all the different names aren't different Gods. They're just different names of the same God. And this relieves us of the responsibility of having to kill all the unbelievers. *Whew!* Instead, we just try to convert them while we try to keep them from converting us. This lets us keep our self-righteousness without having to risk getting nailed up on crosses or burned at stakes or put on the rack. Much more civilized, eh?"

He looked directly at Buzz Kelly. "I can't think of anything sillier than killing someone because you don't like the way he says his prayers, can you?"

Kelly didn't answer directly. He just sort of grunted and shook his head curtly. More a rejection than a reply.

Abruptly, Whitlaw wheeled around to face the rest of us. "So—the question for the rest of us remains. How does a sane and rational and *faithful* human being stay true to God? No, put your hands down. It was a rhetorical question. I'm going to give you the answer.

"You do it by remembering that God *is* the one God. And he—or she—has many manifestations. Many different faces. Whatever may be appropriate for the time and place. Here on Earth, God manifests the way God manifests. On Linnea, God manifests as the Mother of the World. Here, visualize it this way." He held up his hand and wiggled his stubby pink fingers. "This is me, right?"

He pointed his index finger at Da and wiggled it. "Is this me?"

Da nodded.

He waggled his pinky at Auncle Irm. "Is this me?"

Irm said, "It's part of you. Yes, it's you."

"Good." Whitlaw stuck out his thumb at me. "Is this me too?"

"Yes."

"Thank you." He turned back to the rest of the room. "Three different people. Each one has a different experience of me. Index finger, pinky, thumb. But however I manifest, I'm still Whitlaw, aren't I? So if I can show up in different ways to different people, why can't God?"

I started to giggle.

Whitlaw turned to me. "Yes, Kaer?"

"I was just laughing at the idea of God in your thumb."

Whitlaw smiled. "But why not? If that's where God needs to be, and that's what you need to see at that moment, then God lives in that thumb, doesn't he? If God lives everywhere, then God lives in Linnea too. Doesn't she? And if you pray to the Mother of the World, isn't that the name of God on Linnea?" I must have been frowning, because he asked, "Do you think God doesn't manifest on Linnea?"

I shook my head. "I don't know."

"Okay, so imagine this. Imagine a place where God doesn't manifest."

I didn't know how to answer, so I didn't say anything.

"You're having trouble imagining such a place, aren't you? If there were such a place that had no manifestation of God, what would we call it? Want to take a guess?"

"Hell?"

"Right. A place without God would be Hell. So do you think Linnea is Hell?"

"Um...no. I don't know."

"Good answer. All right, so let's go back to Hell for a minute. If you were in Hell, could you pray?"

"I guess so. Do they allow praying in Hell?"

"They might. I'll find out when I get there. I'll send you a postcard."

He grinned. "But even if they did allow prayers, do you think God could hear your prayers in Hell?"

"Um...I don't know. I thought God hears all prayers."

"Well, think about it. If God can't be found in Hell, then God isn't there to hear you, right?"

"Okay, right."

"So if there's a place where God can't hear your prayers, that's Hell too, right?"

I nodded.

"Good. Thanks." He started to wheel away, then turned abruptly back. "So, if you were on Linnea—go ahead, close your eyes, take a moment to imagine yourself on Linnea—and if you said a prayer, do you think anyone would hear it?"

I closed my eyes, imagining. He waited patiently. The answer seemed obvious. I opened my eyes. "Yes."

"Who do you think would hear it?"

"Well, I would."

"Good. Anyone else?"

"And God too."

"On Linnea?"

"Of course. God is everywhere."

"So God *is* on Linnea...?"

I blinked. "Yes." And then I got it. "Yes."

"Good. So that means Linnea isn't Hell."

I nodded.

"And God is there too."

I nodded again.

He wiggled his thumb at me. "And if God needed to manifest as a thumb on Linnea...? He could do that too, couldn't he?"

I felt my smile widening. I could feel a laugh coming up. "Yes."

"And if God needed to manifest as the Mother of the World, she could do that too, couldn't she?"

The laugh bubbled to the surface, a giggle of delight. "Yes, she could." It all made sense, the way Whitlaw explained it.

"So it would be all right to pray to the Mother on Linnea, wouldn't it? Sure it would. Thank you, Kaer." To the rest of the room, he said. "Your prayers are still going to the same server; they'll just be coming in from a different terminal, using a slightly different protocol and operating system. Any questions? Anyone?"

Big Jes stood up. "What if I don't believe in God?"

"That's all right too," said Whitlaw. "God still believes in you."

After that, I didn't mind going to church so much. The service wasn't for Linnea anymore, it was for us. We were learning another way to speak to God. The same God, everywhere. And even if we weren't on Linnea yet, I was sure that the manifestation called the Mother of the World was already listening to us and smiling.

CHOCOLATE CAKE

WE SPENT MY ELEVENTH BIRTHDAY making bricks. The Linneans didn't celebrate birthdays the same way we did, and even though I felt disappointed at not having a party and presents, it wouldn't have felt right. Not anymore. Because we were starting to think like Linneans now.

Our ten acres were down on the flood plain, which would be the hardest place to build a house. The dome had never been flooded yet, but they'd designed it to recreate the Linnean seasons, and if they didn't have a winter flood soon, some of the plants that depended on the flooding wouldn't reproduce. So we had to think about building for flood control too.

The Linneans have different ways of dealing with floods. Mosty they move to higher ground. But on the broad plains, that's not always possible. So sometimes they build their houses on stilts, and sometimes, they build them like boats, and sometimes they sink them deep into the ground and line them with clay bricks and tar, and stick up snorkels, just in case.

But out on the plains, you can't bake bricks out of clay and straw, because there isn't any. And there isn't any tar either. So you have to make your bricks out of rammed earth instead. You start by boiling down a lot of sticky razor grass to make a stinky syrup the Linneans call tarpay. Then you mix some of this syrup in a big pit with the dirt you're going to make into bricks. Then you put the sticky dirt—tarpay dirt—into a brick-shaped box with a wooden top and a lever to press the top down hard. And then you put as much pressure on the wooden top as you can.

Gampa and Da-Lorrin and Irm built a Linnean machine that looked like a big garlic press. Or a nutcracker. There was a ratchet thing, into which the men would push the end of a thick tree trunk to be used as a lever. Three men or one great-horse would push the lever down, locking the ratchet into place, and that would put so much pressure on the dirt in the box that it would harden into a real brick. The machine had nine compartments, so we could make nine bricks at a time. You had to leave the bricks in long enough for the tarpay to solidify, so that meant one machine wouldn't be enough if we were going to finish in time.

After we got the hang of it with the first brick press, the men built a bunch more, so that eventually we had a kind of brick assembly line. Everybody had to help; everybody had to learn how to do everything. Even Gamma. So while the parents were pressing down one set of bricks in one machine, the kids would have already started unloading the finished bricks from the next one in line. The moms would shovel buckets of new tarpay dirt into the empty press until it overflowed the top. Then the men would install the lever into the ratchet and press that one down as far as it would go. We worked in teams, each team moving along the line, one after the other. All day long, we went down the row, filling one press, emptying the next. It was hard work, and at first everybody complained. Everybody's back and legs and arms hurt. And we all took turns giving each other back rubs with stinky liniments.

We had to get up early every morning, even before the sun rose, because that's when the razor grass was the freshest. We'd pack a quick breakfast of hardtack and cheese and sausage to eat while we worked, and then we'd all go out together and cut a quarter-acre of razor grass, because that's how much we needed each day. It grew faster than we could cut it—at least it seemed that way. Then we'd start it boiling down while we stopped for second breakfast—our first real meal of the day. After second breakfast, we'd start digging down to get the dirt for the day's bricks. By the time we had enough dirt and the tarpay was bubbling, it was time for lunch. By the time we finished lunch, the tarpay was ready for pouring.

There was no shortage of dirt—we already had a big pile of it—and as we shaped the walls and dug out extra rooms and storage space, we had more than enough. We weren't going to run out of dirt. It wasn't the same kind of dirt as we'd find on Linnea, but it was close enough, and the experience was good for us.

We worked every day until we ran out of tarpay. We couldn't afford to waste it, so sometimes we worked until after sunset. Any extra tarpay and razor grass we smeared on the hardened walls as a lining. We also had to harden the ramp that Mountain had left leading down into the hole, because eventually that would be our ladder up and out, after we put the roof on.

There was another way too, even faster, but you needed a lot of canvas. You sewed canvas sacks and filled them with dirt, then you made sandbag walls. That's how the forts were constructed. You could put up a lot of wall in a very short time, if you had enough people working. But we didn't have enough canvas, and besides, the purpose of this exercise was to see how much we could do with grass and dirt alone.

After a couple of weeks, we got used to the work and our backs stopped hurting and our muscles stopped complaining. And we had three huge piles of bricks growing around a hole that was finally taking shape as a house. Despite all the hard work, it was one of our happiest times. Or maybe it was because of all the hard work. Like Auncle Irm said, we were all working together—and that was special. We made a game out of it, laughing and singing and seeing how many bricks we could make in a day. On our best day, we made 900 bricks.

We didn't win the brick-making competition, though. We only came in second. The Kelly family, our closest neighbors, only a kilometer away, worked day and night in shifts and turned out twice as many bricks. We rode over there on one of the days we had use of a horse, and they had a long row of brick piles, all neatly stacked, more bricks than they would need for building a house. Unless they were planning to build some kind of warehouse too. And in fact, they were. Their idea was to build a secret underground room outfitted for emergencies.

The scouts agreed that this was a good idea, but all those extra piles of bricks looked suspicious. If they planned to do that on Linnea, they would have to find a way to camouflage what they were doing. They had to hide their extra bricks. A week later, most of the brick piles were gone. They'd put them down in the finished rooms of the house they were digging. It probably meant a lot of extra work, moving all those bricks around, and it made me think of Sokoban, a Japanese game where you have to push little crates around a funny-shaped warehouse until each one is in its right place. But it worked, because the next time we went over there, you couldn't tell that the Kellys were digging a bigger-than-usual house.

The Kellys were Traditionalists. They believed in only one mom and one dad—and a whole bunch of kids. But there were three Kelly families in the Kelly compound. Gamma Mary Kelly had three daughters and each daughter had her own husband and her own children. But they raised them all together, so they were pretty much like a normal family anyway.

I liked visiting the Kellys. When we weren't at church, they were very friendly people. Rose Kelly always had something good-smelling on the stove. Whenever we went visiting, she had oat-bread or oatmeal cookies or pumpkin pie. And once...she made a chocolate cake for Ned Kelly's birthday.

They didn't have chocolate over on Linnea, along with a lot of other stuff we liked, so most of us were learning to do without. But when little Ned cried that he wanted chocolate cake for his birthday, Rose indulged him. Technically, chocolate in the dome was a rules violation. And the Kellys could have been fined a hundred work points for it. But they managed to keep it a secret simply by not using the word chocolate. It was just "Rose's special recipe." Patta Kelly shared a piece with Rinky and me on picnic, but only on condition that we wouldn't tell. I hadn't had chocolate in so long—

We'd all signed agreements, even the children, that we wouldn't do anything Earthlike while we were in Linnea Dome. At first, a lot of it felt like playacting, but after awhile it began to seem real, and Earth was like some place out of a fairy tale or a history book that didn't exist anymore. So anything that came over from Earth looked and felt *wrong* to us now.

But the chocolate cake tasted *soooo* good. And I hadn't had a birthday party of my own and Patta Kelly knew that, otherwise she wouldn't have snuck a piece of cake out of the house for me.

ONE HUNDRED PERCENT

THAT PIECE OF CHOCOLATE CAKE cost a thousand work points for our family and the Kelly family. They got fined for sneaking chocolate into the dome. We got fined because Rinky and I didn't report it. If we hadn't been so close to finishing our underground flood-proof house, Administor Rance would have dropped us from the project.

Rinky and I had to stand up and publicly apologize to the entire dome for putting their lives at risk. I cried a lot. "I have to apologize; Mom-Woo says so. I know I did wrong by not reporting an infraction. But I didn't get a birthday party this year and—"

Administor Rance cut me off. She was very angry and very severe—as if she were a Linnean administor. "We do not celebrate birthdays on Linnea! We do not tempt the demons to rise up out of the ground. Nor do we eat of the demon beans! Who knows what poisons such demon foods contain? Will you burn for the practice of witchcraft, Kaer! You live on Linnea now! You must choose between *chocolate* and life." She made it sound evil.

I started to weep. "I just wanted something for my birthday, that's all."

Administrator Rance's face grew sadder. She came down from the podium and spoke directly to me, "Kaer, do you want to see your family burned alive—all of them screaming in agony, just because you wanted a piece of *chocolate?*"

I couldn't help myself. I broke down completely, falling to my knees on the floor in front of her. Administor Rance ignored me. She walked back up to her podium and waited impassively. "Do you want that, Kaer?" She asked again.

That's when Aunt Morra stood up. "For Christ's sake," she said. "You've made your point. Stop picking on the poor child. This won't happen again. The family has already taken responsibility. You don't have to subject us to an unholy Inquisition!"

Somehow, I stopped sniffling long enough to look up. Administor Rance scribbled little notes on the paper in front of her while Morra went on. "Look," she said. "We've cooperated one hundred percent with this program. We've worked as hard as anyone. And we haven't complained. We've done our best to learn the language, the culture, the traditions. We eat the food, we wear the clothes, we make our own tools, we've built a house and we've planted crops. Doesn't that count for anything? You can't expect perfection."

Administor Rance picked up her paper. "Fifty-point penalty for the use of the word 'Christ.' Fifty-point penalty for the use of the term 'Inquisition.' Fifty-point penalty for the use of the term 'one hundred percent.'" She put the paper down. "Yes, I know this seems harsh and cruel and unfair to you. Especially to you, Kaer. But we cannot allow even the smallest breach in discipline. If we make one excuse for one child's birthday, then we'll make another excuse for something else later on. And another and another, until we've punched so many holes in our integrity, we can use it for a sieve. I take no pleasure in these proceedings, believe me—but better that you learn this lesson *here* than after you arrive on Linnea where anything out of the ordinary can result in an Inquiry by the local administors. I doubt very much that you will like their Covenant of Justice.

"We have had good results with our first group of colonists only because we trained them so rigorously. We will not risk their lives *or yours*. Each and every one of us needs to have a total commitment to the agreements. And that includes the children most of all, because if anything gives you away, it will probably come from the children. I do not apologize for trying to save your life, Kaer." She looked at me sternly. "You must regard all references to Earth as profane, so profane that you would rather die than betray the existence of the home world."

Morra sat down and folded her arms across her chest. I knew that look. She was through listening for tonight. Probably for a long while. Like the way she acted when we first told her we wanted to apply for Linnea. She probably wouldn't say anything at all for a week, and then after she'd thought about it for a while, she'd turn into a real witch—on the side of the agreements. But she wouldn't talk about how she changed her mind; she'd just insist on us keeping strictly to our word.

Mom-Woo said that when you looked up stubborn in the dictionary, you found Aunt Morra's picture. But Morra had spoken up for me, and I'd never seen her speak up for anyone like that before, and I spent the rest of the evening looking at her as if I'd never really seen her before.

Administor Rance then turned her attention to the Kelly family. "By rights, I should drop you from the program here and now. I have the authority to do so. The severity of your infraction leaves very little choice in the matter. And I must ask you now what *other* contraband you've brought into the dome. If you want to continue in this program, I expect you to turn over everything immediately. And that includes that Bible you smuggled in. . . . " She ignored the gasps in the room. "Yes, we know about it, Citizen. It will not go to Linnea with you."

Buzz Kelly stood up. He wore only his blacksmith's apron and leather kilt. Everybody called him Buzzard Kelly because he looked so tall and gangly. But all the hours hammering at the forge had given him arms like tree trunks, so when he stood up, people shut up and listened.

"The Good Lord made all the worlds, not just this one," he said quietly. "He will reign wherever we go. So how can we leave our faith in Him behind?"

Administor Rance didn't like that question. Even I could see that. Probably because it didn't matter how she answered it, someone was going to get angry. She took off her glasses and rubbed the bridge of her nose for a moment before putting them back on. "Dr. Whitlaw has already addressed that. Perhaps you should revisit that lesson. I am not asking you to relinquish your faith, Citizen Kelly. Only your Bible." And then she added in a more thoughtful tone, "As far as we know, Christ doesn't exist on Linnea. Not now. Maybe not ever. We don't know what specifically happened to our lost settlers. Whatever records they left behind may have disappeared when the plagues decimated the continent more than fifteen hundred years ago, almost wiping out all human life. We do know that the Linneans never developed monotheism as we know it. As *you* know it."

She stopped herself. "Never mind all that. For reasons we cannot yet identify, the Linneans have developed a profound hostility to changes in their fundamental belief systems. That may be the result of holy wars in their past. But the practice of any Earth religion on Linnea represents a serious possibility of cultural contamination, with consequences we cannot predict. We can't run the risk of triggering an inquisition, or worse. We can say with certainty that the discovery of religious artifacts among your goods would endanger you and probably everyone you came in contact with as well. The Linneans do not yet have the concept of religious tolerance."

She held up her hand to keep Buzzard from replying. "Consider this, Citizen Kelly. You will have privacy in your own home. And if you choose to use that privacy for the kinds of prayers that succor you, you will do exactly that, no matter what I say here. If you build your home five hundred kilometers out in the wilderness, and if your nearest neighbors remain a two-day ride in any direction, and if you assume that distance equals security—then in all likelihood you will grant yourself the privilege of violating the integrity of your agreement to not practice any Earth-based rituals. And by so doing, your immersion in the Linnean way of thinking will remain incomplete. You will have carved a hole in your integrity large enough for the danger to you and your loved ones to come galloping through like a stampede of enraged boffili. Yes, Morra, chocolate cake by itself carries no danger. Neither does a quiet faith in Christ. But the breach of integrity that such actions demonstrate also proves an intolerable failure to assimilate.

"Had we not already invested so much time and energy in all of you, I would recommend your immediate dismissal from the program. By now, we expect all of you to know better. Administor Moffin gave you high recommendations. This does not give me confidence in any of his other judgments. Nevertheless, based on his prior faith in you, I will withhold immediate judgment and place you on indefinite probation, pending further incidents."

She rang her bell to close the meeting—and exited without saying another word to anyone. That was the way she always did it, but this time it really hurt.

HOME

THAT NIGHT WE HAD ANOTHER FAMILY MEETING around the table. At least we had a table, even if we didn't have a house yet. We were still sleeping in the great-wagon, or underneath it—just like we would do on Linnea someday. And that thought always gave me a curious feeling too, because it meant that someday we'd be leaving this house behind. Even though we hadn't even finished building it yet, it already felt like home.

Klin and Cindy folded the table down from the left side of the wagon, and Rinky and Parra and I put out the tea things: mugs, salt, pepper-rinds, tea and tea-strainers. Gampa lit the lanterns, one after the other, and hung them overhead.

I didn't sit at my usual place. I sat next to Aunt Morra, my way of showing her I was glad she had spoken up, no matter how many points it had cost us. Morra surprised me by putting her arm around my shoulder and whispering into my ear. "Don't you fret, sweetheart. We'll take just so much and then we won't take anymore."

Mom-Woo overheard and looked at Morra grimly. "Don't encourage the children, Morra. We have enough trouble as it is." She brought the boiling pot to the table and began spooning tea leaves into it. One by one, the other adults finished peeing or pooping into the compost pit, finished washing and came to the table. Gamma and Mom-Lu filled tea mugs, and Parra and Cindy started passing them around. Even though no one said anything, I felt so bad about everything, I just wanted to run off into the hills and die. But Aunt Morra still had her arm firmly

92

around my shoulder, so I couldn't go anywhere at all; so instead I just leaned into her and buried my face in her side, pretending I didn't exist anymore.

After a bit the grown-ups started talking, gently at first, easing their way into the subject, and Morra nudged me upright. "No hiding out," she whispered. So I reached out and pulled my tea mug close and stared down into it instead. The salty aroma comforted me. Linnean tea was more like soup than tea. I liked it more than Earth tea.

Across from me, on the other side of the table, Lorrin hunched over his mug too. He glowered diagonally across at Irm. He wasn't angry at anyone here. He was just angry. "Do you still feel the same way, Irm? Do you still think this is such a good idea for us? I can't help but wonder, what have we gotten ourselves into?"

Irm rolled his own cup back and forth between his hands, as if warming his fingers. "I suspect that this conversation will occur in many homes tonight, around many tables." Around us, the howling of the wind had grown. Authority had begun simulating the beginning of winter, and it was a very convincing simulation. I kept my boffili robe wrapped tight around me. Irm said thoughtfully, "What we had before, we still have tonight. We have our family. What we choose to do next, we will still have what we have tonight. Each other." And then he added. "The decision belongs to you, Lorrin—and everyone else who crosses over."

Mom-Woo sat down at the head of the table, indicating that she would take charge of this family meeting. Parra and Cindy finished handing out mugs of tea and took their places down at the foot of the table. They looked strangely silent too.

Bhetto, who hardly ever spoke at family meetings, spoke up first. He said, "I agree with Irm. The decision does not belong to those who will stay behind. But I will tell you this, Lorrin. The more we learn about Linnea, the more I worry. The natural dangers, we all knew those coming in: the kacks, the razor grass, the long winters, the boffili, the range fires, the flooding...all of that. You believed you could handle it. I believed it too. And every day, as they told us of each new threat we might encounter, we included those dangers in the challenge, confident that we could expand our commitment to meet them. But now, we hear that the natural realm represents only the smallest threat compared to the people of Linnea—and I candidly confess that now I worry what other dangers await that they still haven't told us yet." He spoke in Linnean, with flawless rhythm. I actually began to wish that Irm and Bhetto and Morra would come with us.

Cindy, who also didn't speak much at meetings, raised a hand to respond. Mom-Woo nodded, and Cindy, rubbing his new beard thoughtfully, said, "You make good points, Bhetto—but if you stay behind, you won't share those risks, and as Irm just said, whatever risks obtain on Linnea, they belong only to those who choose to cross over. We have to make this decision ourselves, don't we?"

Bhetto agreed. "Yes, Cindy. I know that. But perhaps the time has come for the family to consider an alternative. You know what I mean. We don't have to cross over, and we can still stay a part of this world. Other families have done it—they've chosen to stay on this side as trainers and teachers and reviewers of the material beamed back from the monitors. We could do that, all of us, and we could stay together." Bhetto added quietly, "Sometimes, I feel as if you've already left. And I miss you so terribly. If we stayed here, we wouldn't ever have to say good-bye."

"Thank you, Bhetto," said Lorrin. He reached across the table and patted the older man's hand. "We all appreciate that. But...you know we can't just stop halfway. We set a goal for ourselves. If we won't commit ourselves passionately, and if we don't make a full-out effort, we'll never know what we could have accomplished. And like Morra and Irm have already said—this family cannot survive the stench of a festering dream."

"Well said, Lorrin, as always. But perhaps the family should take another look at this dream. It looked far better in the wanting than in the having."

"The doing, however—" said Morra, surprising us all. "The doing has changed us all for the better. And if we abandon the dream, we risk losing what we've all built together. A closer family."

Bhetto blinked. "But, Morra, I haven't advocated abandonment at all—only that we consider a different realization of the same goal, one that allows us greater freedom and comfort."

"We all understand, Bhetto." Mom-Woo came and sat down beside him. "You don't want to lose us. And we don't want to lose you either. We love you too. And we all of us have days when we look at you and Morra and Irm and the tears fill our eyes because we know there will come a day when we'll have to say good-bye and then we'll never see you again. We'll have messages, yes, as often as we can. But...messages don't give hugs." And with that, she put her arms around Bhetto and held him close, and they both wept quietly in each other's arms.

Watching, I felt good about that. So did the rest of the family. We waited in silence until they broke apart, both wiping their eyes at the same time, and then both laughing gently at each other's tears. Mom-Woo reached across and touched Bhetto's cheek gently, and I realized suddenly that Da-Lorrin had not been her first husband. Finally she turned to the rest of us. "Well, get on with the discussion," she snapped; but I noticed that she sat close to Bhetto for the rest of the evening, holding his hand in hers.

That's when I whispered to Aunt Morra, "I wish you'd change your mind and go with us. I'll miss you. And I like the way you teach. You make the math fun."

An expression of surprise crept across Morra's face. "Why, Kaer, what a wonderful thing to say."

"Come with us? Please? I'll miss you terribly if you don't." Impulsively, I hugged her. I don't remember ever hugging her before.

Morra blinked back sudden tears. "Oh, sweetheart. I wish I could, but you know I can't."

"Why not?"

"Because—just because."

"You can change your mind, can't you?"

Morra looked helplessly across to Mom-Woo. "Can you explain it to her?"

Mom-Woo spoke quickly and quietly, as if this was a subject she did not want to discuss at length. "Kaer, someone has to stay behind to take care of the family's property here. Morra and Irm and Bhetto will do that. If they don't stay, who will take care of our resources?"

"The Kellys hired a company to do that for them. Why can't we?"

"Because we arranged it this way. And we can't change it." She gave me a *drop-this-discussion* look.

Down the table, Lorrin nodded his agreement. "We can't change it. What you said—we've already jumped off this cliff. So let's not have a discussion about whether we want to or not. That'll take us nowhere useful, and we'll still hit the same bottom. More important, we need to consider what we can do in the situation we have."

He lowered his mug to the table and traced out his thoughts methodically. "We've all studied our history. We know about repressive societies and witch-hunts. We know they can't last long. It goes in cycles. And we'll find safety away from the cities anyway, so I think we can minimize the risks, if we take care." Big Jes and Klin and Parra nodded their agreement. Klin looked like he wanted to say something, but then he shook his head; it wasn't necessary to say it. Lorrin put his hand over Klin's anyway, a signal of reassurance or partnership. "No," he said. "I have more serious worries about something closer to home—the goings-on in this dome."

At that, Mom-Woo glanced up meaningfully—at the imaginary ceiling. Her eyes scanned the table, the great-wagon and the surrounding equipment, as if to include them all in everybody's awareness. Nobody knew if the Administor monitored private conversations, but we'd all seen the monitor bugs and we knew how they worked. And we knew that the administors had the right to observe us whatever we did—even going to the bathroom. So we all assumed that the monitors listened all the time and we didn't talk about forbidden things.

Some of the kids assumed that we were safe when we were all swimming naked in the lake. If we were naked, we were away from any monitors that might be woven into our clothes. But we had implants under our skin, and some of us were sure the implants were voice-monitors too. So after a while, we just sort of watched each other and made pointy-fingers whenever anyone said anything they shouldn't.

But Lorrin had little fear of monitor bugs tonight. He said, "Let them hear. So what? If they have monitors here, then they already know how we feel and what we think. We've always been candid in the past, so let them hear that we have concerns and worries tonight—not just about Linnea, but about the way they treat us too." He glanced around. "Does anyone object?"

No one did. "Go on, Lorrin," said Gampa.

Lorrin took a breath. He took another swallow of tea, then pushed it forward for Mom-Woo to refill. I knew that he was considering how to phrase his words in Linnean. Sometimes it was still difficult for us. Finally he said, "The administors have created a repressive society of their own here. Yes, they do it for our own good, but still . . . we live in a world of witch-hunts, informers and totalitarian authority. The administors say that they do this to protect us—and they certainly mean well. Maybe when we get to the other side, we'll better appreciate the strictness of the regimen here. . . .

"But even when I consider all of the mitigating circumstances, I still can't let go of the anger I feel at the way Administor Rance treated Kaer tonight. Over a piece of chocolate cake? A goddamn piece of chocolate cake?" Lorrin glanced up to the imaginary ceiling. "Take the goddamn fifty points, Administor Rance. At least you know how I feel now!"

Irm reached over and patted his arm. "We all feel that way."

"And we all sat there in silence and let Administor Rance get away with it! Didn't we? Have we given up all common sense? Would we let a Linnean administor treat Kaer that way? I don't think so. Indeed, would a Linnean administor even act that way?" And then Lorrin realized something. I could see the look of realization on his face. And so could everybody else.

When Lorrin spoke again, he spoke in English. "Yes, we *are* being monitored. We all know it. But who watches the monitors? Are there that many Linnean-speaking folk in the dome? I don't think so. And I think that those who are here have much more important things to do than eavesdrop on us all the time.

"Yes, we're being monitored—but if we are to use the monitoring of Linnea as a model, then it is the intelligence engines who are listening to us now. They'll flag any serious conversation for review. But who does the reviewing? The trainers? I don't think so. Authority probably has a whole division set up to review anything the intelligence engines spit out. Do the people in that division speak Linnean? I don't think so. They probably depend on translations. But I'll bet that any conversation in English is automatically flagged and reviewed...." He let that sink in for a moment as he glanced around the table. "It's late. They might not hear this conversation until the day shift comes in tomorrow morning and the intelligence engine plays it back for them. Or the night shift might be listening to us right now. The question that I'm wondering about is this: *do they know that the way we're being treated violates the Singapore Convention?* And if so, do they know that no person is allowed to sign away his Singapore Rights, no matter what? And do they also know that anyone with knowledge of a Singapore Rights violation is required by law to report it?" He glanced up at the imaginary ceiling and grinned. Probably nothing would come of what he said, but just as likely Administor Rance would have a couple of uncomfortable moments. And just as possible, we could be expelled tomorrow for not getting with the program.... It was a very dangerous gambit. Even I recognized that. Nobody wanted to respond immediately.

Lorrin finished his tea noisily and made a great show of refilling his cup. He knew that every eye was on him. I could tell that Mom-Woo was annoyed because of the way her mouth tightened. She waited until his cup was filled and he was making a great show of enjoying it, before she spoke herself. And when she did, she spoke in English too. "Lorrin, thank you for that performance. It was very clever. But now let's turn our attention back to the subject at hand. And please—*let's all resume speaking in Linnean.*" She even finished her sentence in Linnean. It gave me an odd feeling to hear English again, and then when she shifted so effortlessly back into Linnean I felt like my brain had been thinking in two separate places. I wondered if that was the "paradigm shift" that Administor Moffin used to talk about.

Mom-Woo said, "Let's talk about our situation. And our choices. What exactly do we want?" That quickly she discarded Lorrin's dangerous path. She turned to me. "Kaer? What do you want?"

Everybody looked at me. I flushed with embarrassment and I didn't want to say anything at all. I stared down into my tea mug, but there was no answer there either. I felt as if I didn't really have a vote anymore. Not after the chocolate cake business. Not after Mom-Woo had told me Aunt Morra couldn't go with us. While everybody else had been arguing back and forth, I'd been wondering if perhaps I shouldn't stay behind with Aunt Morra. But now, Mom-Woo insisted. "Kaer, what do you want to do?"

My words surprised me. "I want to go to Linnea," I said softly. "I really do." And I was terrified that I had screwed it up so badly that none of us could go....

"Why?" said Mom-Woo, in that *voice* of hers that she used when she was speaking for God. Even though I was mosty staring into my mug, I could tell that everybody was still looking at me, waiting for my answer.

I shrugged in embarrassment. "I like the horses," I admitted softly. I knew they wouldn't understand, but I said it anyway.

"Thank you, Kaer." Mom-Woo smiled and patted my hand in a way that suggested that she really *did* understand. Then she glanced down the table. "And the rest of you? Why do you want to go to Linnea?"

Cindy and Parra looked at each other. Cindy said, "We want to become scouts. We want to go exploring—where we have something *important* to explore."

Gamma said, "I want to stay with my family. No matter what." Gampa reached over and squeezed her hand.

Lorrin looked up from his tea mug. He said, "I want to make a difference. A difference that counts."

Big Jes grunted, "I like the work." He thumped Klin meaningfully— Klin grinned sheepishly. "Yeah, that goes for me too."

Mom-Lu said, "What Irm said before. I like seeing this family work together. I like hearing this family laugh. We didn't have that before. I don't want it to stop."

Mom-Trey agreed, "We do best when we do things together. If nothing else, Linnea promises that."

Finally, Mom-Woo spoke. "Well, I guess that settles that. But just to make sure we've considered both sides of the question. Does anyone want to argue for quitting?" She made a show of looking up and down the table. No one did. "Well, let me say this anyway. Even if we wanted to, we've come too far to turn back. Morra and I ran the numbers a month ago—just to see where we are." She smiled with apple-pie satisfaction. "It should please you all to hear that we can't afford to quit. The penalties would bankrupt us. But then again, I hear no one arguing for quitting anyway, so the subject is just another horse turd forgotten on the prairie. Leave it for the dung-mice. Did I say that right?" Everyone laughed, because Mom-Woo was normally so *polite.* She would never use crude language. At least, not in English. "So let's celebrate that we all want to keep going—because we don't have any other options anyway. More tea, anyone?"

Rinky raised her hand then, not for tea, but because she wanted to speak. She was another one who didn't say much at meetings, mosty because she didn't think the moms would take her words seriously; but now she raised her hand now. Mom-Woo nodded to her. "Rinky?"

"Um, it seems to me...that if we can handle anything Administor Rance says or does, then we can certainly handle anything Linnea has in store for us. I mean, what do we care about a few lousy work points? We'll make more bricks and we'll earn them back. Besides, I've got a great new work song! *You deserve a brick today—*"

Da-Lorrin laughed out loud at that, because it was so outrageous-stupid, and then so did everyone else. And that was that. Because whenever Da-Lorrin laughed, *everybody* laughed. Rinky smiled with delight at his guffaws. Whatever tension might have been left at the table, it evaporated in the sound of Lorrin's hearty booming roar. Aunt Morra tittered, Mom-Lu giggled, Big Jes chuckled appreciatively. Administor Rance was no longer a threat to us, just something else to leave for the mice and the beetles. Klin added jubilantly, "Right! We're bigger than any lump in the road—big enough to step over it and keep on going!"

And then, still chortling, Big Jes added that the difference between a horse turd and an administor was that at least a horse turd was useful as fertilizer, and Da-Lorrin roared again. We snickered about that comparison for a bit, with Klin and Parra each adding their own scatological dimensions to Big Jes' joke. The biggest laugh of all came when Klin suggested that Administor Rance would probably have to listen to the playback of this conversation in the same room with all her assistants.

At last, we all felt like a family again—so Mom-Woo adjourned the meeting and ordered everyone to bed, because we still had to get up early the next day. We had a lot of bricks to make before winter set in.

But it wasn't quite over for me. I went over to Da and put my arms around him and just held onto him, smelling his wood-and-sweat smells, and told him how sorry I was for all this trouble. He held me close and patted my head softly and told me not to worry about it anymore, and that was all I needed to hear. I started crying again, but this time with relief.

CULTURE SHOCK

A FEW DAYS LATER—and we had no way of knowing if it was part of the larger program or if it was a suddenly decided result of the chocolate cake incident—the Dome Authority started a new series of seminars about life on Linnea.

Instead of our regular instructors, we now had real scouts coming in to speak to us. Now we started seeing pictures that weren't released to the public, and a lot of it wasn't very pretty. But then, I guess, a lot of pictures taken on our world wouldn't look all that wonderful to someone from the other side either, even with an explanation, so it probably wasn't fair to judge all of Linnea by just this little bit.

It wasn't unusual to have scouts leading the seminars. Scouts came back for intensive debriefing as often as they could. Most scouts stayed on Linnea no more than six months at a time, but some had gone on extended explorations and traveled for more than eighteen months before getting back to Earth. Whenever scouts came back, the administors had them speak to the trainees. The scouts spoke a lot more candidly about conditions on the other side than the instructors, and most of us appreciated their honesty, because they didn't try to hide the uglier side of the things they'd seen. Mom-Woo fretted that some of this might not be good for the "children" to hear, meaning me in particular; but by now, I had grown into a pretty *old* child. And what the scouts said fascinated me.

During the second week, three scouts came in we'd never seen before. They'd just come back after a long time on the other side. All three wore boffili robes over Linnean kilts and aprons. The women were solid-muscled and leathery and they had their hair cut so short they looked like boys; one was short and stout, the other was tall and rangy; and they had weather-hardened faces.

The man had the same built-from-bricks appearance. He had a beard and eyes so dark they were beautiful in a scary sort of way. He wore a silver earring with a single red feather hanging from it. The way he stood, he looked important—not like a boss or a leader or someone like that, but like someone who *knew*. If I were ever in trouble, I would want him on my side; not because I liked him, but because I *didn't* like him and didn't ever want someone like him angry at me. I thought of him as the Man with the Silver Earring.

These three had come back to Earth to debrief and then go back through the gate. If everything went according to plan, they would lead a small group of families up to the northern plains. Several of the families ahead of us had just passed their certification exams; we knew some of them, the ones who had worked as teachers and trainers for us while they waited to cross over; but the Gate Authority had abruptly delayed their departures without saying why. People asked the scouts why the delay, but they just shook their heads and said that the administors still had things to discuss.

Smiller, the stout woman, had been one of the first scouts ever to cross over. She'd gone to Linnea even before Novotny, our language instructor; and while he'd spent most of his time studying videos and deciphering the language in a lab, she'd spent her time actually speaking it—and at far greater risk. She didn't talk about it much, but later we found out that Smiller had spent more time on the other side of the gate than almost any other human alive. She'd gone all the way to the south continent and back, and she'd traveled to seven different cities on mapping expeditions. She'd planted thousands of remotes and monitors all over everywhere. Whenever anyone had a question that no one else could answer, they took it to Smiller. Even Novotny acknowledged her as the primary authority on the nuances of the Linnean language. She had trained most of the language instructors and more than half of the active scouts—over two hundred people.

But it didn't seem like she wanted to train us. She glowered angrily as she watched us file into the room. And with her first words she laid it out clearly. "I'd rather get back to my work on Linnea. Administor Rance told me of your sorry progress—I told her to make sure you pack your shovels. I expect you folks will dig a lot of graves before you learn—if you ever learn at all. I don't think you have what it takes. I'd just as soon drop the lot of you and start over. And don't anyone assume that we have too much invested in you to do that. We don't. You can consider these sessions our one last attempt to salvage you."

Behind her, pictures began flashing on the display wall. She didn't bother to explain any of them. "Let's talk about Linnea now. You don't understand how much difficulty you will have trying to think like a Linnean. You will slip, you will speak of something that doesn't exist over there or something they don't know about yet—like the speed of sound or the speed of light—and the people around you will blink in sudden confusion, wondering what you just said. And you won't even understand what you just did, not until you go back and replay the conversation in your mind. Do that enough times and the people around you will begin to think you a little bit odd. And after they've decided that you're odd...then it's a very short step to the accusation of maizlish behavior. And if that happens, you lose everything you've worked for. If you survive...if you escape to the west and go into exile, don't think about starting again in some new location. The word will go out to every settlement. It may take a while, but the news will travel. We have several families in exile now. We may have to bring them back, we may try to build a settlement of exiles as a halfway station. We don't know yet.

"I cannot understate the seriousness of the effort required. Just as we have concerns for your safety, so do we have the same concerns for the Linneans. You will have an effect on the people you meet. If you endanger yourselves, yes, we will make every effort to get you out safely; but we cannot rescue the people you endanger around you—the innocent Linneans who will have the misfortune to befriend you, and who will suffer the same consequences you will, when you fail.

"We have grave concerns over the cultural contamination of Linnea. More so as we have learned the dangers. We have had these concerns for ten years—from the very first day we discovered that people lived on Linnea. It took us four years of unseen monitoring to learn the language and the culture and the day-to-day behavior of the people well enough to risk penetration. That first contact represented an enormous gamble—and the risk increases with every subsequent contact.

"In the six years since first insertion, scouts have brought back books, newspapers, all kinds of artifacts, anything we could buy, borrow or steal. We've had a lot of difficulty gathering items that you now take for granted. Think about it. We arrived with no money, no identities, no credential of any kind. We had some boffili robes we thought we could trade. We had some gold nuggets in reserve, just in case. We thought we understood the market—but what if a tradesman asked us for a license or a permit? Or any kind of document?

"So we operated on the fringes for another two years. We penetrated their society slowly. We acted with careful deliberation, and we made few assumptions. Circumstances have repeatedly proven our caution justified. Look at these pictures behind me. We've found a lot of fear and suspicion in the Linnean culture. These people live a hard life—not a joyous one. They see danger everywhere. Something in their history has made them fearful. Do you wonder why we put you through such rigorous training?

"Five years ago, we began moving the first family groups over, only a few, and we kept them away from the cities. We put them on the trails west and let them join whatever wagon trains would have them. Two of our wagon families disappeared within a month of insertion. Their monitors stopped working, and we have no idea where they went or what happened to them. Another family was expelled from the train they had joined; we still don't understand why. But three of our families did complete their westward trek and have since settled in as members of flourishing communities.

"That small success encouraged us to insert another dozen families. Seven of those families took root. Two returned for additional training. Two others ran afoul of the Authority; we were able to pull one of those families out. The other retreated into the high mountains. Our contact with them remains sporadic, and we have considerable concern about their mental state; but they have refused our repeated offers of extraction and we remain hopeful we can get them back into the mainstream at some point, or build a halfway station around them. The last family simply disappeared, possibly killed or captured by hostiles. We don't know what happened, but as a direct result of these missteps we decided to increase the coverage of our monitoring technology. Despite the increased risk of detection or contamination, we judged the additional coverage absolutely necessary for the protection of the next set of families crossing over.

"For the most part, the increased monitoring has worked. Our ratio of successful insertions has improved. We now have sixty-three families on the western Linnean continent. And until recently, we felt confident that we had achieved a critical mass of information necessary to train families for full assimilation. Until recently. . . . " Smiller paused uncomfortably, like she had a very bad taste in her mouth. "Then we started getting conflicting data."

The displays behind her showed pictures of the different kinds of probes. I recognized some of them—the robot animals, the kites, the high-altitude satellites, the ones like that; but I didn't recognize the rest—things that looked like rocks or beetles or pieces of tree trunk. But I did like the Linnean doll with button-camera eyes. The screens showed a lot of different satellite-planes; most of them had transparent wings and bodies.

"As expected, once we inserted more probes, the number of UFO sightings in the coverage zone increased." Smiller looked very unhappy as she admitted the next part. "Yes, I know that sounds unlikely to most of you. We've told you repeatedly how we've built the probes out of transparent, non-reflective material. The specifications demand silent operation and invisibility to the naked eye at heights above 100 meters. Nevertheless, despite our stringent specifications...glitches do happen. Mistakes get made. Machines fail. A circumstance occurs that we didn't foresee. Perhaps someone on a cliff top looks across a valley and sees a spybird passing only a few meters away. He can't tell its size or speed; he has no referents. He can't even describe what he saw because he has no words in his language. Or maybe a spybird loses its calibration due to weather conditions or inaccurate maps and dips too low. Or maybe it crosses the sun, or a trick of the light gives it a sparkle or a reflection or a shadow. We can't foresee every possibility; we've always had a margin of uncertainty.

"As we feared, we started hearing stories about Linneans in the target areas seeing things in the sky. The reports contained enough specific descriptive detail—culturally adjusted, of course—to cause us enormous embarrassment. Although most of the individuals involved eventually came to believe that they had seen one of the eufora, even that doesn't let us off the hook, *because these incidents simply do not match the established tradition of euforan contacts.*

"What troubles us in particular, the sightings have created a new meme in the Linnean culture, and the ripples have spread. Yes, most of these sightings have met with the same kind of skeptical dismissal as you or I might give to a report of a Martian spacecraft landing in the outback, because those reports came from individuals with little credibility. But some of the reports have attracted attention because they came from otherwise reputable individuals.

"Regardless of the believability of any individual report, the continued sightings have created a widespread awareness of a *different kind* of euforan manifestation. The Linnean perception of the eufora *has changed*. Let me give you an example." She stepped up to the podium and picked up a piece of paper. She read slowly, to allow for the archaic style and unfamiliar words:

"'After three days in the wild, without hope of rescue or succor, I resolved to die in the same manner as I had lived—with my family uppermost in my thoughts. As I had lived to honor them, so I would die to honor them. I finished the last precious drops of my water and arranged myself upon the rocky ground as comfortably as circumstances would allow. I stared up into the evening sky, once again struck by its awesome beauty, and the gift of awareness that the Mother has given to all of us so that we may apprehend such wonder. With that thought, I realized that I should list for myself all of the grandest moments in my life that I could recall—my own way of acknowledging Mother Linnea's great gifts to me. I could not die ungrateful, you understand. As I contemplated my blessings, the heritage of my parents, the love of my good wife, the blessings of my children, my pain began to ebb and a great sense of peace began to fill me, as if I had left my body behind and now floated on an ocean of humble sanctity. I felt overwhelming joy. It swept through my body in a rush, a physical wave of sparkling sensation, and I wept with the beauty of it. I felt as if my substance had changed—had somehow lost the earthly chains of weight that held me down upon the ground, so that the slightest gust of wind could lift me bodily into the air like a gossamer veil of spider-silk. I saw myself as if from above, translucent and filled with the glowing light of Mother Linnea's love. I knew then that the Mother had blessed me yet again, infusing me with the spirit of her own eufora. Yet through it all, I remained exquisitely alert and aware of every sense. Each new sensation registered itself in both my feelings and my thoughts. No act of physical love had ever swept through me as powerfully as the Mother's grace. And through it all, as if the Mother herself were speaking to me in her own voice, I kept hearing one word only—a single thought that finally came laughing out of my own mouth, the word '*Yes!*' Mother Linnea's blessing came to me as a simple profound acknowledgment. She sent me her grace and her agreement that we, her children, should celebrate our joys together. And by that mandate, we achieve forgiveness for our missteps and mistakes.

"'When at last, the feeling finally began to ebb, I wept again, neither in sadness nor relief, but only as a joyous and exhausted aftermath, as one who has spent the evening consumed by an act of exquisite congress finally sighs in the humble acknowledgement of the gift of ecstasy. I felt cleansed by the Mother's tears as well as my own, and the peace that enveloped me was the peace of an infant safe in the arms of its parent. At last, I fell into a deep slumber. When I awoke, dawn had lifted the curtain to the east and as my eyes popped open, I laughed with the memory of my blessing. I knew also that I would live, because the Mother wanted me to return to the bosom of my family and share with them what she had shared with me. So I stood and began walking toward the rising light. And that, dear listeners, concludes the tale of how I got here...."

Smiller didn't comment on what she read. Instead she returned that paper to the podium and picked up a second page. This time, she read: "'The eufora had great wings, outstretched. It looked like nothing of land or sky or sea. It glowed with the color of the day, and it flew neither as a bird nor an insect. It did not flap or buzz, it made no sound, and yet it moved directly through the sky as if along a track that only it could ride.'" She grabbed a third piece of paper. "This one troubles me the most. 'I don't know why I looked up, but the Mother must have intended me to see her spirit. She wanted me to know. I saw a glint of light coming toward me. Like a shooting star, but in the day. As it came closer I saw that it had wings, perfectly straight, and by the manner in which it flew, also straight, I knew that I saw a true manifestation of the eufora, for no human endeavor could have produced a device of such elegance and beauty. I prayed then for cleansing, that I might find forgiveness and enlightenment—that I might receive the blessing of the Mother's grace. But the messenger passed, and although I felt awe at what I had seen, I felt nothing in my soul. I felt inconsolable sorrow, for I knew that if the Mother intended me to witness the passage of her euforan manifestation without partaking of her blessing, then she must have intended me to know that she found me unworthy of her grace. I pray that I will find forgiveness at least in the hearts of my children.'" Smiller paused a moment, then added quietly, "The author of that committed suicide. The words I just read you—she wrote them in the note she left behind."

SUPERSTITION

QUIETLY, SMILLER PUT THE PAPER BACK on the podium. She looked around the room at us with an expression that could have curdled milk. "I hope that you can begin to understand the shift in thinking these accounts represent. Prior to the events described in the last account, the eufora *never* appeared as a physical manifestation. Prior to these events, the Mother *never* withheld her grace from anyone. The Linneans used to experience the eufora as personal revelation—contact with the eufora always occurred through the emotions, *not* through the senses."

"Excuse me, Scout—?" Buzzard Kelly stood up. "I don't understand. Why do we concern ourselves with the pagan superstitions of these people?"

Smiller didn't answer. She glanced over at the Man with the Silver Earring. He grunted softly. Without moving from where he stood, with only that single soft sound, instantly he had every eye in the room on him. He gazed across at Buzzard, and even though his face had no real expression, I knew I never wanted him to look at me that way. "So you think your superstition should outvote theirs...?"

Kelly didn't get it, although everyone else seemed to. "They believe in spirits and demons and mother-goddesses. My faith lies in the one true God."

The Man with the Silver Earring nodded. It was not a nod of agreement. "So you *do* think your superstition has more importance than theirs."

108

"My faith—" said Buzzard Kelly, bristling slightly, "—comes from God." As if that settled it. "I have His word. I have the Book. At least, I did until Administor Rance took it away. But I still have my faith in *here*." He rapped his chest hard. "I have the *truth*. You can't take that away from me."

"Nor would we try," said Earring. "But the Linneans say they have the truth *too*."

"They have superstition! You said so yourself."

"Ahh, they have superstition...." repeated Earring. "And you have the truth...?" He paused as if considering this as a moment of enlightenment, then turned his attention back to Buzzard. "Hmm. Just one thing. Do you know what they would say if you told them of your faith? They would say what you just said—that *you* have superstition and *they* have the truth."

Kelly sputtered. "You know what I mean."

"Yes, exactly. You mean that *your* superstition should outvote theirs."

"Don't play word games with me, Scout!"

"I do *not* play word games, Citizen! I challenge you to consider this question. What makes your *truth* more true than theirs?"

"I have the Bible—the revealed word of God."

"And they have their scripture—also the revealed word of God." Earring held up his hand. "No, stop there, Citizen. I do not want to chase this wabbit—and neither do you. You need to understand only one thought. And if you get it, it will change the way you look at *all* thought."

Earring moved across the room to stand directly in front of Buzz Kelly. He moved like a force of nature—like something that does what it wants without regard for anything that gets in its way. And he spoke to Buzz Kelly in a voice that God probably borrows when handing down commandments: "From the inside, it *never* looks like superstition. From the outside, it *always* does.

"No—" Earring held his hand up to stop Kelly from replying. "Don't say anything, Citizen. I did not invite you to discuss it. I did not invite you to negotiate with it. I did not invite you to argue with it. I only want you to *get* it. Over on Linnea, the people live inside a different truth than you do—and they have the same strength of faith *in their truth* as you have in yours. If you wish respect for your beliefs, then you *must* respect the beliefs of others, lest you reopen wounds that will not heal easily. Not here, and definitely not on the other side."

He stepped past Smiller to the podium. "These sightings"—and he swept the entire stack of reports off the podium; they slid across the floor in a cascade of paper—"create *external* evidence. These sightings take faith out of the equation. They change the relationship of the Linneans with the eufora, and by extension, with the Mother as well. This creates an enormous danger, to us as well as the Linneans.

"Faith always demands proof to justify itself. The insecure believer constantly seeks validation. The creation of *tangible* evidence always petrifies faith, turns it into dogma. It proves to some people that they believe right—and it will damage others by demonstrating that they believe wrong. This *will* create widespread ripples. Some people will inevitably feel abandoned by the Mother, alienated from a spiritual source that they have invested a great deal of energy in. That kind of disaffection.... Well, we have already seen some of the possible consequences.

"Last month, two children—a twelve-year-old girl and a thirteen-year-old boy—saw one of our probes in the final stages of failure mode. It lost altitude, then vaporized itself. The children reported what they had seen, but they had no credibility. Even worse, they reported no feelings of the Mother's grace. Instead, they could only say that they had seen one of the eufora drop from the sky and die—an unthinkable concept in Linnean terms—so the authorities declared their sighting a maizlish—an 'evil mischief.' They castrated the boy and exiled him. They executed the girl to prevent her from bearing any maizlish offspring.

"I cannot begin to tell you how much this particular incident hurts. It has devastated the spirits of the scouts." Earring glowered at Buzz Kelly, and then at the rest of us as well. "Do any of you here want something like that on your conscience? No? I didn't think so. But we have that now, and we continue to run that risk every time we send anything through the gate."

A HOUSE

FOR A WHILE IT SEEMED LIKE we were spending every night sitting around the table and talking about what had happened in the evening's seminar. I didn't mind. I got to stay up late and sit in on all the meetings, and it felt good being treated like an almost-adult for a change. And it gave us a lot of good experience speaking in Linnean because we had to talk about a lot of different things besides gathering boffili chips and making bricks and building houses.

But talking didn't accomplish anything, and there didn't seem to be much to say anymore. The family quietly decided to give the Kellys a wide berth. For a couple reasons. Mosty because they still wanted us to come over to their place for private Sunday prayer meetings and we felt that was a bad idea—because it meant not thinking like Linneans—but also because we didn't expect them to last much longer in the program anyway. Although we did spend a while speculating on how they'd gotten approved in the first place. Irm said they must have bribed a congressman to get in; Da-Lorrin growled at that. We'd had to do it the hard way. But it didn't matter how many congressmen you bought, Big Jes said, you still couldn't buy your way over to Linnea if the Dome Authority didn't trust you.

But after that evening with Smiller, it seemed like the Kelly family settled down anyway. We didn't hear any more about Bibles or chocolate from them, so maybe they had gotten the message, but even if not, I was through being Patta Kelly's friend. She'd already gotten me in trouble

111

once. I wasn't going to get my family in trouble a second time. I had a hunch we'd used up all our second chances. All of us.

But it didn't make too much difference anyway because we were too busy building our house. We had promised ourselves that we would make good on our work points as fast as possible, so we just went back to work. After a couple of long, hard days, we fell back into our old routines. Almost.

Only now, everything felt different. No one would say for sure, but everybody knew that something serious had happened over on Linnea. The scouts looked grim and the administors acted busy and preoccupied all the time. We figured it had something to do with cultural contamination, but nobody would say. Lorrin even asked Smiller about it, but she rebuffed him and told him to concentrate on getting the house finished before they started winter. "You'll have plenty of time to talk around the fire."

Originally, we had planned to build the house without any wood at all, because we wouldn't have any wood on the open prairie; but then we realized that on Linnea we'd have at least two great-wagons to dismantle, so we petitioned for an amount of wood equal to the planking in a single wagon. We pretended that we were taking one wagon apart and used the wood for shoring up the sides of the house before putting in the bricks.

We had dug a great round hole in the ground, almost five meters deep. It was deeper than a swimming pool. Then we dug chambers off of it, like the petals of a flower. Six chambers in all; each with one wall of shelves and one wall of shelf-beds. It would be cramped, but at least we'd have a little privacy when we needed it.

We packed the dirt as solid as we could, both walls and floors, and then we painted everything with layers and layers of tarpay and mats of razor grass, until everything had a hard, sticky surface as thick as two hands laid one on top of the other. We hoped this would make a permanently watertight layer. Lorrin had figured worst-possible case for the weather and then doubled it, but we had no way of knowing for sure until the flood.

Even before the tarpay dried, we began laying bricks—two layers across the floor and two rows up the walls. We dipped every brick in tarpay, rammed it into place, and painted it again with even more tarpay. As we built the first row of bricks up the wall, we painted it again and pasted it with more mats of woven razor grass, then we rammed the second wall of bricks hard against it.

Next to the house, we'd dug a wide, shallow hole with a bottom slanting away from the house. After we painted it with tarpay, we installed a double lining of bricks; that would be our water tank. We built a sloping brick pipe from the house to a point halfway above the deep end. When I asked why not to the very deepest part of the tank, Big Jes explained that we had to leave the lowest place for sediments to settle; we didn't want to drink that stuff.

On the other side of the house, a safe distance away, we dug another pit which we painted, but didn't brick. That was the winter latrine. Later on, next spring, we'd dig a summer pit. At the end of every day, we'd drop all of our garbage and refuse into it and put a layer of razor grass and a couple of shovels of dirt on top. When it came time to plant crops in the spring, Big Jes said we would pull up buckets of rich stinky fertilizer and the crops would grow twice as tall.

If we had actually been on Linnea, we'd have had to dig out a barn and a root cellar and a fuel cellar as well, but the house we built proved that we knew what we were doing, so that was enough. The Dome Authority didn't want us building things we weren't going to need or use here.

We did have a small fuel cellar, though, which was a much politer name for it than it deserved. At the end of every day, Parra and Cindy and Rinky and I had to go out and gather up all the dried out manure we could find. Either horse manure or boffili manure would do. Sometimes we went over to the corral, and sometimes we looked along the trails, but usually we had to go over to where the herd was grazing. We couldn't take a great-horse, but we could take a wheelbarrow, and we had to bring it back full. The manure had to be completely dried out before we could toss it in the fuel cellar. In the winter, this would be our only source of fuel for the fire.

If we had started earlier, we would have harvested razor grass and dried it, rolling it up in bundles and pressing them in the brick presses to make fuel bricks for our fires. But we needed to concentrate on building the house first, so the brick presses were mosty busy. After we finished making bricks for the house, we did make some for the fire, but we were quickly running out of time.

We stored as many fuel bricks as we could make, but Da-Lorrin had calculated how many we'd need per day, and we knew we wouldn't be able to make enough to last through our first winter. And we'd already used most of our grass making tarpay. In future years, we'd start earlier and store a lot more fuel bricks; but for now, we kids had to take the wheelbarrows and go out looking for manure.

When it came time to put a roof on the house, we used the heavy axles from the wagon as cross beams. And we used the chassis boards too. Then we laid the rest of the planks across them to support a ceiling of bricks and earth. Then we laid more planks, more bricks and more dirt. The roof had to be strong enough to support the weight of a bof-fili stampede and thick enough to insulate us against a range fire. The scouts had told us that two meters of ceiling should be enough, but Irm and Bhetto had both been trained as engineers and decided that an extra meter of thickness was worth the extra effort.

One week after tossing the last shovelful of dirt onto the roof, we saw the first sprouts of razor grass poking through. That was good. The root system of the razor grass was a tough interwoven mat. Give it a few months to grow and it would knit the dirt of the roof into a strong solid piece.

That evening it started to snow.

It was almost like it had been waiting for us to finish.

WINTER BEGINS

IT STARTED WITH A COUPLE DAYS of light flurries while they tested the snow machines. Then we had two more days of gentle snow that drifted down in feathery drifts but didn't really get in anyone's way.

We had already moved most of our heavy stuff underground, but we still had a lot of little things to pack away for the winter, and we had to make sure that the ventilation chimneys were clean before we socked in for the coming storm. Linnean storms usually lasted a week at a time, sweeping across the plains like great avalanching blankets. We'd seen simulations of the way the storms formed up in the great northern ocean before they came rolling inexorably south, so we had some idea what to expect. The arc of the Desolation Mountains wouldn't let them spill west, so they angled eastward, meeting the hot air of the prairie and creating great walls of lightning and rain in the summer and smothering white in the winter. We wouldn't have satellite access on Linnea, at least not for a while, so until then we'd have no idea how long any storm would last. So we had to assume and prepare for the worst.

The snow continued intermittently while the Authority ran various weather tests, and we used the time as best we could. We wrapped ourselves a little warmer and concentrated on the last few chores we needed to do. We had to put canvas covers over everything we wouldn't be taking down into the house and we had to pull all the rest of our winter supplies down out of the wagon we had been living in. It was cold and nasty work, and Mom-Woo drove us all harder than ever. She fussed and fretted and nagged, and a couple of times she even raised her voice impatiently at Da-Lorrin.

Maybe it was just the tension coming from the administors in the Dome Authority. And maybe she knew something in that secret way that mothers always do. And maybe it was just winter. The days had turned bitter-cold and everybody had to work long hours, and we were all cranky and hurting all the time.

Mosty, it was because we didn't know how long winter would last. On Linnea, sometimes the snow stays on the ground for as long as six months. They say they get a gut-buster like that every seventh year. Administor Rance hadn't given us any idea how long we would have to stay underground, but Mom-Woo assumed that was part of the test and she acted like we had to lay in half a year's supplies.

For that, we'd dug a snow locker—another underground room—and after the snow came down, we filled it with as much ice as possible. On Linnea, we would hang emmo or boffili carcasses there and keep them frozen for as long as the ice lasted; if the snow locker was big enough and deep enough, a family could have ice all spring and most of the summer.

Gampa said we could smoke the extra meat if we wanted to dig a smokehouse too. But the only fuel we had for smoking meat was boffili chips, which didn't really appeal to anybody, so we talked about pickling the meat in clay jars instead. Gamma said she could make a pretty good corned beef out of boffili, and next year we'd have cabbages and potatoes to go with. But those were decisions we wouldn't have to make until we got to Linnea. Here in the dome, we didn't have to build a whole ranch, just demonstrate that we could when we got there. On Linnea, we'd gather grass all summer and make fuel logs for the winter.

But here in the dome, this first time, it wasn't going to be a long or a severe winter. Mosty because it was more a test of the weather machines than anything else. They wanted to see how everything worked, so they could see what kind of problems they might have. Drainage was one concern; humidity was another. But the authorities also worried about the lack of sunlight and something they called "winter depression."

Living on Linnea, spring was spent planting; summer was about digging and repairing and gathering; and autumn was for harvesting as much as you could, as fast as you could, and getting it safe underground. Winter—that was about hunkering in the cold dark earth and waiting for spring, so you could start all over.

Not that the winter had to be an unhappy time, but it was definitely cramped. Older families on Linnea would dig one or two new rooms every year. Sometimes more. Some of the oldest families had grand underground villas, sometimes even four or five levels deep. Whatever you were willing to dig.

At first, most of us kids thought living underground would be fun. Nona and Shona and the toddlers played at being bunnies. They crunched Linnean carrots and asked each other, "What's up, Doc?" They never tired of it, but the rest of us soon found it boring, even annoying.

As we settled in, we discovered that there are lots of advantages to living in a burrow. For one thing, once you're underground, you don't have to worry about heat and cold the same way you do aboveground. Da-Lorrin explained it. Because we roofed over the rooms with the natural insulation of dried razor grass, we created a kind of underground umbrella, and once you get deep enough, the surrounding soil temperature is pretty much the same in summer or winter. Ten degrees Celsius or fifty degrees Fahrenheit.

Because you heat the house with a firebed, the whole dwelling acts as a heat-radiator in the ground, and eventually, the surrounding soil starts to warm up, maybe a degree a year. It takes a lot of time and living to heat up a home. The scouts said that some of the older burrows actually get up to a comfortable twenty Celsius or sixty-eight Fahrenheit, and really old dwellings sometimes need to open extra ventilators.

The firebed was like a big flat brick oven. Big Jes and Klin had taken a week to build it. The top was a platform as big as a king-sized bed; underneath was a deep firepit with a chimney up on each side. Every morning we started a roaring fire in the pit and by the time we'd finished the rest of our chores, the top of the bricks were hot enough for the moms to cook breakfast. The center of the platform was always hottest, and the edges were the coolest, so you could boil things in the middle or just keep them warm on the sides. After breakfast, the moms would start lunch and dinner stews in different pots and leave them to cook slowly all day. As the fire ebbed, the pots would get pushed closer to the center. By bedtime, the firebed was comfortably toasty, so we'd stretch out our sleeping pads on top of it or next to it and we'd be warm all night. It was kind of like camping out, only forever.

We had originally planned separate sleeping rooms, but as we finished the burrow, we realized that wouldn't work for a couple of reasons. First, we wouldn't have enough room for everybody, and second, the rooms would be too cold. Big Jes and Klin tried it the first night and they both woke up shivering and moved back in with the rest of us, so they could be closer to the fire. Next evening at dinner, we decided we'd use these rooms for when anyone needed private time, because sometimes people just need to be alone. But more important, *real* Linneans don't have separate bedrooms. Linnean families all sleep together on firebeds. So we would too.

By morning, the firepit was always a dark smolder, and the air in the burrow would be as crisp as dawn, so mosty I tried to stay under the snuggly blankets until Mom-Lu roused everybody up for chores. There was a lot to do. We had to light lanterns, stoke the fire, empty the night-pots, hang the beds and sheets to air, get the little-uns up, help fix breakfast and clean up afterward. My job was washing the dishes in a big tub over the firebed. I didn't mind because it was the warmest job in the burrow. Big Jes and Klin had to go upstairs every morning and bring down buckets of snow, so we could have fresh water for washing and cooking. They said they didn't mind, but later on, when the snow got deeper, I figured they might change their feelings about that.

Over breakfast the second morning, I asked Da-Lorrin if we'd have to stay underground the whole winter, or if we'd be allowed to go up and play in the snow. Mom-Lu and Da and Aunt Morra all looked at each other and I got the feeling that they knew something that they weren't going to say.

"Might as well say it," Morra said. She put down her tea.

Da nodded. "Should have told you before." Everybody sitting around the table went silent and waited for Da to continue. He didn't look happy. "They've let the kacks out."

"All of them?"

Da nodded. "We have only three kacks in the dome, but one of the females is pregnant. That's why they opened the canyon. She'll need to feed her litter. They get hungrier in winter and have to hunt more. They have to eat as much as they can as fast as they can, before the snow buries the kill and it freezes solid. By springtime, they can get fairly hungry; when the snow starts to recede, the kacks feed on the carrion as it thaws. They've got great noses for sniffing out meat. And near as we can tell, they're pretty good at remembering where their own kills were frozen and how deep."

I must have looked impatient, because Da smiled at me. "Yes, Kaer, I know that you learned all this already. But Mom-Trey missed that class, so I have to retell it for her benefit, all right?" I knew he wasn't telling the exact truth, because Mom-Trey had sat beside me in that class. I remembered it because every time the scouts talked about the kacks,

Mom-Trey would make those little fear-noises that she does in the back of her throat. So I figured Da was talking for the microphones more than anything else, because we knew they were watching all of us a lot more closely now.

"We *think*—we do not know—that because the kacks are hungrier now, the implants might not work." Birdie had told us that all the kacks were implanted so if they got too close to a human, they would get an unpleasant nerve-jolt. But it had never been tested. And we hadn't seen Birdie in months anyway—not since we'd moved into the Linnea Dome. So she wasn't the expert anymore—we were. Da held up a hand to keep anyone from interrupting. "We've had an incident in the north ranges. Nobody got hurt, but for a few moments, it looked serious.

"Three scouts went in for a close-up examination of a bunny-deer kill. They needed to take samples. They could have dropped a probe from overhead, but Authority uses the dome for training scouts too, not just families, so they have to attend their own exercises. While they were cutting slices from the kill, the kacks came circling. The scouts have trained well, so they knew what to do. One runs the growler, the noisemaker; you've seen how that works, haven't you, Kaer? It makes a very loud noise. Loud enough to make a kack slow down and study the situation. Long enough for the other two to mount their horses and arm their crossbows. Then they stand guard while the first one climbs up. Kacks have great cunning; they don't just run in. They circle slowly and stalk their prey first. Their hunting strategy is to worry the prey to exhaustion.

"Great-horses can't outrun a pack of kacks, but we've always assumed it unlikely that three kacks would take on three horses. We assumed wrong. Even though a recent kill still lay on the ground, the kacks kept advancing on the scouts. Not a good thing."

"Didn't the implants work?" Big Jes asked.

Da nodded. "They did and they didn't. The scouts could see the kacks shuddering with the shock of the nerve-jolts. But they still kept advancing. Nobody wants to say for sure why, but apparently the winter-kill instinct overrules everything else. For a moment, the scouts feared they might have to kill the kacks."

"What happened?"

"The horses. When a great-horse rears up and comes down hard, it makes for a remarkable sight—impressive enough to make a pack of kacks back off. The horses put on an astonishing display, whinnying and snorting and even shrieking—a noise we've never heard them make before. Scared the maiz-likka out of the scouts. And the kacks too. They retreated. A strategic withdrawal. You'll see the video next time we have a meeting. Irm thinks we could build a growler that makes the same kind of noises, but nobody on Linnea has done that, so we can't either. But maybe we can; we don't know yet. Maybe Linnea can do it with native technology, maybe we can print the electronics into the carvings on the outside; we have to look at all the possibilities. But this gives us two dilemmas, you know—what do we do on Linnea, when our lives get threatened? Do we use our advantages and risk giving ourselves away as aliens? Or do we not use our advantages and put ourselves in physical danger?

"But we will consider those questions over time. Right now, we have three hungry kacks running loose. We do not have enough bunny-deer in the dome to feed them for a full winter, so we will have to continue to provide Earth-meat for them. The thing is—all the Earth-meat they've been eating, the kacks have developed a taste for it. The administors think that's why the nerve-jolts didn't work. Perhaps the animals' nervous systems have changed. Unless we dissect one, we won't know for sure. But that question has to remain for another time as well.

"More important, we now face the same problem that the Linneans do. We have hungry kacks prowling the grasslands. The boffili can live off their fat for a while, but the kacks need to eat at least once a week. We have to assume that they will prowl the whole dome—"

I knew I shouldn't interrupt, but I couldn't help myself. "What about the horses? They'll go for the horses, won't they?"

Mom-Lu started to shush me, angry that I had spoken out of turn; but Da reached over and touched her arm. "No, dear, please. Let the child speak. We all share Kaer's fears for the great-horses." To me, Da said, "The scouts have already moved the horses behind the stockade walls of Callo City. They will have to live off hay and oats for a while, but they will suffer no further attacks."

Mom-Woo nodded. "A very wise precaution, Lorrin. How soon do they plan to return the kacks to their canyon? How will they accomplish that task?"

Da looked surprised. Hadn't Mom-Woo understood? "They have no plans for that," he said quietly.

"Then they intend to kill them? I don't understand. I thought the administors intended to duplicate life on Linnea as much as possible."

"Yes, exactly," said Auncle Irm. He got it. "Linnea has kacks running wild. So do we. The kacks will continue to run free, right, Lorrin?"

Da nodded. "Yes," he said, his voice still soft. "That means that we cannot allow anyone, especially the children, to go up alone and unguarded. We will have to take special precautions from now on, every time someone has to go upside. The children may have chances to play in the snow, but only when we have certainty that we have no kacks anywhere near."

SNOW

AFTER A FEW MORE DAYS OF INTERMITTENT FLURRIES, the sky darkened over and stayed dark. We only went up in groups, and all the grown-ups carried whistles and crossbows now. Several of the scouts had ridden out to all the farms and delivered additional supplies, including extra weapons and bolts. The administors had decided that the kacks represented too big a danger; they'd have to break their own rules. When we'd entered the dome, they'd told us that we would have to build our own equipment. Big Jes had built one crossbow, but it hadn't turned out well and he had planned to use the winter to try again. In fact, he intended to keep at it until he got it right. He said he'd build as many as necessary so that everyone in the family would have protection. But with the kacks running loose, we couldn't afford to wait.

Most of the families had turned angry when they heard about the kacks. Buzzard Kelly wanted to hold a special meeting to demand action. He wanted the Authority to either capture and contain the kacks or send the scouts out to kill them. But on this point, the administors dug in their heels. We had to learn to live like Linneans, and that meant with Linnean danger too. Buzzard never got his meeting; not enough families wanted to risk the journey across the dome.

In the evenings, we could hear the kacks howling. Sometimes they yipped and called to each other across the darkened prairie. Maybe the great roof overhead bounced the sounds back down. Little Klin tried to explain about standing waves and focus points and reflectivity. The curved walls and ceiling could made the kacks sound closer and louder if you stood at the right place.

I didn't think the kacks would come sniffing around our burrow. Mosty they stayed close to their den in the north. But one morning, I went up with Big Jes and Klin and Da to help gather snow and we found big splayed paw prints all around the half-disassembled wagon. The kacks had visited during the night, sniffing and inspecting. We found a lot of tracks around the entrance. And we found more tracks around the ventilation shafts, where they must have sniffed the air rising from below.

Da and Big Jes told me to stand at the entrance and hold the wooden doors open for them; they circled the camp slowly, pointing out paw prints to each other. The kacks had sniffed our cold firepit, our brick-lines, our latrine, everything—like a burglar checking out a house before he breaks in. Not a good sign. When Da and Jes came back, they went back down and had a quiet hurried conference with Irm and Bhetto and Cindy. Then the five of them went back up topside and rebuilt the doors to the burrow; they made them bigger and heavier. After that, nobody went up for the rest of the day. And not for a couple of days after that either.

At dinner that night, Da said that we would not fear the kacks, but we would respect them. I couldn't see that much difference, but I wouldn't argue the point either. Because the kacks were running loose, it meant everybody else would have to stay in their burrows or travel only in large, protected groups. To compensate, despite their policies against dependence on electronics, the administors increased the number of hours of online access from two to six, and we settled in to take our classes off the wall instead of trekking in to Callo City.

Klin had hidden the projector inside a wall, not in the main room but in one of the rooms we used for private time. He'd dug out a hole, slid the tube into it, then packed the dirt back in around it. Then he'd hung a grass-totem in front of it. Linneans respected representations of the grass-mother, and they would be unlikely to look behind the mam. After he finished, he said he wanted to find a better way to hide a projector; but Big Jes said he didn't think it likely that any Linnean with average curiosity would even know to look for one. Nevertheless, Little Klin still thought the installation too vulnerable—what if we met a Linnean who had more than average curiosity? So he wanted to talk to the scouts about it.

But for the moment, we had video; we had a window on the world, and that helped take away some of the buried-alive feeling. Mom-Woo had us all playing different games. One day, we were journeying to the center of the Earth, the next we turned into bunnies hiding from the wolves, the third we pretended that we lived under the sea. The burrow became a spaceship, a submarine, an igloo, a secret cave hidden from horrible monsters. Sometimes we dressed up in hats and shawls. But my favorite of all the games we played, we turned the burrow into a vast underground complex and we became the secret defenders of the whole world, sending forth armies of super-agents and robots and spies to fight the monsters who lived on the far side of the sky. On days like that, the burrow felt safe and warm.

But we had just as many days when we all felt cramped and cranky. We stopped talking to each other and withdrew into ourselves, into our private selves, into the most secret and sometimes most lonely places of all. On those days, we'd turn on the video and do a scan to see if the kacks were prowling anywhere near. If not, we'd all go up as a group; we'd keep close to the burrow entrance, but at least we'd see the sky—or at least something that looked like a sky. The dome ceiling was high and far away.

But most days, we couldn't even do that. The snow kept falling, kept piling higher and deeper. Sometimes, even on days when it paused, we couldn't go up. And when we finally could, the snow lay everywhere in huge drifts that rose taller than Big Jes. We wanted to dig tunnels in it, but Da wouldn't let us; he feared that the snow would collapse down on us. But he did allow us to dig out a clearing, and eventually trenches, and the more water we needed below, the longer and deeper the trenches became.

After a few weeks, going up meant standing around in a deep hole or digging a little further in a rising trench. We could look up at the dome sky and see it as a bright yellow sliver. Sometimes blue, sometimes greenish, but mosty amber because of all the micro-dust in the air. Well, on Linnea, it would be micro-dust. On Earth, it was tunable light-panels.

We didn't spend a lot of time studying how the dome worked, but our enforced captivity in the burrow gave us a lot of time for talking, and we needed to practice our language until it was second nature. Most important, we had to lose our accents. Or learn how to fake Linnean accents. Aunt Morra explained that to all of us, more than once. She said that every language has its own rhythm, its own set of inflections and idiosyncrasies. Most tricky, she said, every language puts the emphasis on different syllables. Hungarian puts the emphasis on the last syllable of the word, German puts it on the first, and the French speak all syllables with equal emphasis. Not only that, but you can hear this emphasis reflected in the music of each nation, because song comes from speech. "If I had a piano here, I'd show you," she said. And then she sighed. "I miss my music. I could never give up my music." Then she remembered what she intended to say, shook her head as if to brush away the memories, and continued. "We all speak Spanglish. That has a very lyrical set of rhythms and inflections, inherited from at least two distinct languages. When we speak Linnean, we don't realize it, but we add those inflections and rhythms. We need to unlearn our Earth ways of speaking, and match the Linnean sounds instead: the drawl, the slur, the way the vowels and the consonants are pronounced, and most of all, we need to match the rhythms and emphasis of Linnean speech. Otherwise, our language will give us away. If even one person with a Spanglish accent gets caught as a maiz-likka, then every other person with that accent will immediately come under the same suspicion. So let's do our language exercises again. Our lives—I mean, *your* lives," she corrected herself, "will depend on it." She seemed suddenly embarrassed by the reminder that she would not be going to Linnea with the rest of the family.

Little Klin had become fascinated with the mechanics of winter in the dome. He and Bhetto argued about it for hours. Days. Where had the water come from to manufacture all this snow? That part was easy, of course. Authority had a gate open to a frozen world. They could pump in as much frozen H_2O as they needed. But Klin and Bhetto were more concerned with the engineering. Did they pipe it in as liquid or solid? If liquid, that meant expending energy to heat it on the frozen side so it could be piped over, and then more energy on this side to freeze it again for the dome; but if solid, that meant cutting the ice into blocks or shaving it into particles and moving it through different kinds of tubes. Neither of them ever convinced the other, and the question remained unanswered because Authority had long since made it clear that they would not reply to any questions about the mechanics of the dome. You could lose work points for asking. We had to behave as if no such place as Earth existed, as if we lived only on Linnea. We must focus ourselves on the sea of grass and nothing else.

Linnea has longer days than Earth, about three hours longer. At first, we thought that the dome had a translucent ceiling and the rotation of the Earth determined our days and nights; but after a month or two,

Mom-Trey remarked that the days and nights seemed unnaturally long. Then the rest of us began to notice it too. Very quickly we realized that the dome was gradually shifting to Linnean time; on one of the few occasions that the administors talked about the workings of the dome, they actually admitted to adding two minutes a day—one minute to the day and one to the night. In just a little more than six months, the cycle of life in the dome would match the day-night cycle of Linnea. If we stayed on Earth long enough, it would eventually happen that our days and nights would be totally opposite those of Earth, before creeping back toward a semblance of synchronicity.

Of course, that created another argument between Klin and Bhet-to—how the dome managed to successfully create the illusions of day and night skies, especially sunrises and sunsets. They each had theories about projectors and light panels, and insulation against Earth-daylight too. But most of the rest of us paid little heed. It had become much easier to accept the cycle of light and darkness that we saw.

After a while, the snow stopped falling. We had reached midwinter, a time when the whole world sat quiet and waited. The snow lay on the ground and the few animals that hadn't "migrated" crunched their way from place to place, leaving broken trails through the icy crust. That's how we knew that the kacks were prowling close again.

We didn't go up as much as we wanted to. When we did, we all went, and every grown-up had a crossbow. Big Jes had offered to make a smaller bow for me, but Da-Lorrin had quietly vetoed that. Just as well. I wasn't sure I liked the idea of weapons. I could see their necessity, I just didn't want to be the person who carried one—because I didn't want to be the person who might have to use it.

We'd all hike up one of trench-ramps to the surface and crunch our way around through the snow, packing down the old, and breaking the crust of the new. We'd wrapped our feet in boffili skins; the soles of our boots were cut from wooden planks. By midwinter, we'd made Linnean snowshoes; bit thatches of grass, frozen solid. Once we built a snowman, but we didn't know for sure if Linneans built snowmen, and none of the scouts could answer that question either, so we decided not to do it again. The Linneans didn't make representations the same way we did; they had totems instead.

We all decided that the long midwinter was the hardest part of all. The nights were silent and dark and lasted forever. Twenty hours of night to ten hours of day. Everyone grew sullen and cranky, even more so than usual. We stopped playing games, we stopped pretending our adventures, and we simply stayed in bed and slept longer than usual. Even the videos from Linnea failed to arouse our interest anymore. We just wanted winter to be over.

And then, one day, the snow started to melt. Not a lot, just a little. We noticed the icy crust on the snow and the glistening drops that hadn't quite solidified. We noticed that the bite in the air didn't burn as sharply as before. So of course, Bhetto and Little Klin started arguing about where all the water would go and how long it would take to drain the dome. For some reason, Linnean math is twelve-based, so when they started scratching out their numbers on the grass paper Mom-Trey had made, they would sometimes stop to curse in frustration at having to think in a different number-base. Of course, they got used to it eventually, but for the rest of us, the sight was always funny. Sometimes, we'd have to go into another room in the burrow to laugh; otherwise, they'd both get angry and that could start an argument that would leave everyone upset for two or three days. Or until Mom-Woo made her special honey-cake. Eventually, we renamed it "forgiveness cake" because while you're dipping cake in honey-sauce you can't stay angry about anything—and if you tried to stay angry, then Mom-Woo wouldn't let you have any cake anyway, at least not until after you did the silly-dance. You had to do the silly-dance until everyone was laughing. And then, if you could still stay angry after doing the silly-dance, then you had to have a snow-bath, administered by the whole family. Nobody ever wanted a second snow-bath. So we usually resolved all serious quarrels before the end of the silly-dance. The best silly-dance we ever had, nobody remembered the argument that started it, but we all remembered joining hands and dancing in a big circle around the firebed and singing, "Ding dong, the bricks are red...." At least until we realized we couldn't sing that song at all. Nobody on Linnea sang that song, so we couldn't either. We'd have to find a Linnean song. Aunt Morra said that she would research that. And all the rest of Linnean music too, even though we didn't have very much of it to work from. The scouts said that Linnea had a rich heritage of folk music, but not a lot of it was written down and they hadn't been able to record as much of it as they wished. Not yet anyway. Some of the researchers thought that a large part of the culture was embedded in the music, because it was an easy way to codify information and pass it down from one generation to the next; if that was true, then we had a great big blind spot and not a lot we could do about it.

As the thaw continued, the ice and snow above the burrow turned to slush. It was treacherous footing and not very safe, even for the grown-ups, even when they wore snowshoes. And it really wasn't much fun for us kids either. Linnea doesn't have a lot of trees. Not on the sea of grass, anyway, so we stayed downstairs and played dress-up, or we went upstairs and got wet and muddy, or we just lurked on the stairs halfway between and felt bad because we had nothing interesting to do. At least until one of the moms got tired of listening to us whine and put us to work.

The moms kept us busy, and we had lots to do every day. Not just our daily chores, but all the others too. We had cloth to weave and clothes to sew. And we had to make new boots and repair old ones. Authority had given us three boffili skins to work with, and a side of boffili to last through the winter; we hung it in the snow locker to age, but it was nowhere near enough meat for all of us. Just like the administors promised, we were going to go hungry—unless we rationed ourselves. The moms argued about it for three days before finally settling on a schedule of four small meals a day. Seven hundred fifty calories per adult for breakfast and supper; 500 calories each for lunch and dinner, with half-rations every third day. Bhetto did the math and said we still wouldn't have enough food to last until the first spring crops; so we revised the numbers down by 100 calories per meal. We might make it, but we were all going to look a lot thinner, come thaw.

Of course, Aunt Morra had something to say about that too. Aunt Morra always had something to say. Big Jes once said, behind her back, "That woman has a mouth like a torn pocket. Everything just spills out." Mosty, everyone ignored her comments. But this time, it was a cranky day for Mom-Woo, so when Aunt Morra said, "You could stand to lose a few," and then went on to comment on everybody else's weight as well, it started a three-day uproar. And no amount of silly-dancing was going to stop this family riot. Even Da-Lorrin's expression grew harder than usual.

Aunt Morra meant well, in her own clumsy way—I'd figured out that much about her—but she didn't have any sense at all about how to deal with other people. Sometimes she said what needed to be said, but mosty not. Or maybe she shouldn't have said it that way. I couldn't always figure her out. But she was smart and she was a hard worker and nobody ever faulted her for not carrying her share of the load. I used to wonder how she got into the family, until Mom-Woo told me she came in when we merged with Irm and Bhetto, and that sort of explained a lot.

The funny thing is Aunt Morra was right. Most of the moms could stand to lose a few. And Bhetto and Irm too. Maybe Big Jes, but not Little

Klin. Da-Lorrin always looked just right to me. We'd all hardened up quite a bit during the digging, but none of us looked as thin as real Linneans. Not yet. So maybe the administors had planned it this way. They needed to starve us down.

The thing about hunger, real hunger, it hurts. Not a hurt like being punched in the arm or the belly, because that hurt goes away after a while; no, this is a hurt like something nagging inside that doesn't go away, a kind of nervous emptiness that makes you all jittery and tired at the same time. The moms insisted that the little-uns get full rations, and that included me too.

I felt bad about having a full plate when everyone else didn't, except that some of us didn't need as much as others, and a couple of us, like Big Jes, needed more. So even after Mom-Trey served out the stew or the beans or whatever, some of us would quietly shove part of our supper on to the plate of whoever needed it more. I'd always give some of mine to Da or Jes. I'd pretend I'd eaten my fill and I'd say I wasn't hungry and didn't want any more and it would offend the Old Woman in the Grass if it went to waste and I'd shove it onto the nearest other plate faster than Mom-Woo could argue. She knew what I was doing and she always gave me a disapproving look, but I think inside she felt proud that I was trying to take on the responsibilities of a grown-up. Even if it meant going hungry. During the day, we'd chew on bits of boffili hide, and that helped a little, but only a little, not very much. One day, Big Jes' trousers slipped off his waist, all the way down to his knees, and that made everybody laugh; but it also showed how much weight we all were losing. Mom-Trey made some noises that this couldn't be good for the babies, but Mom-Woo took her aside for a private talk and after that, she kept quiet about the food.

We had rice and beans and Linnean noodles. We had potatoes and carrots and Linnean corn. And we had a lot of different spices too. Plus we had a couple of bales of dried grass, which could be used to make soup or tea, depending on what you wanted to call it. You could fill your belly with it, even though it didn't have a lot of calories. So we had the winter-hungries as Mom-Woo called them. We were all nervous and jittery and cranky and we all tired easily and slept long. By midwinter, we were even wondering why we'd signed up for this and if it was ever going to be worth it.

Bhetto and Irm and Jes and Klin got into a week-long argument about that. "Why not just send in a couple of divisions and take control of Linnea? Why not just go in and tell the descendants of the original explorers what happened? We could bring them medicine and technology and education. We could make their lives so much better. That would be the quickest solution. So why should we go through this whole silly game of pretending to be Linnean natives, just so we could infiltrate their society and study them?"

Da-Lorrin wisely kept away from that discussion. Even Aunt Morra uncharacteristically kept her mouth shut, though Cindy and Parra foolishly spoke up more than once. At least, until they learned better. I thought that Bhetto and Irm made some good points. Why didn't we just go in? But the more I listened to Big Jes and Klin, the more I realized that there were two very good reasons why we shouldn't.

First, we had no idea how many people were over there. We knew that there had been at least three major plagues in the past three thousand years, but we still believed that there were at least three million people living on Linnea, maybe as many as ten million. That was just too many. Even if we had a million-man army, it wouldn't be enough; because we would never be able to find them all.

And second, it wouldn't be fair. It wouldn't be right. These people had lived their whole lives in a society that had adapted itself to life on Linnea. If we took it away from them, the cultural shock could be as devastating as when the first European settlers invaded the African and American continents. Plus, if we came in with force to take over their land, their world, then we'd be establishing a precedent that it was all right for the next guy to come in with force and take it away from us.

There was a third reason too. The sociologists had never had an experiment like this. They wanted to see what kind of society the Linneans had invented for themselves *before* it was tainted by contact. I could see the value in that, but I didn't agree with it. Human beings aren't experiments. Of course, that point came up too. Little Klin said it. And that's when the argument got really interesting—because that's when Bhetto replied, "If human beings aren't experiments, then why did Authority build this dome, and what are we doing in it? We're an experiment too. The only difference is that we know it."

Nobody really had a reply to that. The conversation sort of trailed off into the whys and wherefores and justifications for invisibly integrating scouts into Linnean society, and besides, it's too late for the pebbles to vote after the avalanche has already started.

MORE SNOW

JUST BEFORE MIDWINTER ENDED, we had another three weeks of snow. That wasn't fun. The burrow was cold and damp, and we couldn't dry it out. We didn't have enough fuel. We had to damp the fire by noon to save wood and grass-bricks and boffili chips. We all had runny noses all the time, everybody had a cough, and if we hadn't already been vaccinated against seven hundred and fifty-seven different possible infections, we probably would have all died of quadruple pneumonia.

Bhetto and Little Klin were sure they'd figured out why we got this sudden unexpected storm. The Arizona farms needed more water. Authority could have piped the water directly from the frozen world, but Arizona wouldn't need the water for another two or three months, so what better place to store it than inside Linnea Dome? Some of it would raise the local water table, but most of the runoff would go directly into Lake Linnea, with the overflow getting piped westward as the water level rose. So the more overflow, the more water they'd have to sell. Whether or not that was the reason for the midwinter snowstorm, that was definitely where the snow would eventually go.

None of us were very happy about it. The snow piled up higher than ever, and we went from cold and damp to bitter-cold and sodden. We'd peel off our clothes and do our best to wring them dry, lest they be frozen into boards by morning. We'd lay them on the edge of the firebed and hope for enough heat to turn the damp to steam.

Finally, in frustration, Mom-Woo scheduled a curse so we could all rage at how angry we were about everything. Everybody took a turn; we went round and round the circle, with each person standing up and cursing all the different objects of his or her rage, everything we could think of. You couldn't leave anything out, and nobody could interrupt. Everybody had to curse. And it wasn't enough just to shout your anger—you also had to be inventive.

We started out heating ourselves up with our irritation and annoyance about the snow. We didn't have a lot to say about the cold and the wet that we hadn't said a hundred times already, so very quickly we moved on to the folks who'd ordered the snow. They hadn't given us enough food, enough fuel to keep warm, enough time to prepare for the winter. So we started cursing the administors, listing all the things we'd like to do to them, all the things we'd like to see happen to them.

"I wish they'd get their heads caught in the hind end of a boffili."

"I wish they'd all get eaten by kacks—except kacks would spit them out because they don't like the taste."

"I wish they had to live in burrows like us."

"Oh, that's cruel—"

"If the administors had to dig their own homes, they'd have a lot more appreciation for what we have to do out here."

"How do you know they don't? I thought the administors had to have served as scouts."

"None of them had to suffer winter. Not like this."

"No, only on Linnea, where it gets worse—"

"Hey!" interrupted Mom-Trey. "Did you forget? We made this circle to curse!"

"Oh, yeah, right—" Big Jes picked up the thought. "You know what I don't like about the administors? I don't like their little beady eyes and their narrow little mouths and their nasty expressions."

"And don't forget those ugly earrings they wear," added Little Klin.

"I hate their shoes," said Mom-Lu. "They look so uncomfortable."

"No taste," agreed Aunt Morra, clucking her tongue. "You'd think with all their authority, they could at least have some sense of style."

"Maybe they could wear scarves. Bright red to go with their blood-shot eyes?"

"A feather boa," said Little Klin.

Auncle Irm laughed out loud. "I'd like to see that!" And then everyone began laughing. And then it got even sillier. "And the scouts. Have you ever noticed that the scouts all look constipated?"

"It comes from drinking all that grass soup and eating all that grass salad."

"It comes from eating too much boffili."

"It comes from having to deal with administors."

"No," said Da. "It comes from being so tight-assed, they just can't poop."

Big Jes laughed. "Even when they want to poop, they can't. It all plugs up inside. That's why they all have brown eyes—the internal filling showing through."

"If they want to poop, they have to stand in a high wind with their mouths open and let it all get blown out the other end."

It went on and on like that. Most of it was pretty silly, some of it was just plain stupid. But it made us feel better to say it. We didn't end up any warmer. It didn't fill our bellies. And it didn't dry us out. But we ended up feeling just a little bit better, and that was something anyway. And even for a few days after, all that anyone had to do was mention the scouts or the administors and we'd all start smiling in remembrance of the most outrageous remarks.

But we all knew the biggest joke of all—that we had *chosen* this. That was what made the rest so funny and proud at the same time. Because we could resign any time we wanted. All we had to do was take a family vote and call a scout. We could have hot food, clean sheets and steaming baths in just a couple of hours. And as the winter dragged on, we heard that a few families had done just that. I think it was baths I missed the most. *Real* baths. We all kept clean, after a fashion, but it wasn't the same.

Every sixth day, Mom-Woo would make us bathe. We'd boil up a big tub of hot water and everybody would line up. When each person's turn came, they'd strip off their clothes and the moms would scrub them all over with hot soapy lather. Then they'd rinse them with hot wet rags. Then they'd wrap the shivering victim in a boffili robe to dry off, hairy side in. The thick fur of the boffili mane worked better than a towel. By then, the moms had already started scrubbing the next person in line. We could wash everyone with just two tubs of water.

We never got as clean as we wanted, so in addition to feeling cold and wet all the time, we also felt dirty. And as the fuel supplies dwindled, we started bathing every ninth day. It was just too much, and one afternoon I started crying in Da-Lorrin's lap that I didn't want to do this anymore. I just wanted to go home. Da tried to comfort me, but I couldn't hear him, I felt so bad. I ached all over, I was shivering and hungry, and I felt dirty and ugly. As Da patted my head, I could feel how stringy my hair had become.

That night, Da called a family meeting. Everybody knew what he wanted to discuss. Everybody had seen my outburst. Everybody sat around the inside of the burrow, on the benches we'd carved out of the dirt. The little-uns huddled on the firebed between me and Cindy. In the flickering lantern light, we all looked like strangers. Mom-Woo, Da-Lorrin, Big Jes, Little Klin, Rinky, Auncle Irm, Bhetto, Aunt Morra, Gamma and Gampa, Parra, Mom-Trey, and Mom-Lu. I'd never thought about why all these separate people had come together as a family; I'd always assumed that we were family because we all fit together. But tonight, everybody looked different, like a group of people who'd just met for the first time. I couldn't imagine them staying together. Maybe Big Jes and Little Klin. Maybe Gamma and Gampa. Maybe Da-Lorrin and Mom-Woo. But the rest? I had the strangest feeling that if we left this room tonight, we'd all scatter like embers in the wind, quickly burning out in the cold night.

Da spoke quietly. "We have to think about the children." He said it in English.

"I thought we were thinking about the children when we signed up for this misadventure," Bhetto replied, always the first to sink his teeth into the argument.

Da nodded. "We thought that life on a new world would be better for everyone. I think most of us still think that. Maybe Linnea isn't the right world. Maybe we miscalculated. Maybe we underestimated the difficulties. And maybe we're not suited for pioneer life. I think we've all had our doubts. Maybe we should talk it out."

Big Jes, who hardly ever argued with Da, shook his head. "How many times do we have to talk this out? We've been having this conversation for months. It always ends the same way. We have to stick it out. Because that's who we are. We're bigger than our problems. We're not quitters. Blah blah blah. And every time we remind ourselves of that, we're good for two days, and then something else happens and we have to have the conversation again. We've spent how many months now trying to convince ourselves that we want to do this? Either we're in this or we aren't. So either we quit tonight or we stop pissing on ourselves."

A couple of people applauded, but not for very long. Everybody looked to Da for his response. "I could just as easily have made the same speech, Jes. And I probably would have, under other circumstances. But you saw Kaer this afternoon, everybody did. I've never seen such anguish in any child, and for the first time since we began, I actually felt guilty for putting Kaer and all of the rest of us into this."

"You didn't do it alone. We all voted. We all came willingly."

"But—well, yes. But I still feel that—" He trailed off.

"Lorrin," said Irm. "For you, of all of us, to have doubts, it's startling. Because you're the one who always stood firm. You've always been the strength. Whenever any of the rest of us felt frustrated or weak, all we had to do was look to you and remind ourselves what kind of strength is possible. We weren't going to let you down, we weren't going to let each other down. And speaking only for myself, I have to say, there have been times when I've wondered if you were truly human inside. Sometimes you've seemed so obsessive that I wondered if you had lost all rationality. So I have to admit, for you to express doubts now—well, it's refreshing. It kind of confirms how bad things have gotten in this hole. Finally, even Lorrin has misgivings. Thank the Old Woman in the Grass. Lorrin has revealed he has feelings. But—so what?" Irm smiled grimly. "More than once, you've said to the rest of us that the emotional reason is the single stupidest reason for doing anything. Yes, we can have our emotions—you've said it over and over—but our emotions don't control us, we control our emotions. So what's it to be, Lorrin? Who's in charge here? Us—or our feelings?"

Da smiled gently, that slow thoughtful expression that reveals nothing about what he's thinking, only that he's listening, hearing and considering. He finally responded, "Yes, of course. And that's why I asked for this meeting. We've had months to live with our feelings. Now, perhaps it's time to apply our logic. Will it be good for us to continue this way? Are we the right people for this job?"

"If we aren't," said Big Jes, "then who is?"

"Eh?"

He nodded toward the other room, where we gathered for video classes. "You've seen what the other families are up to. They're clumsy, they're undisciplined, they're sick and weak. They all have lousy accents, they're cold and wet and hungry. They're badly trained—"

"Just like us," Parra said, shivering in the robe she shared with Rinky.

"No," said Jes. "Look around. We've trained ourselves better than any other family, and we work harder than anyone else in the dome. We look like Linneans, we talk like Linneans, we eat like Linneans—"

"—when we eat, which isn't very often anymore—"

Jes ignored it. "If we're not capable of doing this job, then nobody is."

After he said that, there was silence in the burrow. Because he was right.

"We can't run away from the responsibility," Jes continued. "Authority has invested over a million dollars in us by now. Maybe ten times that much. We don't know. But if any of this is going to work, we're the ones who have to make it work, because if we can't, no one can."

Da nodded and looked across at Jes. "What if you're right? What if no one can?"

Jes snapped back immediately, "What if no one *tries?*"

"Why do *we* have to be the ones?"

"Because, once upon a time, when we still lived under a blue sky and not a yellow one, *we* said that we were the ones. We gave our word."

Da continued to nod. "I hear the words. I hear all the words. I've said them myself, many times. Not only in family meetings, but out there in the fields, in the dirt and the snow—I've reminded myself over and over again. But this afternoon, with Kaer crying in my lap—I felt helpless."

"So you would give the entire decision to Kaer?"

And in that moment, every eye in the room turned to me. And I suddenly realized this meeting wasn't about Da, had never been about Da, had always been about my frustrated outburst. I felt strangely detached. I felt like an alien in my own home, as if all of these people had suddenly become something I couldn't become, couldn't even comprehend. I felt *left behind*. That feeling of being in a room full of strangers came back stronger than ever.

I wanted to get out of this hole, more than anything. I wanted out of this burrow. I wanted to stop being cold and hungry and wet. I wanted a bath, a cup of hot chocolate and big fat hamburger smothered in juicy red relish. I wanted a root beer float with vanilla ice cream. I wanted clean sheets and a soft nightshirt. I wanted everything we'd left behind—everything we'd said we wanted to get away from. I wanted to quit.

Mom-Woo asked softly. "Kaer, darling? Do you remember why you wanted to come to Linnea? Because of the horses. You said you wanted to go to Horse World. Remember? Every time you talked about the great-horses, your eyes lit up. The first time you saw the horses, your whole face shone with wonder. You radiated such sheer happiness, everyone in the family laughed with joy. You love the horses. More than anyone else in this burrow, you're the one who wanted Linnea the most. I don't want to say that your love of the horses was the only reason we chose this world, because it wasn't, but it was certainly one of the important reasons. None of us had ever seen you so happy ever before in your life. When we all sat down to make our final decision, Da said it for all of us, 'There are lots of places we can go, and there are lots of good reasons for choosing any of those gates; but I think we should add one more question to our discussion. I think we should choose a world that makes the children happy.' So if this world isn't making you happy, Kaer, we want you to say so."

By now, there were tears rolling down my cheeks, probably leaving dirty streaks in the ever-present soot and grime that we all wore as burrow-makeup. I shook my head. "I don't want—" I started, then stopped. I choked on the words and tried again. "I don't want to be the reason anyone quits or stays. I don't want it to be my fault."

Mom-Woo nodded. "What do you want to do, dear?"

"What I want—?" I shook my head, I choked on the words. All of these strange people, these orange jack-o-lantern faces, lined and drawn, with rings and paint and hair in the Linnean style. Like American Indians, like the Inuit, like the natives of some small forgotten village in some dark southern jungle. All these aliens. These natives of Linnea, asking me if I wanted to go home. All I had to do was click my heels three times and wish—

But all these people had worked so hard, so long. We couldn't quit now. It would all go to waste. Well, no—it wouldn't go to waste. We could continue on as trainers. Or atmosphere people, living in Callo City, helping others to learn how to become Linneans, so they could take our place and go on through the gate and actually live on the new world and...and...ride the horses. No, we'd worked too hard, we couldn't give it up. We couldn't quit. I knew the speech as well as anyone.

"I don't know what I want," I said. "But this isn't fun anymore. We're all hurting too much. I just want the hurting to stop."

Mom-Woo looked across at Da-Lorrin. "Kaer is right about one thing. This isn't fun. We are not having a good time."

Big Jes said, "That's no reason to quit."

Mom met his eyes. "That's not what I said. That's what you heard." To the rest of the room, she said, "This stopped being fun a long time ago. We have no holidays, we have no treats, we have no joy down here. We have nothing to look forward to except the possibility of escape. We've imprisoned ourselves. Maybe this is part of the training—maybe the administors have to do this to sort us all out, so that only the toughest of the tough will survive the training. Maybe this is how we harden ourselves for the trials still to come." Abruptly, she laughed. "And maybe this is the *easy* part."

Everybody groaned at that thought. And then, everybody laughed because everybody had groaned.

"Nonsense," sniffed Mom-Lu. "This is the hard part. And we're handling it as well as anybody."

"You think so?" asked Irm.

"Certainly. If I can survive one of Morra's farts, I can survive anything."

This time, everybody laughed except Morra, whose expression tightened in annoyance. "I don't fart," she snapped, almost embarrassed even to say it.

"Right, and you don't snore either," said Mom-Trey. This time, everybody roared and howled. Morra turned red in the face. If this hadn't been a family meeting, and if she'd had someplace to go, I felt sure she would have left the room angrily.

Morra looked like she wanted to say something about Mom-Trey's bean stew, but Irm put his hand on her leg and visibly squeezed it hard. Her words choked in her throat. That was *interesting*. We had all turned into different people here in Linnea Dome. We'd all grown stronger and harder. I wondered what I looked like to them.

Da spoke up then. "We do not have to make a decision tonight. Perhaps we should all withdraw from this discussion for a bit and each consider it in the privacy of our own souls. Let's resume this discussion in three days or six. When everybody's clear about their own feelings. Does that work for you, Kaer?"

I nodded, swallowing hard, grateful to wriggle off the hook of this moment.

"Then, we shall do it that way," Da said. And everyone agreed, relieved for the moment not to have to confront the decision. We could survive another few days, and another few after that, if necessary.

DECISIONS

So, OF COURSE, EVERYTHING GOT WORSE. The weather got warmer, then colder—warm enough to turn the snow to slush, cold enough to freeze part of it to an icy crust. The ground seeped constantly and the burrow got wetter. We ran low on fuel, and cut back the fire again, so of course everybody got sick. Not just sniffly-sick, but lay-down-and-die sick. We all huddled together on the firebed and slurped at soup and tea and took turns throwing up.

Whatever it was, we couldn't shake it. We coughed, we shivered, we vomited. We cried with the endless pain of diarrhea. The thing—that's what we called it, the *thing*—ricocheted through the family, infecting and reinfecting. Some of us relapsed two or three times. It was hardest on the little-uns, Nona and Shona—and none of Mom-Woo's medicines did much more than ease the pain for a few hours.

We reported our status to the administors every morning and every evening, but they offered us little acknowledgment and less advice. We understood that they were trying to teach us that we were on our own, but it didn't make us like them. Mom-Woo started muttering under her breath. I didn't recognize all the words, but I did catch something about ancient ancestors and untouchable night-soil collectors.

Da-Lorrin had gone all stoic again, which meant he was angry. Angrier than usual and not letting it show. When the *thing* got to him, he even threw up in silence, rinsed his mouth, then crept back to bed without comment.

139

On the fourth day, Cindy and Parra bundled themselves up and headed for the ladder up. Big Jes roused himself enough to say, "Where are you two headed?"

"Callo City. We're going to demand a doctor. Or at least some medicine that works."

"They won't give you anything. They'll just send you back."

"They can't do that. They don't understand how bad this has turned."

"They most certainly do—they're watching everything we say and do. We've all got monitors implanted. They know what we've got. If they thought the situation serious enough, they'd have sent someone out already."

"It *is* serious. We're all on the verge of pneumonia. And the toddlers are sickest of all."

"This is a test. We have to solve this like Linneans—"

"I see. That's a great way to show our commitment—bury a baby or two!"

That stopped the conversation. The only thing that broke the silence was Aunt Morra's cough.

Finally, Big Jes said, "It's too dangerous. If you don't get eaten by kacks on the way in, they'll certainly get you on the way back."

"We've got crossbows," said Cindy. "And clubs."

Da said, "I'll go with you—" But Mom-Woo pulled him back down. "You're not going anywhere. Not in your condition."

Big Jes was already pulling on his boffili robe. He pushed Little Klin back into bed. "No, not you." Little Klin started to protest, then rolled to the side of the bed and vomited into a bucket.

Auncle Irm spoke up then. "Why don't we try phoning first?"

Cindy, Parra and Big Jes looked at him as if he'd just arrived from Mars.

"I mean it. Call for help. Use the code-phrase. 'Elvis has left the building.' They have to respond. It's in the contract."

"Elvis leaving the building means we leave the dome," croaked Da-Lorrin. "It's a one-time deal, not negotiable. It's the rip cord on the parachute. Once we pull it, we're done."

"Maybe . . ." whispered Mom-Trey quietly, "Maybe, we *should* pull it." Everyone turned to look at her. "I mean, if we have to choose between going to Linnea or saving Shona's life, then . . . then I say, *fuck* Linnea."

I put my hand over my mouth to keep from giggling. This was serious—but it was so startling to hear *that* word out of Mom-Trey I wanted to laugh. But at the same time—*fuck* Linnea? Now? After everything we'd been through?

Big Jes pointed at me. "Kaer, come up with us. I want you to pull the hatch closed after we're gone."

I guessed that was it then. Fuck Linnea. I felt bitter and alone and betrayed. And a little bit relieved. Okay, yes, this was the easy way out. But so what? We weren't Linneans. We couldn't be expected to live in holes like gophers. They should have warned us—

No, that was wrong. We'd known what we were getting into. From the very beginning, they'd told us how hard it would be. They'd said it over and over. "No matter how hard you think it's going to be, it's going to be harder than that. It'll be the hardest job you ever loved. So you'd better love it, or you won't get through it."

I guessed we didn't love it enough. Fuck Linnea. I wondered how long it would take to get out of here. If they'd send a bus for us. If we'd sleep in real beds tonight. I wanted a hot bath, even a shower. I wanted to be clean again. Even clean underwear.

I wrapped myself in Da's robe and followed them up the ladder steps. We had a kind of foyer dug into the ground and half covered over with planks, a good place to put on snowshoes and outer wraps before finally stepping up into the world. We were out of the wind, but swirls of snow and ice kept floating down. I waited while the others wrapped themselves against the cold. As bitter as it was, it was also refreshing to get out of the stuffiness below. Big Jes put a hand on my shoulder and leaned in to my ear, "Everybody's feeling cold and hungry. They're all saying things they don't mean—"

"Yeah, I know." I hugged him. So I wouldn't have to say, "But they do mean it."

It took a few moments for everybody to tie up their leggings and fasten their snowshoes. Then it took even longer to wrap them tightly in their robes so the heat wouldn't escape out any loose folds. And then we had to hang their weapons on them, their crossbows and clubs. And finally, their great wooly gloves. By then, my ears were burning from the cold. It would be worse just a meter up—the full force of the wind would whip ice crystals into their eyes. Just before dropping their snow-masks over their faces, Cindy and Parra both gave me hugs. Big Jes too. Then he clapped me on the back and said, "All right, we're ready. We'll be back as fast as we can. Be sure to secure the hatch on the inside."

The three of them turned to go. They climbed the last few steps up to ground level, picking their footing slowly and carefully. Cindy and

Parra first, then Jes; at the top, he hesitated. Parra was pointing at something. They leaned their heads together to talk, but the wind whipped their words away. I wasn't dressed for this, but curiosity got the better of me. I pulled the hood of Da's robe over my head and wrapped it close around me, then climbed the last few stairs to the top. What were they looking at? Kacks?

Something bright in the distance. For a moment, it didn't resolve. Rolling across the snow, it flickered like a star. It was something from Earth. *Alien.* What the hell was it doing way out here on the Linnean steppes? I blinked, confused—right, we were still in the dome. But just the same, an air-car? Here? No, not a car—a chopper-bus, coming in low.

"They must have heard us—" said Cindy. "It's a rescue."

Big Jes poked me. "Kaer, get downstairs." Then he poked me again. "Kaer, get downstairs and tell them. *Now.*"

I slipped-stumbled excitedly down the stairs, down through the hatch, and down the ladder steps. I made so much clatter that everyone stopped what they were arguing about and turned to look at me. "They're coming! They're coming for us! A chopper-bus. It's coming!" And then everyone started talking at once, grabbing for robes and blankets, and scrambling up topside. "They're taking us out—"

And inside, part of me was screaming, "We've failed. We're quitters. We're no better than Tildie's family, or any of the others who flunked out. We're just another bunch of almost-made-its. I climbed back up the ladder steps with sinking heart—up in the bright yellow air again, just in time to see the chopper-bus clattering down onto the snow. It whirled up great flurries of white. Its pods crunched into the crust and sank deep, bringing the body of the aircraft almost down into the snow. A rollaway ramp unspooled toward us and two white-suited scouts picked their way carefully across. They crunched off the end of the ramp down to where the snow was packed harder. One of them threw back her hood. It was Birdie! Beautiful Birdie! She looked like an angel from the sky, with her long blonde hair and sparkling smile.

She spoke fluently, and she spoke only Linnean to us; her accent was flawless. She offered ritually correct greetings to everyone, but especially to Da-Lorrin. She bowed before him and offered her services. If they were here to rescue us, this was very puzzling. Then she straightened and became much more businesslike. "I offer sincere regrets at interrupting your winternap. You have my apology and the apology of the administors as well; but I must impose on your hospitality this evening.

In the *machine*—" There was no word for aircraft in Linnean, so she used a phrase that meant machine, though a more accurate translation would have been 'constructed tool.' "—In the *machine* we have guests from another world, a place called *Orth*. They represent *the authority that owns and controls*. They have asked to *admire-inspect-investigate*. They want to see how a real Linnean family lives. They want to see your home, your tools, your manner of dress and speaking. This has much *importance-value* for all of us, so please show us your best selves."

A *real* Linnean family?!

Then they weren't here to rescue us. I almost laughed. I almost cried. We weren't going home at all. I didn't know what I felt, disappointed or elated.

Da started to protest, started to explain, but Birdie cut him off, laughing and pretending that she was saying something else. "Please," she said to him Then to all of us, "Give me your trust. You must speak only Linnean. Say nothing in the old-tongue." She looked around to all of us—almost with a sense of pleading.

Mom-Woo got it first. This was a surprise inspection, and there was a lot at stake for everyone; not just us, but the whole dome, perhaps even the entire project. Mom-Woo stepped forward and made a ritual bow, with outstretched hands. "Of course, we welcome you. We welcome all of you as our guests. The long journey across the plains must have exhausted you. Please bring yourselves into our home. I shall make soup-tea." She poked Rinky. "Go stir up the fire, get a kettle, and gather fresh snow—"

"Thank you for your kindness, mother; but we have no need of soup. We have many other things to see today. Please? May we proceed?" Birdie looked to the rest of us and repeated, "Remember, you don't speak English, only Linnean."

English? Why would I want to speak English? I'd stopped thinking in English a long time ago.

Mom-Woo nodded acquiescence and stepped aside. Birdie nodded to the other scout and he spoke into the headset he wore. "All right, we're good to go. Bring them out."

The strangers wore bright colored clothing—red and blue and gold. Narrow pants and vivid jackets. They glittered and shone. A kack would have spotted them easily against the snow. An effortless meal, all of them. Two men, three women. Something about their manner—the way they walked, the way they looked at us, the way they sniffed the air— not just something, *everything* about them unnerved me.

They approached us warily, as if they feared us—as if they thought us savages. They didn't bow. They didn't offer handshakes either. They just stared. They didn't realize that they looked just as odd to us in their thin clothes, with their short hair and beardless, unleathered faces. Without braids or face-paint they looked naked. Their skin was too soft, they looked weak and fragile. Birdie made introductions too fast for any of it to register. "*Representative* Rich, *Senator* Snowden, *Secretary* Muller, *Chairman* Vocineck, *Advisor* Barx." She introduced all of us as well; she remembered all of our names.

Birdie spoke in English to them. I could understand what she said, but it sounded strange, not familiar. "This is Da-Lorrin, head of the family. Mom-Woo, the number one wife; yes, their family arrangements are similar to our own contract-family structure, but the work-roles are much more disciplined. They have a greater degree of gender assignment. No, the Linneans don't have mutable genders; they have no biological sciences, no science at all as far as we know; we're not sure why. It's almost as if they foreswore it. The tall one is Rinky; Big Jes and Little Klin are partners within the family. Gamma and Gampa—Gampa has a patriarchal role, he's the family advisor, and Gamma is the historian, maintaining the oral history of the family and teaching it to the children. Yes, that's Kaer—the one from the videos. Morra and her family are allied; Morra and Mom-Trey are sisters from a previous contract—" When she finished, the strangers just nodded to her, as if we weren't here. As if we were exhibits in a zoo:

The woman in the bright red jacket asked, "Do they just live out here in the snow?" She pointed at what was left of our great-wagon, a looming ramshackle shape. "Do they all sleep in *that?*"

Mom-Woo stepped forward then. She spoke directly to the woman; but she spoke in Linnean. "We should all get out of the wind and the cold. Would you like to come below where we have a warm fire?"

Red Jacket blinked; she looked to Birdie.

Birdie said, "She's invited you to see her home. They live underground."

The woman made a face. As if she couldn't imagine it. "In a hole in the dirt? Like animals? Why don't they have real houses?"

Birdie's response was quiet and dispassionate. "They don't have a lot of wood. But they do have a lot of dirt. You use what you have. I think you'll find it quite interesting. This way, please." I offered a hand to help one of the women steady herself as she picked her way down the stairs, but she didn't want me to touch her. She pulled her hand away as if I was dirty.

Down in the burrow, they didn't behave any better. Mom-Lu had stoked the fire with precious fuel we couldn't spare. She had water boiling in the pot and was already stirring in grass for soup. The three women made faces. "It stinks down here." I looked at Mom-Woo, she looked to Mom-Lu, and she looked to Mom-Trey. The real stink down here was Red Jacket's overbearing perfume. Mom-Trey coughed into her scarf, then turned away. She went into one of the other rooms and watched, peeking around the door.

Both of the men kept their expressions stiff, but all the visitors looked uneasy, as if they'd rather be anywhere else but here. I wondered if Birdie was embarrassed; if she was, she didn't show it. She kept up a steady stream of chatter, explaining all the details of Linnean life, like a travelogue on TV. "If you'll notice, the walls are made of rammed-earth bricks. The Linneans also use sandbag construction as well; that's often faster and easier."

The men ran their hands over the walls like masons inspecting an old building; but the walls were weeping with condensation and possibly slow leaks—Big Jes and Little Klin had been arguing about that since the first day it started. The men wiped their hands distastefully and mumbled something to the women. None of the women touched the walls. They looked around as if they were visiting a prison cell. They peeked into the other rooms of the burrow, but made no move to explore them.

Birdie tried to show them the boffili robes, how carefully we'd sewn the separate strips of fur into warm comfortable garments; they weren't interested. She showed them the painted clay jars packed with rice and beans and noodles, the pickled meats and vegetables, the root cellar, the dried and smoked provisions—all the good things we'd put away for the long winter. They tried to look polite, but the man in the black jacket poked the others. The senator, I think. "You'd have to be really desperate to eat this stuff. Or really hungry. A good steak in the evening, that's all I want."

"Why do people live like this?" Red Jacket asked Birdie. "Don't they know any better? They don't even have a bathroom."

Before Birdie could answer, the man in the blue jacket replied. "Don't be so harsh, Tasha. This is a step up for these people. Maybe the first time they've had a real roof over their heads. Look at them, they're proud that they can put food on the table every evening. Probably for the first time in their lives. For them, this is luxury."

The woman next to him, the one in the gold jacket, added her own shovelful. "You have to understand how the program actually works. The Gate Authority deliberately seeks out the poor. These people had no chance in the real world. They can't survive in a technology-based society. The Authority teaches them basic survival skills and then sends them through the world-gate. It's economic empowerment for both sides. They get a simpler world to live in, and we get rid of that class of people who can't or won't work in ours."

"You're being too polite, Tasha. We're deporting them for their failure, for not keeping up with the world."

"Whatever. It's good for them; it's even better for the rest of us." Behind them, Rinky had a hand over her mouth, trying not to laugh out loud; she covered it with a coughing fit. Mom-Trey turned her back to the rest of us and pounded Rinky's back. Aunt Morra looked angry, but Irm had had a strong hand on her shoulder, squeezing hard and holding her back. Da was looking at the ceiling, as if studying a bug. Big Jes was rummaging in a corner for something; I couldn't see his face.

To her credit, Birdie kept a straight face. She looked to us and spoke quickly in Linnean. "Yes, they are boffili droppings. Please regard them as *strange animals* in a *place for strange animals*." That triggered another coughing fit from Rinky, and even Da had to smile.

"So where do they all sleep?" Red Jacket asked bluntly.

Birdie indicated the firebed. "Usually, they all sleep together on top of the brick stove. It conserves fuel. In larger burrows, they might have two or three beds, but this is fairly normal."

"They all sleep *together?*" Both of the men and all three of the women exchanged glances—as if Birdie had just suggested we regularly practiced incest, cannibalism and theocracy.

"It's the Linnean custom," Birdie said. "You cannot judge any of this by the standards of Earth; Linnean culture has evolved for the conditions found on Linnea." She started to explain that Linnea had a much more limited ecology than Earth because only a subset of Earth plants and animals had been imported—

And then, suddenly, I got it. I looked across at Da and said excitedly, "Da! These people think they're really on Linnea. I bet they insisted on a trip through the gate, but the administors couldn't allow that, so they brought them into the dome and told them they're on Linnea. They think we're colonists. I bet I'm right."

Da's reaction of surprise and recognition ricocheted around the room. The angry expressions of the rest of the family softened immediately. The joke was on *them*, not us. Rinky even giggled aloud.

Birdie interrupted herself, stopped in the middle of a discussion of the versatility of the genetically enhanced grass, to look to me specifically. "Very smart, Kaer. Not quite accurate, but close enough. Thank you for understanding." She winked, then turned back to the guests and dryly resumed a dissertation on what a marvelous evolution lab Linnea had become. The rapid spread of known species into new niches had startled even the most radical of theorists, and therefore the people emigrating to the new world were pioneers in the truest and bravest sense.

The visitors stood around uncomfortably and listened to Birdie's lecture with ill-concealed impatience. At last, one of the women raised her hand, "Yes, yes, we know all that. What I don't understand how can they live in this *squalor?* Don't they know any better?" I thought Mom-Lu was going to spill soup on her, but instead, she turned away and handed the bowl to Birdie.

Birdie—bless her soul—took the bowl held it high and gestured north, east, south and west, each time thanking the Old Woman in the Grass; then, appropriately, she took a sip and passed the bowl to the guests. "You must each take a sip. It's an enormous insult if you don't accept their offer of hospitality." The visitors took the bowl and sniffed, but despite Birdie's instructions, only the men sipped at the soup. The women made more faces. "Do you think it's safe?" "It doesn't look safe." "God knows what's in it." I wondered if they'd been born women, or if they'd chosen to be such witches.

I looked around at the rest of the family. Big Jes was sanding the edge of his axe, as if it were some chore he'd been meaning to attend and only now had gotten around to, except the rest of us knew better; whenever he was annoyed, he sharpened his axe. Little Klin leaned against a wall, arms folded, eyes narrow. Bhetto had gathered both the little-uns into her arms and had turned away from the guests to rock them. Mikey hid behind her skirt and stared. Cindy and Parra glowered from the top of the steps. Gampa and Gamma simply left the room. Irm and Morra looked furious, but I wasn't sure at who. All in all, we must have looked seriously ferocious to these poor stupid tourists. Only Da and the moms wore their company faces, but I could see it was a strain even for them. Despite the joke. Despite their ignorance. Despite Birdie's fervent words. These people were abusing our hospitality. They were bad guests—because they weren't letting us be good hosts.

The senator pulled out his pocket-machine and looked at it. "We're running late. We've fallen way behind schedule. We'd better be moving on. Come along, people." He started ushering them toward the ladder steps. Birdie wisely fell silent and followed them up. I followed Da and Big Jes and Mom-Woo. I wanted to hear what they would say to Birdie. Or what Birdie might say to us. Nobody stopped me, so I went right up after.

Most of the visitors were already picking their way along the ramp toward the chopper. Blue Jacket and the senator were talking quietly to Birdie, adamantly shaking their heads. "I'm not sure these people made all that good an impression on the committee. Perhaps you should have chosen a more appropriate family?"

"You said you wanted to see a real Linnean home, Senator. We showed you a real Linnean home."

"Well, perhaps—but this isn't as inspiring as we'd been led to believe. These poor people—couldn't you have done better for them? This is shameful."

"This is Linnea."

"Well." The senator glanced around, looked up at the yellow sky, the endless plain of pink-glowing snow. He wiped his hands together as if rubbing the last of Linnea off his shining gloves. "If this is your way of saying you need more money, you've made your point. I'm not happy about this." Next to him, Blue Jacket pulled off one of his gloves and reached inside his coat, reached deep, pulled out a thick wallet and extracted a fat wad of bills. He crunched a few steps over to Big Jes and pushed the money into his huge gloved hands. "Here. Maybe this will help. You deserve better."

Big Jes stared at the money, the green and peach bills, then he held the cash aloft, laughing. "Look everyone—toilet paper! We have toilet paper!" Even Mom-Woo laughed out loud. Da guffawed. Rinky and I slapped each other's shoulders, laughing. Little Klin shouted, leapt backward into a snowbank and kicked his feet up in the air.

"See?" Blue Jacket said to Birdie. "They understand what's important."

That set off a new round of laughter. Joyous, raucous, uninhibited, silly laughter.

The senator agreed. "Well...they may be simple people, but they're happy. I can't argue with that. Maybe they know something the rest of us don't."

Pleased with himself, Blue Jacket turned and began crunching through the snow back toward the chopper. The senator followed close behind. I wanted to wave my hand and call "Thank you," in English, but Rinky must have read my mind; she put a hand on my shoulder. Birdie looked at us, at our merriment, and realized there was nothing she could say.

"Wait," said Mom-Woo, touching Birdie's arm. "The babies need medicine. We need help out here—"

"Yes, we know. But you know the rules. You agreed to the rules. We cannot bring you help. You have to survive on your own. Or not at all." Mom-Woo hung her head, dejected, but Birdie caught her before she could turn away. She pointed toward a stack of boxes the pilot had unloaded while we were all below. "But we have imposed on your winternap, so we have brought you gifts of gratitude. Administor Rance sends her most gracious appreciation for your help and cooperation. And we hope you'll find the contents a lot more useful than... all that toilet paper. Toilet paper, yes. Big Jes has the right attitude." Shaking her head bemusedly, she followed the senator back to the aircraft. A few moments later, it clattered up into the air, turned in the wind and headed back toward Callo City.

REAL

IT TOOK TWO OR THREE TRIPS, even with each of us carrying one or two boxes at a time, but we got them all safely downstairs. Da wouldn't let us open any of them until everybody was unwrapped and warming themselves with soup. The first package was the smallest, but it was filled with medicines, all kinds; a note was included. "The red syrup is for the babies. One spoonful every morning for three days. Everyone else should take one yellow pill every day for three days. This is an update to your vaccinations."

Da made a face, and muttered something under his breath. Something about God arriving in a constructed tool. Whatever.

The bigger boxes contained slow-burn logs. Enough to last for two months, if we were careful. Two others had warm blankets and some clean clothes.

"I thought they weren't supposed to help us," said Bhetto, grumpily.

"This isn't help. It's a gift. There's a difference."

"A difference of words, not results."

"Maybe this is their way of admitting that they scheduled winter too soon, that we did not have enough time to properly prepare, starting from scratch," said Rinky. "By the time we finished digging our burrow, we had no time left for anything else."

"It will be that way when we get to Linnea," said Big Jes. "Now we've learned our lesson."

"When we get to Linnea?" asked Cindy. "I thought we had decided to quit."

"I dunno," said Little Klin. "After all those stupid things those stupid visitors said, I'm just angry enough to stay. They insulted our *home*."

"I feel the same. Who wants to stay on the same planet with that ugly old bitch in the red jacket? She had a face like an elbow wrinkle."

"And a mouth like a torn pocket," said Morra. "Even worse than me." Everybody laughed. Even Irm looked at her in surprise. Big Jes went a little pale. "Uh, I didn't know you'd overheard that—"

"Oh, hell, dear—I hear everything. This family has no secrets. I thought you knew that." She patted his arm. "For a moment there, I thought you were going to use that axe. You certainly polished it hard enough."

"If he didn't sharpen the axe, he would have had to use his bare hands. And I don't think he wanted to dirty himself."

"Um, there is that," said Mom-Trey. "For all their shiny cleanliness, they felt like the dirtiest people I'd ever met. I wanted to wash the whole nest as soon as they climbed out—to get rid of their stink. That awful perfume. I still want to wash this room. I can still smell it." She wrinkled her nose and put her bowl aside. "It makes the soup taste soapy."

"Poor Birdie," I said. "She tried so hard."

"I thought she would choke when Blue Jacket handed Big Jes all that money. How much was it, Jes?"

Big Jes shook his head. "I didn't even bother to count it." He took it out of his pocket and handed it to Da. Da riffled through it, then laughed. "Two hundred and sixty. Even their generosity is stingy. Here, Kaer. Next time you see Birdie, tell her to send this back to them."

"*After* we use it as toilet paper...?"

Da laughed. "Imagine the looks on their faces."

"They wouldn't see it as an insult, you know," Mom-Woo pointed out. "They'd just think we're too stupid to recognize money."

"There is that," said Da. "Kaer, just give the money to Birdie and tell her to buy herself something nice."

"Speaking of Birdie," Parra added, "I liked what she told them. She called us *real* Linneans."

Cindy poked him. "Well, we are real Linneans. Thanks to the visitors, we now distrust Earthers."

"And that brings up another reason why we have to stay," Mom-Woo said. "If we quit now, it would certainly embarrass Birdie. And I think she has already suffered more than enough embarrassment for one day. Perhaps we should wait and embarrass her next week." Everybody laughed at that. Mom-Woo didn't really tell jokes, but many times the things she said had the same effect.

Then she looked at me. "Kaer, what's that look about?"

"We can't quit next week either. We can't quit *ever*. If we did...we'd still have to work off our contract. And they'd probably give us Birdie's job. Or one just like it where we'd have to spend all our time with people like the stupids."

Everybody looked at everybody else—and then everybody laughed out loud. It was funny. Uproariously funny. And that was the last time we ever talked about giving up. Now that we knew who we were, we knew where we belonged.

Inside the last box we opened, we found packages of spices, all kinds. More than anything, that brought cheers from everybody. And even a few short arguments what we should prepare for dinner that evening. Sweet butter pudding? Bean pie? Jerked boffili savory stew? Mom-Lu ended the argument when she said, "All of those things would bring us great delight. And more. But if we make the food too delicious, we will eat more of it, and we will run out of food before spring. We must make it last." She took the box of spices and put it away on a shelf. "We shall give ourselves a hint of flavor, just a bit, but we shall delay the real feast until we have something to celebrate." And then, just to make sure that everybody understood that she was not inviting them to argue the point, she added, "I have spoken." And even though everybody laughed, it was a laughter of agreement. It was what a *real* Linnean family would do.

After that, life in the hole didn't get easier, but it stopped being hard. It was just life in the hole. We were still cold and hungry and cramped, but we weren't crazy anymore.

And something else, too.

We were Linneans now, *real* Linneans. Not just because Birdie said so, but because we did. And that made everything different. We felt different. We acted different. Even the way we talked to each other changed; we stopped acting the various rituals and started *meaning* them. Even the blessings over tea became important. The Old Woman in the Grass became a real person to us. When we celebrated Winter Solstice, when Da actually got up from the table and opened the door to the world and invited the Old Woman to join us, I half-expected to see her come toddling down the stairs wearing a long grass cloak and a happy smile. I felt her spirit arrive, but I was genuinely disappointed she had not sent her corporeal self as well.

Now that we had become *real* Linneans, our studies also became more serious. There was still too much to learn, so many things that you could only know if you had lived all your life on Linnea—like knowing to look both ways before crossing the street, that red means stop and green means go; like knowing that the black beetle colonies are mosty harmless, but the bright red ones have a nasty bite; like knowing how to find your way through the grass when it's taller than you. That last one—well, I never really figured it out. The best I could ever do was backtrack along my own trail of crushed stalks until I got back to my starting point.

Sometimes, it felt like we had double vision. We had to learn about Linnea from the inside, as if we had always lived there; but at the same time, we had to learn about Linnea from Earthside too. It felt like an avalanche of facts, as if all that information was pummeling us. It seemed the more we learned, the more we had to learn.

Like all gate projects, the design for Linnea had started with the design parameters for Earth; then the scientists widened the criteria. You couldn't find an exact duplicate, but if you widened the criteria to allow for slight differences in gravity and atmosphere, you would increase the likelihood of actually finding a useful world. They knew the planet would need a moon, not just for its tidal effects, but because the gravitational influence of a moon would keep the planet stable on its axis, instead of wobbling like a top losing its momentum. The planet would have to circle its star at a livable distance and exist within a specific temperature range. The star couldn't be too old or too young and it had to have a usable spectrum of light. The planet would have to have a strong magnetic field, useful metals, available water, not receive too much radiation, and would have to be old enough to be geologically stable. It couldn't be all volcanoes. Everything had to be the right age, the right size, the right color—or close enough that it wouldn't kill you. Linnea had turned out better than most.

From Earth's point of view, the best thing about Linnea was that it could be terraformed. You drop in some anaerobic bacteria, close it up, and come back in a hundred thousand years; next you add aerobic bacteria and wait another hundred thousand years. Now you've got the beginnings of an atmosphere. And if evolution has done its job, you might even start seeing some lichens and fungus; but if not, you add some. You can start putting in other ingredients too; maybe some plankton and diatoms. Maybe even some grass seeds. Put the top back on, shake well, and come back later. The time-slip effect made it possible to do real-time evolution on a whole world.

Eventually, Linnea had a whole subset of Earth's ecology: basic bacteria of decomposition to feed the grass and trees, the flowering shrubs, the vines and ferns; then insects and spiders and beetles, bees and ants, worms and mollusks and slugs, lizards and mice and birds, all the little creatures that lived off the plants. And finally, the animals. Wolves, buffalo, horses, antelope, emus, camels, dogs and cats. And in the ocean, cod and mackerel, yellowtail and tuna, salmon and sharks. And eventually dolphins and whales too. The oceans on Linnea were almost as salty as the oceans on Earth; most fish would survive.

But Linnea wasn't Earth. It was different—just different enough that life had to adapt. Because Linnea had a slightly lighter gravity, plants could grow taller, animals could grow larger; but that meant that all the other parts of the ecology had to adjust as well. A taller plant means that water has to rise higher to nurture the leaves or blossoms. That affects the composition of the stems. And that ultimately affects the teeth of the creatures who feed on the plants. Insects could grow larger, but that would affect their ability to "breathe." Insects don't have lungs; their ability to take in oxygen is a function of their size. If they get too big, they need bigger hearts and that means more oxygen and that affects the shape of their chitinous shells. The larger animals too—they could leap higher on Linnea, but coming down put a different kind of stress on bones and muscles.

Earth animals are designed for Earth gravity, for Earth sunlight, for Earth atmosphere; on Linnea the stresses occurred differently. And sometimes, those stresses would occur in ways that put more strain on different parts of the system. Until the necessary muscles grew and the reflexes adapted, Earth-born creatures could be at serious risk for broken legs. *This means you, stupid.*

Earth gravity requires Earth-walking. You have to lean forward, shifting your center of gravity, almost falling, and put your foot out to catch yourself, shift your weight onto that foot, continue almost falling, and put the other foot out to catch, shift your gravity forward again, and so on. On Linnea, with less gravity, you have to lean farther to walk. You walk with a different gait. An Earth gait won't work, because you aren't shifting your center of gravity far enough forward. Running is a whole other problem. On Linnea, you have to run falling down.

But that part was still theory for us. We wouldn't know it until we actually got to Linnea. Even the few days we spent in simulators wasn't enough; it only gave us a sense of how much different our physical activities would become. The good news was that we'd be able to lift heavy things with less effort. The bad news was that all our muscles would ache in unfamiliar places for the first two or three weeks until we adjusted.

Some of this interested me, some of it bored me to exhaustion; but the arguments and discussions over dinner always held my attention, because I not only got to hear what different members of the family thought, I got to hear a lot about their past lives and experiences, things I never knew before. Aunt Morra had been a dancer. In a club. Earning money for school. That's where she met Irm and Bhetto, who were also students, already in a partnership contract. Rinky, who was my favorite sister, had been adopted by Big Jes and Little Klin before they joined the rest of the family. Big Jes and Little Klin had been in Little Klin's family, they met Rinky in the system; when their previous family rejected her adoption, they moved out and started a new family, but they couldn't get the adoption approved without guarantees of continuity, so they joined Da's family. Da only had two wives then, and only Gamma and Gampa—except Gamma and Gampa had never been partnered. Gamma was Mom-Lu's mother, and Gampa was Mom-Woo's father. Mom-Trey came along later, with Cindy and Parra from her previous marriage.

I knew a little of this from before, but now I was getting a lot more details—because now we were inventing new histories for all of us. Linnean histories.

Once we got to the other side, we couldn't just pretend we'd been there all along. People would ask us questions—things like, "Where did your Gampa meet the Old Woman?" which was kind of like asking, "What church do you go to?" And that was always a tricky question because every church kept records of every birth, death and marriage—so we couldn't just claim to have come from some city here or some church there, because if anyone checked those records and they didn't find our name, they'd know we were lying, and that meant that if we weren't part of a known church, we weren't recognized as human, therefore we were demons. Maiz-likka. And therefore dead.

So we had to have backgrounds that were consistent, but couldn't be checked—like if the church burned down and the records were lost. Or maybe we were the lost survivors of a family that had emigrated west a hundred years ago. Or, if we wanted to live really dangerous, we were wildlings—folks who had left the Church without permission. Except that was really, really close to being maiz-likka. Some places tolerated wildlings. Places where they needed extra hands to bring in the crops. Others drove them away.

Human beings had only lived on Linnea for three thousand years, Linnean time. They had mosty forgotten that they had come from Earth. The anthropologists weren't sure how that had happened—there were a lot of theories. The theory that everybody liked the most suggested that some kind of catastrophe had happened that had decimated the settlements. It had probably happened early. Maybe in the first two or three generations, before they had a chance to establish a sense of permanency. This was logical; Linnea's history since then recorded three major plagues and seven lesser ones. Maybe the survivors of the first plague no longer believed in Earth. I could understand that. If you're living in a mud hut, it's hard to believe in towering cities and silver airships. I remembered how strange the chopper looked when it came clattering over the snow. Maybe the tales of Earth seemed so fantastic to the generations on Linnea that they became fairy tales. Maybe the fairy story of the Old Woman in the Grass made more sense to them. Da said it best; it's a lot easier to believe in the Old Woman in the Grass, when you have old women and grass in your experience. Lots of grass. And probably lots of old women too. That's when Mom-Woo slapped him. Not hard, but hard enough to make everybody laugh.

Linnea has two large sprawling continents, each larger than Asia, and four small ones, about the size of Australia. She's got two big oceans, one larger than the Pacific. For most of her history, Linnea had people only on the western edge of one of the big continents, with settlements creeping slowly east. About a thousand years ago, settlements were established on two of the smaller Australia-sized land masses. A hundred years ago, or so, the Linneans finally reached the eastern edge of the large western continent. That was the one we were learning how to live on. Most of the settlements were young, it was a frontier situation, and most of the people were grudgingly tolerant of each other, because there was too much work to do and not enough hands; they couldn't afford to waste anyone. At least, that's what we were counting on.

Some of the scouts thought that it might be easier to infiltrate the bigger cities on the eastern continent, but Authority was reluctant to take the risk. Observations of even the smaller towns suggested a frightening level of theocratic control. Linnean society was in a kind of dark ages. Although we weren't allowed to see the pictures from the remotes, the scouts reported that witch-burnings had become common in some of the larger settlements. We couldn't take chances.

Some people on this side thought we should just send in an army. We had bullets, bombs and beams; they had rocks and crossbows. We had tanks and armored troop carriers; they had great-horses and wooden wagons. We had VTOLs and choppers, we had satellites and robots and probes; they had . . . what? Nothing.

Da told us of one of the seminar series he'd sat in on, where the possibility of repossession—they didn't want to use the word *invasion*—had been discussed. The military experts said that a relatively small strike force could capture the average Linnean town in a single day. It would be like Martian war machines invading medieval France or frontier America or pre-colonial Africa. There would be no resistance. It would simply be a matter of rolling in and taking control.

The real problem would come *after* the invasion.

The Linneans would simply disappear into the surrounding countryside; ten meters into the sea of grass and you're invisible. The result would be at least three generations of culture shock, occupation, continued resistance, guerilla warfare and terrorism. The effectiveness of the resistance would not diminish with time; it would grow—especially as the Linneans learned the nature of Earth technology. The Linneans already knew how to build catapults and fire-bombs. They would be determined, angry and ferocious. They would see the invaders from Earth as monsters and demons; for them, it would be a holy war and they would fight to the death.

Da said that was why even the most optimistic of the military planners advised against any kind of direct intervention. We had no real understanding of the psychology of the Linneans, only a few broad strokes and educated guesses. It wasn't just culture shock, it would be cultural destruction; it would be genocide. It would be one more failure to learn from the lessons of history.

The problem was that there were people in Authority who were impatient. They didn't want to do this the slow and careful way; they wanted the land and the lumber *now*. They said that the Linneans would just have to be assimilated one way or another, but the need for the new world had become critical. The Gate Authority had adamantly refused; the charter made the Gate Authority an independent agency, but the funding governments were now making ugly noises about decertifying the charter and replacing the Authority. The administors were threatening to shut down the gate entirely if that were done. Da didn't know if they were bluffing or serious, but he said that the political situation had become delicate.

We talked about that for a while. Gampa, who hardly ever said anything in these discussions, cleared his throat politely, and suggested that this might explain the attitudes of our recent visitors. Gampa didn't speak much, but when he did, he always said something important. If the visitors had already made up their minds what to do about Linnea, they would not want to see Linneans as people worthy of respect. They couldn't dare to see Linneans as having any dignity at all—because the moment they recognized that, they would also have to recognize the essential immorality of any plan for repossession. Invasion. Destruction. Genocide. That made us angry all over again. Twice over. Because if the repossession plan went through, then all of us would be drafted as interpreters. We would be forced to betray the people we had learned to identify with. That realization left us with an ugly simmering resentment.

But whatever the funding governments intended to do in the future, right now we were still down in a hole, still drinking grass soup and eating grass stew and sleeping under grass blankets.

KACKS

Shortly after that, we began a new series of classes. Seminars. Exercises. Workshops. The snow had halted and a great-wagon came out from Callo City. It was one of the big ones, two stories high, with two stoves and sealed glass windows, and actual velvet curtains; the best part, it had padded seats. The whole family bundled up, climbed up the steps into the wagon and bounced and jostled together all the way into town.

Gamma and Gampa and all three of the moms rode down below in the enclosed section of the wagon, all wrapped in blankets and huddled around the stove, taking turns rocking the babies. Morra and Irm rode with them too. The rest of us sat up topside and cheered the melting snow and slush, the promised end of winter.

The air still felt bitter-cold on our cheeks, but we all looked rosy and bright, happy to get out of the cramped burrow, even for school. We laughed and passed around flasks of hot spice-tea. We sang defiant songs, daring the winds and the kacks to howl; we would just howl louder. The great-wagon rolled and bumped and skidded across the frozen ground; the great-horses snorted and stamped. The wooden bells on their harnesses klacked and klonged.

The road cut round the whitened hills; the snow glowed amber in the day. We'd gotten a late start, but we still expected to reach Callo City before nightfall. We'd have a hot dinner at the inn and even a community bath; then we'd bundle up in warm soft beds and sleep without care, so we could all rise fresh and ready for tomorrow's sessions. But an unannounced set of flurries had dropped a few more fingers of snow on the road in late afternoon and that slowed us down, putting us perhaps as much as an hour behind schedule. The great-horses crunched slowly through the fresh white blanket, picking their steps as carefully as old ladies. Already the westering sky shone pink and rose. Big Jes and Little Klin no longer argued about the mechanics of the show; they simply appreciated it in silence.

Twilight on Linnea lasted an hour longer than on Earth. The snow glistened, the magic hour sparkled. Soon the lanterns on the wagon would cast a warming glow, and we'd bundle across the plain in a pool of bright. This time, we had two of the smaller great-horses pulling the wagon; Kilter and Kale. Usually, we had the larger, older horses; but Kilter and Kale had not had much chance to exercise since winter began and they had become restless in their stalls. The trainers felt that perhaps the time had come to let them earn their apples the old-fashioned way, working for them.

Kilter and Kale looked proud. It even seemed as if they jingled their bells deliberately. They were the first two great-horses born on Earth, and they had more monitors implanted than most of the scouts and trainees. The scientists wanted to know what would happen when Linnean life-forms returned to Earth-normal gravity. Could they survive, or would the additional strain on their bones and muscles shorten their life spans? Would they die young? Would their offspring gradually dwarf back to Earth-normal sizes? And if so, how many generations? Even more important, could they crossbreed with regular-sized horses to create new Earth breeds of greater size and strength? We had few answers, but we made up for it with extra questions.

Abruptly, the horses whinnied and stopped. The great-wagon skidded as the driver leaned on the brakes. I didn't know the driver, but we had two of the younger scouts with us, riding lookout. Willow and Burr. We knew them from class. Both of them had been to Linnea, and both had met real Linneans. They had even visited the real Callo City, but only for a one-day walk-through. Neither had engaged in any lengthy interactions. Next visit, perhaps.

Da called forward. "Why did we stop?"

"The horses—they've called a halt."

"Yes, I see that. Why?"

"They do that sometimes," said the driver. "They don't like the gravity here."

"Did they say that?"

The driver didn't answer. He began rummaging through the warm blankets at his feet, looking for his own flask of hot spice-tea. "You can't work these horses too long in Earth-gravity. It puts too much strain on them. They don't have the same endurance as they would on Linnea. Every so often, they have to stop and rest. So they stop when they feel like it."

"How long?"

"Fifteen minutes at least. More likely thirty. You might as well go down below and keep warm."

"Perhaps we should," said Da. "Will you come in with us?"

"No, we can't. We have to keep watch." He glanced to me, then added, "For kacks."

"Do you think they'll come this far south?"

"It depends."

"On?"

"On the size of their litters, how much food they've had, how much their bellies growl." Driver shrugged. "Kacks—hard to say. Kacks always have room for another meal. Even if they've just eaten."

Willow put a hand on Driver's shoulder. "Enough of that talk, you'll scare the children."

Driver grunted and drank from his flask. He pulled his boffili robe closer around his shoulders.

"Nothing to worry about," said Burr. "We've got growlers. And if the growlers don't work—" She held up her crossbow.

"The administors have given you permission to shoot them?"

Burr hesitated. "Only as a last resort. But we have tranquilizer and taser weapons." She patted the bulge under her robe. "You didn't hear that from me. Those kinds of things don't exist on Linnea. But only if those don't work will we use the crossbows. We had a hard enough time capturing those damn kacks, all to make the dome more realistic. I understand the argument—we need to keep the pig-mice and bunny-deer populations in check—but sometimes I think we have given ourselves much more trouble than we need."

"Have you seen many kacks out here?"

"Kaer," Da patted my back. "You ask too many questions."

"I don't mind," said Burr. She smiled at me. "Yes, we've seen kacks out here, but only from a distance. They haven't come near the wagons."

"I heard—well, Patta Kelly said that kacks followed their wagon almost all the way to their burrow."

"And when did Patta say this happened?"

"Last Nineday. After last class."

Willow and Burr looked at each other, then both looked back to me. Willow shook his head. "It didn't happen. At least, not like Patta tells it. They saw kacks, yes. But the kacks kept their distance."

"Do you think we'll see any?"

"We've already seen them," said Willow. "You probably can't make them out from here—they keep well beyond the circle of the light—but if you had eyes sharp enough to see through yellow twilight, you would have already spotted three large kacks hunkering low on those hills over there. Watching us." He inclined his head north.

"How do you know?"

He opened his robe and pulled out a tablet display. "See? Those three red blips? Kacks. The green blip? Us."

"How far?" I gulped.

"Far enough," Willow said. "They track all the wagons now. They've done it for several weeks. They've learned the roads. We think they've begun teaching the pups to hunt."

"How many pups?"

"Only four. The little one didn't make it. We haven't implanted them yet, so we have to track them with overhead probes and cameras. The pups all have white fur, so that makes it even harder to spot them against the snow. But the infrared should give us good targets." He started tapping at the display. "Ahh, we've got them now. They've spaced themselves out along the ridge. Hunting behavior. They don't have the endurance of the great-horses, so they run a relay to exhaust their prey. We haven't seen the pups do this before." He unclipped his phone and punched for Authority. "Yeah, Willow here. We might have a situation. Have you got us on monitor? Look at the positioning of the pups.... Yes, definitely a shift in behavior. No, they haven't moved yet. But look at their readings—they look more intense than usual. I don't think we can count on them holding back much longer. The flush of adrenalin could push them over the edge. And remember, we haven't implanted the pups yet. What do you advise? Yes, we have a kit. I think. Wait a minute, we'll look." He motioned to Burr.

Burr came back to the passenger area of the wagon and motioned for me to get up. I stepped forward while she pushed the cushion aside and lifted the seat to access the compartment beneath. She pulled out a large plastic case. "I've got it," she called. She opened it up, looked and added, "All current." Inside the kit, I saw various medical supplies, but also a few things with metal and straps that I didn't understand.

Willow spoke to the phone. "Yes, we've got a kit. Everything current." Pause. "Actually, I'd prefer not. We've got a full house here." Another pause. "Yes, I understand. Yes. All right. If we can. But I won't endanger any lives. Yes, all right. Thank you." He clicked off and pocketed the phone. He said a word I didn't recognize.

Da climbed forward to the seat just behind him. He put a hand on Willow's shoulder and leaned forward. He spoke quietly, but I stood close enough to hear. "What did they ask you to do?"

Willow's breath made clouds. He said, "They want us to capture a pup, if we can. Tranquilize one and bring him in so they can do a full bio-scan, implantation, the works."

"That sounds risky."

Willow nodded. "One pup doesn't represent any danger. The rest of the pack, however...they might defend it." He turned half-around to look at Da directly. "Don't worry about it. We'll only attempt it if they approach. As long as they keep their distance, so will we. Every minute that passes favors us. As soon as the horses have rested, we'll move on."

A few moments later, Kilter and Kale began snorting impatiently, shaking their heads and clattering their wooden bells. Driver picked up the reins and shouted loudly, "All right, move it! Ye stubborn great beasts!" The wagon jerked and slid and we headed on toward Callo City.

MOCKS

Depending on the course, we would spend two or three days in town before heading home again. We did this one triad out of every three, once every nineday.

It was both training and test to see how much we'd learned, how well we'd mastered the Linnean way of being. The way it worked, the trainers would assign us a situation, a job of some kind, and then we'd try to do it the same way native Linneans would. The other people in the cast would watch us carefully; if anybody did anything that was wrong or stupid or just inappropriate, a loud ugly buzzer would sound.

We had to learn every tiny detail of how to behave in public as well as in private, when it was polite to turn away and when it was not. Don't sneeze or touch your nose in formal company, it's a bad omen. Don't use your left hand at the meal table, it's unclean. Don't use your left hand to wave, it's an insult. Don't use your left hand to lift your tea to the Old Woman, it's sacrilegious.

If we had thought the training difficult before, now it became rigorous to a degree we had not imagined. As Birdie had told us on the very first day, "It will not only be harder than you imagine, it will be harder than you *can* imagine."

We had to learn how to barter in the store, the greeting rituals, the blessings, the polite way to negotiate, achieving the right combination of generosity and self-interest. We had to learn how to order a ritual meal in the inn, how to eat with respect instead of hunger, how to treat the innkeeper as an informal agent of the Old Woman, how to request lodging the evening and what to expect and how to behave inside the shared sleeping chambers. We had to learn how to respond to the ritual greetings of the local authorities, especially the churchmen. Every relationship had strict rules of conduct; even something as simple as a casual greeting on the street required specific symbols of respect depending on how well you knew the person you were greeting and whether the relationship was formal or business or...or a whole bunch of other things we still didn't understand. Nobody understood. Because the scouts hadn't determined it yet, and neither had the probes provided the information to decode that part of the Linnean semiotic.

You couldn't just watch and imitate the behavior of others. That didn't work, because adults had different levels of courtesy and familiarity, based on relationship, trust, gender and caste. Children had to talk to adults different than adults had to talk to children. Men and women had different ways of speaking to each other, depending on how they knew each other, what they were discussing, whether one or the other or both were married, if they had children, and so on. The Linneans had a lot of specific words and phrases, some just for men and some just for women—and no language at all for inbetweens or unchosen or recently-chosen or chose-backs. When you spoke in Linnean, you had to think Linnean—and the thinking sometimes hurt, because you knew that there were things that didn't exist in the language, that you couldn't say, couldn't describe and couldn't even imagine, unless you switched back to thinking in English. And that would be dangerous.

To put it bluntly, not knowing all the correct words and phrases and rituals meant you couldn't function in society. Not polite society, anyway.

Impolite society, however...that was our access. Out on the frontier, folks spoke the "rude tongue," a kind of catchall language that let folks who had just met exchange information without first having to go through several days of negotiations and discoveries. Not just useful, but necessary—especially if you wanted to warn someone of an impending boffili stampede.

We had several sessions where we had to learn various children's games. Even the adults had to learn the games, because on Linnea, they would have grown up playing these games. Not knowing slither or runaround or little dog would have seemed as suspicious as not knowing football or soccer or baseball back on Earth.

But the hardest exercises were the "mocks"—the simple conversations between one person and another. How do you answer even the most innocent-seeming of questions? I liked the pretend games; I hated the ugly buzzer. Bzzzt. Wrong. Thanks for playing. Please step over here so we can burn you to death in the firepit.

The scouts and the trainers continually tested us. Suppose, for example, you had information from a weather satellite that a dreadful storm would strike in a few hours. How do you warn your neighbors? Bad weather is maizlish, the work of demons stirring up the wind. Anyone who predicts bad weather must have spoken with maiz-likka. So how do you warn people? I had to think about that one for a bit. I raised my hand. "My gamma fears the demons work tonight."

"Why do you say that?"

"Because she always gets a terrible itch just before a dust storm hits. And she has that terrible itch now. She fussed all morning."

"You think we'll have a dust storm?"

"I don't know, but I intend to lock up everything tight just in case. I think you should too. When Gamma gets fussy, you don't want to listen to her say, 'I told you so.'"

Whitlaw was one of the trainers. He nodded, "That one works. But what other problems might it create?"

"If Gamma gets itchy before every storm, that starts to look like a kind of magick," said Rinky. "It might make people think Gamma a witch."

"But Gamma is a witch," said Gampa. "That's why I married her." Gamma smacked him, but not hard; everybody laughed.

But Whitlaw took it seriously. "Yes, you have that danger with any prediction you make. A successful prediction makes you look maizlish. So how do you defuse that?"

"Make some wrong predictions?"

"Make them guesses?"

"But that still makes you someone who pretends to have knowledge of the future. Do you really want others to regard you that way?"

Da raised his hand. "You have to get caught unprepared a few times too. Lock down what you can't afford to lose, but sacrifice a wagon or a corral to show that you had no special advantage."

Whitlaw nodded. "Yes, that works. Let's try another. A neighbor has a sick child. It's only a mild infection, but it could become pneumonia. What do you do?"

Gamma raised her hand. "Bring over chicken soup, laced with antibiotics."

"Yes, that will work. And how many neighbors will you have to cure before they start wondering if you practice witchcraft?"

"But if it saves their lives—?"

"Yes, some of them might overlook it. Some of them might have genuine gratitude. But fear overwhelms gratitude nine times out of ten. Do you really want to start a witch-hunt? And what happens the first time you fail to save someone's life? If people believe you have the power of life and death, then a failure is regarded as deliberate, even malicious."

"Oops."

"Yes, oops. That can earn you a quick trip to the firepit."

"So...?" Mom-Woo raised a hand cautiously. "Does that mean we must let people die?"

Whitlaw shook his head. "Think of every situation as a place where you must apply careful judgment. You must hold it as your most important responsibility to take care of your own well-being first. Otherwise, you have nothing to give to anyone else. Sometimes, you will have to withhold your own generosity, because in the long run that might ensure your own survival. If you ever get to the point where the people around you begin asking you for help, because your cures always work, then it will be time to disappear and disappear quickly. We do not want you to have to do that."

Whitlaw suddenly turned around and pointed to me. "Kaer. Where did your Gampa meet the Old Woman?"

"Huh? You mean Gamma—?"

Bzzzt!

"Huh? What did I miss?"

"The story of the Old Woman and Her Promise."

"Um. What story is that?"

"Warm up the firepit. We just caught a maiz-likka." He stepped down off the dais and grabbed my arm and started dragging me toward a taped-off area that we had from time to time identified as the penalty box. Now we called it the firepit. Others in the room started chanting, "Burn the demon-child! Burn the demon-child!" For a moment, I almost started to cry.

"What? What did I do wrong?"

"The story of the Old Woman and Her Promise."

"I never heard that story! Nobody ever told us that story! How can you punish us for not knowing what you didn't teach us?!"

Whitlaw stopped and stared straight into my eyes. "Exactly, Kaer.

Ignorance does not excuse you. The Linneans will burn you for not knowing."

"But—but—nobody told us that story."

"Yes. Nobody told you that story. That does not give you a get out of Hell free card. If anything, it only proves that you and your whole family stand outside the Law. So off to the firepit."

I said a word. A Linnean word. The closest translation was, "That's not fair." The other word I said referred to a certain body function.

Whitlaw shrugged. "Who promised you fairness? I didn't. The Old Woman didn't." Then he added, "We didn't withhold the story out of maliciousness, but so that you would realize how much exists on Linnea that you don't know, that we don't know, that we couldn't teach you, that you will have to find out for yourself. And you will have to find out without letting anyone know that you don't already know. You may go back to your seat now. We will burn you to death another time, when we run out of firewood and need a warm blaze."

A moment later, Whitlaw turned back to me. "Why do you cry, Kaer? Did I say something to upset you?"

"I'll never learn all this, I'll never remember it. I'll make a stupid mistake and we'll all end up in the firepit. I can't keep up."

Whitlaw sat down opposite me. He took one of my hands in his. His hands were huge and rough, but gentle. He said, "All this feels so difficult to you, sweetheart, because you know that other possibilities exist. You've lived in a world that has much wider horizons, a world filled with a greater richness of flavors, colors, textures and experiences. You've flown through the sky, you've visited faraway places and soared through worlds of imagination that the Linneans could never conceive. You know so many more possibilities of life. What you feel now—the pressure of cramming your great big life into a very small container—it hurts, it frustrates and it saddens. Do you think no one else before you hasn't felt this? We've all felt it. All of us. Over and over.

"Do you want to know the saddest part? We feel for the Linneans, for the trap they've built around themselves. If we could break them out, we would—but we can't, we just can't. I can't even begin to tell you all the reasons why it doesn't work; but think of it this way. You cannot help a baby chick out of its shell, or it dies. It has to peck its way out by itself. It has to learn that life only happens when you attack it aggressively. If you help it out of its shell, it never learns that lesson, so it just lies there and waits for life to happen; it lies there until it dies.

"We can't help the Linneans out of the shell they live in, because they don't remember how they got into it. They have no memory, no experience, of anything else. Someday we'll know enough; we'll find a way to get them back to where they once belonged. But we can't do that until we know more. We just don't know enough yet." He paused. "Y'know, sweetheart, I think that's the exciting part. Think of it this way; every new thing you learn about the Linneans—no one else will know that until you tell them. You will have the first bite of every new apple you pick off the tree of knowledge. Oops—I can't use that phrase, can I? 'Tree of knowledge.' That doesn't exist on Linnea. Shame on me. Off to the firepit I go. Come on, we'll go together this time. We will have an honorable death together."

That should have been frightening, but it made me laugh. And everyone else as well. Somehow, we always felt better after attending class, no matter how hard the work had been.

THE OLD WOMAN AND HER PROMISE

A VERY LONG TIME AGO, in the time before time, an old woman left her village and went out into the world. She took nothing with her but a knife and a song. As she walked, she sang of the sun and the rain and the good dark earth. And the sun shone, and the rain fell, and the shoots of grass came up fresh in the ground. She walked for a very long time, and wherever she walked the grass came up at her feet, happy to grow in the sun and drink in the rain.

She lived in a little hut on the edge of the world and gave her songs to the sky. The wind carried her songs to the far ends of the world. She sang of birds and beasts and children. And the world gave birth to birds and beasts and children. They sprang forth from the earth, all the birds, and all the beasts, and all her beautiful sons and daughters.

The old woman loved her children. She loved all her sons and all her daughters, and in the fullness of time, all her sons and all her daughters loved her as well. She taught them to sing of the sun and the rain and the good dark earth. And in the fullness of time, all of them knew joy.

But soon, her little corner of the world grew crowded, and some of her children began to quarrel; so the old woman gathered them all together, blessed them and told them all how much she cherished them. Then, she sent them out into the grass so that they would each have their own place in the world and would not have to quarrel with each other.

"But," her children cried, "we will never see you again. If we travel to the far corners of the world, how will we ever see you again? How can we love our mother if we live too far away to visit?"

The old woman patted the heads of her children and made them each a promise. "You will never go so far away that I cannot come to you. I will visit each of you in your life. I promise you this: when you most need me, I will come to you. I give you my word; now go out to the world and sing of life."

And her children did just that. All her sons and all her daughters went out into the world, singing. They grew plentiful and joyous and they had many beautiful children of their own.

The old woman kept her promise—not just to her children, but to her children's children, and her children's children's children, and unto all the generations thereafter, because she believed in her children; but not all of her children believed in the old woman. Some of them turned bitter and angry. Others became cynical and skeptical. And when the old woman came to them, they did not recognize her. And when she offered them her love and all the gifts that came with it, they rebuked her and turned her away. The ungrateful children had become even too selfish to accept the love of the old woman. They grew bitter in their lives, never knowing that the faults they found in the world grew first in their own hearts.

The old woman saw this and felt sad; but she did not grow bitter. She had an endless love for all her sons and for all her daughters and for all their children everywhere in the world and even if they did not recognize her, she always recognized them. And even if they did not recognize her gifts, she always gave them anyway, freely and without question. Because she believed in them, she blessed their hearts and souls; she sang of their joy and their fulfillment.

Once in every life, the old woman comes to visit. She never breaks her promise. Will you recognize her when she comes to visit you? Will you welcome her or turn her away?

THE RIDE HOME

WE COULD HAVE SPENT ONE MORE NIGHT at Callo City, but the administors had scheduled a major storm and wanted everyone back in their own burrows, so we all bundled back into the wagon and lurched off into the evening. Twilight ran late and both the moons shone high and bright, so we rolled through a silent blue-green world. I felt as if we had gone underwater, to some magical realm of faeries. Except Linnea didn't have faeries. Linnea had little grass people. But we didn't know much about the little grass people; the scouts hadn't had the temerity to ask.

This time around, the classes had exhausted us. The trainers even acknowledged the exhaustion, telling us not to worry at it; this particular set of classes always frustrated trainees. "Don't try to understand it; just sit with it awhile and let it sink in. You'll get it." I didn't like that answer; there was still so much I didn't understand and it seemed like neither did anybody else, and even though the trainers explained it over and over again, sometimes the explanations just didn't make sense. It felt like a game of Hide the Potato. They wouldn't tell you where the potato had gone, only where it hadn't.

So when we rode back this time, we didn't sing or cheer or even howl. We just huddled in our robes and blankets and wished the ride would end as quickly as possible. We had boxes of firebricks and even a case of fresh meat we'd picked up at the commonstore. The moms planned to make sweet-stew with it. Maybe it was the scent of the meat that drew the kacks to us—

173

We had Kilter and Kale pulling the great-wagon, and they always stopped to rest at the bottom of Little Hill. It looked little to us, but we sat high in the wagon. Perhaps, to Kilter and Kale, pulling the wagon, the hill didn't look as little.

Willow, as usual, pulled out his tablet and studied the display. Without comment, he pulled out his phone and called the monitors. I could see by the look on his face that he felt the situation had turned serious. I sat too far back to hear him clearly, but I made out enough. The kacks no longer watched from their usual place on the northern slopes. They had moved southward, arranging themselves along the road ahead. The horses stirred uneasily, stamping their feet and snorting.

Burr leaned over her shoulder and the two of them whispered together grimly. Any change in kack behavior stopped everything. So far, we'd all taken extreme care, regarding the kacks with enormous caution and giving wide berth to their hunting grounds. Although we'd had numerous sightings of kacks tracking great-wagons, as yet, we'd had no serious attacks. Not on humans, not on horses. Everyone wanted to keep it that way.

Authority wanted the dome environment as realistic as possible; the trainees could not regard Linnea as safe. We had to stay aware of the risks, every moment. Wildfires, floods, cyclones, kacks and other humans. But while Authority could control the threats of fire, flood, wind and human behavior in the dome, the kacks remained a wild, unknown quantity—an uncontrollable danger. Despite their implants, the kacks had become much more aggressive, and almost everybody believed that they would soon start attacking travelers on the main road. Even the scouts used the word "inevitable."

Despite demands from some of the trainees, Authority remained reluctant to act. With three adult kacks and four surviving pups in the dome, the administors wanted to see how a wild kack pack behaved. And, if necessary—if the kacks attacked a wagon—they were willing to sacrifice one or two of the animals to see how well humans could defend themselves using only Linnean weapons. Crossbows. But those had to be a weapon of last resort. And if those didn't work...the wagons carried other devices, things the scouts didn't want to use at all.

The dome was more than a training ground. It was also an experiment. And this part of the experiment was the treacherous part. This was the one thing that everybody argued about the most. It was an unnecessary risk—it was a necessary risk. The argument raged without end. And now, tonight, it looked like we would have to test it.

"No," Willow said, before Da could even ask. "We won't try to capture a pup. Not tonight. Not here. Not without an entire team. We've talked about it, all the scouts. We can't afford the risk to the trainees. As much as we want you and your family to have the experience, not here, not now. Perhaps some other time. If the Old Woman sings true, we may never have the need. In the meantime—" He climbed back to the passenger part of the coach and started pointing around. "Kaer, do you know how to work the growler? Good. I want you to come up forward. No, don't start cranking yet. Wait until I tell you." He began opening up compartments and handing out weapons—crossbows, trank guns, taser-darts and even a couple of things I didn't recognize. "I don't want to use the crossbows. But we've never had a real confrontation with these things, and if nothing else works, I will take them down. I'd rather lose the entire pack than a single one of you."

We'd performed this drill before. All of the adults already had their defense positions assigned. Burr opened the hatch to the compartment below and handed weapons down. But this time, it wasn't a drill.

When everybody had taken up their posts, Willow and Burr stopped for another quick conference. They pointed to Da, Big Jes, Little Klin, Bhetto, Parra and Cindy. "The six of you, the two of us. We'll walk the horses up the hill."

"Wouldn't we be safer staying in the coach?"

"We would, but the horses would not. You three, with me on the right. The rest of you, take the left. Kaer, you and Rinky ride next to Driver. Rinky, don't fire unless I tell you. Kaer, do not turn the crank on the growler until I order it. We don't want to panic the horses. All right, let's move." They didn't wait to lower the steps; they went down the ladders on the sides.

Driver tossed a couple of dark sacks down to the snow. Willow and Burr opened them and pulled lengths of leather-wrapped chain down to the ground—hobbles for the horses. We couldn't risk having them bolt in fear. They could easily topple the wagon. The sacks themselves unfolded to become blackout hoods. Willow tapped Kale's neck with a baton, reached up, grabbed the strap at the bottom of the horse's bridle—it had a handle on it that looked like a subway handle—and pulled down hard. The great-horse obediently lowered his huge head so that Willow could throw the sack over the top of his skull and cinch it tight, tight enough that Kale couldn't shake it off. Then he helped Burr do the same with Kilter.

We couldn't keep the horses calm, but we could keep them from seeing the danger. We could keep them from running and hurting themselves and us. If they ran, the kacks would run them to exhaustion and surely bring them down.

Now the scouts hobbled the horses with the leathered chains. Burr hobbled Kilter, Willow hobbled Kale. Both the horses stamped and snorted, shook their heads unhappily and made ugly threatening sounds. When an animal the size of an elephant makes noises like that, most people step back; but the two scouts just poked the horses hard in the ribs with their batons, harder than I would have, hard enough to make them both go *oof*, a great punch to the belly. "Shut up, you great noisy sack of potatoes. We have too much work to do to listen to your complaints. Damn, I hurt my hand."

Then, each of the scouts went back to the lead, reached up and grabbed the handle straps hanging from their horses' bridles—and began pulling the animals forward. One lumbering step at a time. "Come on, you lazy things. Let's go show the kacks who really runs this world." It took a couple baton pokes. Once I would have thought it cruel, but to the great-horses, those pokes must have felt like gentle nudges.

The wagon was 600 kilograms lighter now. At least. Probably closer to 800. Assume eighty kilos per person, not counting boots and robes and weapons and ammunition; figure another ten per person for all that. And even more for Big Jes and Da. Okay, 700 kilos. Enough to make a difference. The horses grunted—more for show than out of any real sense of weight. I'd already learned that great-horses love to complain, especially in Earth-normal gravity.

Up the slope we headed. Rinky had the tablet display and held it so the driver could see. So far, the kacks hadn't moved. I could hear the overlapping conversations coming from the speaker. A lot of unfamiliar voices. It felt strange to see an electronic device here on Linnea. For the first time in a long time I wondered how many people were watching us.

"Do you need backup?"

"Dunno. Probably wouldn't hurt—"

"We've got you all on the ceiling cameras. And we've got armed sky-balls moving in. We can scare off the kacks with shock-grenades—"

"That might frighten the horses." A pause. "We need to see how well the growler works."

"The growler works, we know that—"

"We don't know if it will keep them from stalking prey. We need to find out."

"You have the call on this one."

"Keep the choppers on the ground."

"You sure?"

"So far. Position?"

"Still holding. Inching forward. How do you think they'll come in?"

"Sideways across the slope. Halfway to the top. They'll want to exhaust the horses quickly by forcing them to run uphill."

"The kacks have the same disadvantage—too large for Earth-gravity."

"Yes and no. We don't know. We've hobbled the horses. We'll stand and fight. If we don't run, it could confuse them."

Burr's voice now. "Use your rangefinders now, people. Get a sense of the distances across this hill. You won't have time later." She pointed. "See that stand of leftover summer grass—too confused to lie down and die—right, the tall one. Halfway between here and there, anything farther than that, you won't make the shot. Wait till they cross the halfway mark."

Willow picked out a similar landmark on the right. "Everybody clear? Don't fire until I say. If you don't have a clean shot, don't waste your bolt. Tranks and tasers first. Crossbows only on my command. Kaer, stand ready—"

He yanked the handle he held; so did Burr. Kilter and Kale lurched forward, grumbling and complaining. The wagon jerked. I heard a couple of unhappy remarks from below. One of the babies had started crying and Mom-Lu couldn't comfort her.

"I see them." That was Da. He pointed across the snowfield to the edge of the slope.

"Got it," said Willow. Almost immediately, the others confirmed. I could barely make out the dim black shapes shifting in the darkness.

The kacks didn't come running in. And they didn't come in howling. They moved easily across the snow, barely breaking the crust. Sitting high on the driver's bench at the top of the wagon, I could see everything. The kacks came in on the right. Willow and the others spread out sideways, putting themselves between the kacks and the horses. Burr and her squad moved forward of the horses, to provide crossfire and keep the kacks from flanking the team.

"Kaer! Hit the growler!" I began cranking as hard as I could. The sound started low, like a deep scrape; then as I turned harder, the sound became louder and higher-pitched. It became a siren, then a scream, then an incredible banshee howl. The kacks stopped, uncertain. They cocked their heads. They stepped sideways, as if trying to figure this new thing out.

Beside me, Rinky turned her lantern like a spotlight, focusing it toward the approaching beasts. On my other side, Driver held up what looked like a flare gun and fired a stink-grenade. It arced up high, reached its peak and came down trailing a billowing plume of smoke. Strange perfumes filled the air—musky, rotten, repugnant, a fruity mix of pheromones and flavors. For a moment, I thought I might vomit.

The horses caught their scent then—of the kacks or the stink-grenade, I couldn't tell—but it upset them. They whinnied and stamped and snorted, suddenly eager to get away. Driver held the reins tight and made comforting noises. "Easy, girl, easy—" but they ignored him. Da had hold of Kilter's bridle strap, and Big Jes had Kale's now; leaning in with all their weight against the great-horses' urgency, forcing their heads down and keeping them from bolting in fear.

Disconcerted by the noise, by the brightness surrounding the wagon, by the sudden confusion of strange smells—the kacks hesitated. Rinky focused the glow of her lantern on the largest.

I'd seen pictures of kacks, lots of pictures. Big-screen, high-resolution pictures. Pictures more vivid than reality. Close-ups from the probes and overhead shots from the sky-cameras. I'd always thought them beautiful, impressive. I'd always felt a kind of nobility in these predacious giants. But not tonight, not now—this was different. This was *real*. I could smell the creatures; they stunk of sourness and rotten meat—a stench of carrion and rot. Whatever nobility I'd imagined, that had been an illusion; these were stinking death-machines.

The adults were as tall as bison. The pups were the size of ponies. These things were just too big—all meat and bone and muscle. Their skulls were oversized, their jaws were long and distended, their heads were all teeth. And each of them had two large incisors that curved down below its lower jaw—saber-tooth wolves, huge and hungry, white eyes glistening in the moonlight, fur bristling, low throaty growling—

I turned the crank of the growler and the kacks stared up at me, unblinking, curious, focused intently, studying, examining, weighing—

"Easy there, easy . . . ." I didn't know if Driver was talking to the horses or to me. I turned the crank, afraid to stop, afraid to look away. Beneath us, Willow's squad took careful aim—

And then it was over. Two of the kacks were down. And the rest were retreating up the slope, hesitant, unsure, each one pausing to look back, then resuming the strategic withdrawal, following its fellows. Too fast.

So fast, I wasn't sure exactly what had happened. I'd have to see the pictures from the ceiling cameras.

Slowly, carefully, Willow and Burr approached the fallen kacks. They stood off a distance, Burr surveying each with a scanner. Satisfied, they turned and waved to us. The animals were tranquilized; they'd each be out for hours. A bio-team was on its way to retrieve the animals, take them back to the labs and properly implant them.

Willow and Burr unhobbled the horses, then removed their hoods. They reassured the animals, giving each a dozen apples. Kilter and Kale were not assuaged, but they ate the apples anyway.

Da climbed back up into the wagon and pulled me into his lap. He wrapped his great arms around me, and I should have felt safe, but I didn't. I wanted to cry, but I didn't know why. "Shh," said Da, stroking my hair. "Save it for later."

A few moments later, we were on our way again. We got home just as the first flurries of snow began to fall. There really wasn't much to say anyway. This was Linnea.

NEWS

THE CALL CAME IN THE MIDDLE OF BREAKFAST. We had fifteen minutes to get dressed and get upstairs. By the look on Da-Lorrin's face, we knew it was urgent. By the time we got up the ladder, a tractor-bus was already crunching across the plain from the direction of the Kelly farm, leaving harsh tracks in the snow.

The Kellys were already aboard and as we climbed up into the warmth of the cabin, they hailed us warmly. We hadn't seen anyone for a while, so even the Kellys seemed like good company now. I sat down next to Patta and we started chatting as if nothing bad had ever happened between us. She told me that they were going to be listed on the next crossover schedule, and I nodded politely without saying anything at all. I wondered what Da-Lorrin would say when I told him; nothing repeatable, probably.

All the moms were talking about the snow, how real it looked—of course, it was *real*—and Patta and I just rolled our eyes upward. All the dads and uncles were talking about this emergency meeting; not exactly speculating, but not hiding their concerns either. Whatever had happened on Linnea to make the Dome Authority so darkly secretive, we were about to find out. I felt as much dread as anticipation.

The main auditorium was almost filled by the time we got in, and Administor Rance was already at the podium impatiently ringing her bell and demanding that everyone take their seats as quickly as possible. Da-Lorrin led us down the aisle toward our assigned section. We

180

saw families from all over the dome, a lot of people we hadn't seen in months. I wanted to wave hello, but Mom-Woo pulled me down onto a bench and hushed me up quickly.

Administor Rance looked like she'd swallowed a frog. She rang the gathering sternly to silence. "We have some information for you," she said, and then stepped away from the lectern. A scout named Byrne stepped up to the podium and began speaking immediately. At first, I didn't understand why we needed to hear her story, but as she talked the enormity of the situation became apparent.

Byrne had been traveling across the western continent on the Linnean rail lines. The Linneans didn't have real railroads, not with locomotives. They didn't have an iron industry and they hadn't invented steam engines yet. But they had rails, sort of. They made bricks—the same kind we made—and used them to build heavy roadbeds with raised edges like rails; then they ran horse-drawn wagons along them. The wagons looked a lot like the ones we used, except they had wheels shaped for running on the rail-edges.

A horse-drawn wagon could go fifteen kilometers a day over dirt, but three or four times as far on rails. The Linneans didn't have rail lines across the continent yet, but they were building steadily, if slowly. The railroad extended all the way to Callo City now, the real one.

Byrne and two companions had boarded at Callo City and traveled as far east as anyone had yet dared. Their instructions were to turn back at the first funny look, but they had gone all the way to the eastern seaboard, and then north as far as the wall of glaciers. Beyond the glaciers, the mountains looked as sharp as knives, so they turned south and west again, working their way back to Callo City through the northern wastelands and scrub forests. That took a while because there weren't any railroads there. Few Linnean families lived that far north and those that did kept mosty to themselves. The people held their trust close and did not talk easily to strangers who might be outcasts or hostiles.

But the scouts did attend a few county fairs and local celebrations and other gatherings where few questions were asked. They listened to conversations everywhere they went—"everything from preaching to speeching to barroom screeching," as Byrne put it. They went to church services and town meetings and market days. They traded boffili robes and beaver pelts for copper and iron coins. And once they'd traded a gold nugget for paper banknotes printed by the Church.

Wherever they traveled, they always learned new things about the Linneans; but this time, they had noticed something *different* in the talk of the people, especially as they worked their way back westward. They discovered not just a growing awareness of strange sightings in the sky, but stories even more worrisome. A new mythology had sprung up, about another world just beyond the wall of purple mountains lining the western edge of the continent: a world called Oerth.

The people of Oerth weren't like the people of Linnea; they were sort of like elves, tall and thin, pale and emotionless—and they had mysterious magicks. They lived a hundred years or more and they never fell sick. They flew to the moon in fiery chariots. And they dove under the sea in ships of metal. The pale folk of Oerth had mirrors that let them look a thousand miles away and oracles of captured-lightning held in glass that gave them answers to any question they could ask. They built bridges ten kilometers long and towers a kilometer high. The cities of Oerth shone with magical light all night long, and carriages without horses ran through the streets. Paintings of the dead could talk to their grandchildren. And eeriest of all . . . some of the faerie-folk of Oerth lived under a giant bowl twenty kilometers across and pretended to be Linneans, practicing for the time when they would move unseen among the Linnean people for purposes of their own. . . .

When Byrne told us that last part, an audible gasp swept through the auditorium. Her words shocked us. It was like what Gampa said about a bucket of cold water in the face. It wakes you up. Well, we were definitely awake. What dismayed us the most, I think, was the terrible realization that somebody who had gone through the same rigorous training as the rest of us had betrayed his silence and put everybody else at risk. We couldn't believe it.

Byrne said that most of the stories she'd heard were told as fantasies for children—too outlandish for the Church to consider them "evil mischief." But lately, some Linneans had begun warning their children that the unreal-folk of Oerth were roaming the land, looking to steal the souls of good Linneans. And even more lately, some folk had begun wondering aloud where such stories had come from and what they really meant. . . .

THE MAN WITH THE SILVER EARRING

THEN BYRNE RELINQUISHED THE PODIUM to the Man with the Silver Earring. He ignored the lectern and started talking even before he got to the center of the stage. He was just as brusque as ever. "We've known about these rumors for several months now. They seem to have started in the west and traveled east with returning caravans. Because the Linneans have a great deal of curiosity about what lies in the unknown regions of their continent, any story—no matter how outlandish—gets repeated endlessly.

"Now, the Linneans don't believe all the fabulous tales of Oerth, but many of them do believe that a great and prosperous land lies beyond the western mountains—and some Linneans believe that the Oerth-folk will work evil mischief to keep honest folk from finding them. They talk of a secret pass through the mountains, which they call the gateway to Oerth. We know of several Linnean explorers who have announced their intentions to search for that gateway."

Earring continued, "You all know that we've had families disappear. Perhaps the stories started with them. Maybe bandits or hostiles captured one of those lost families. Perhaps the family tried to bargain its way to freedom. The other possibility..." He rubbed his nose distastefully. "We suspect that the families that disappeared...may have vanished *deliberately*—that they intended all along to colonize Linnea at cross-purposes to the Gate Authority's goals. If so, they have put us all at danger."

Earring held out a hand to silence the cries of horror and anger, but for a moment, everyone was too upset to calm down. A lot of hands went up then; some people stood up and shouted for attention. Earring just stood his ground, looking from face to face with those dark eyes of his, and after a moment, people began sitting down again.

Everyone but Da-Lorrin. He remained standing even after Earring turned to glower at him. "Maybe I don't know how to ask this correctly," Lorrin said slowly. "The Linneans have only mysterious tales, no real evidence. Ignorance always breeds distrust. It seems to me that if they actually encountered one of the Oerth-folk, they might have so much curiosity about Oerth and how to get here that they would treat any Oerth-person as an important emissary."

"We had always hoped for that," said Earring. "It doesn't seem to have worked that way."

"How do you know this?" Da-Lorrin challenged.

Earring hesitated, but Administor Rance spoke up from the side of the stage. "Go ahead and tell them."

He looked to her, unhappily. She nodded curtly. A whole conversation passed between them in that instant. Earring turned back to the rest of us, and when he spoke, his voice had gone more sour than ever. "The Linneans hold Administor Rance's son, Jaxin, and three other scouts as prisoners in the Callo City confinement. Someone identified them as Oerth-folk the day they arrived in the city. We don't know who made the identification. We don't know how or why.

"We do have contact with the scouts. They have monitors in their shoes and belts, and in the buttons on their clothing, so we know that they remain safe for the moment. We have two other teams in the city, undiscovered and observing from a safe distance, and they have confirmed this information. And we have a chain of spybirds keeping the channels open, so we have near-instantaneous communication. We have a pretty good sense of the situation in Callo City.

"Apparently, a panic has swept the city. The city administors don't know what to do. They've sent a petition for an Inquiry by a High Church Council—*not a trial*, but an Inquiry. To determine the intentions of the Oerth-men. I should point out here that the Linneans do not consider maiz-likka human, so the Church restrictions on torture do not apply."

He held up his hands for silence and pushed on, raising his voice to be heard above the rising shouts. "If the High Council accepts the petition, they will travel to Callo City and convene an Inquiry. If they reject the petitions, then we don't know what will happen. All kinds of speculations have circulated. We fear that our scouts will lose all protection against the frightened crowds—so we hope that the Council will accept the petition. Considering the significance of the matter, acceptance of the petition seems the most likely course of action. We expect the Council members to send word back to Callo City as quickly as possible, and then follow on themselves a few days later. We estimate travel time will take at least twelve days, probably more. It depends on the weather and the rail conditions."

Someone called out. "What crime will they charge the scouts with—?"

"No crimes," said Earring. "Remember how the Linneans think. Only humans commit crimes. To commit a crime, you have to know the difference between good and evil; knowing the difference, you still choose evil; that defines a crime—only humans can know the difference, so only humans can commit crimes. Maiz-likka, on the other hand, cannot know the difference. By definition, they come from evil, they only know evil, so they can only do evil. Choice plays no part in their actions. They come from the dark between the stars, not from the Mother—they hate the Mother. Therefore the maiz-likka and all who practice maizlish ways can expect no mercy, only the full wrath of the Mother's children...."

The Man with the Silver Earring paused a moment to let us consider what that might mean. For a peaceful religion, the Linneans had demonstrated some horrendous ways of keeping the peace. Apparently the Mother's love was only a stone's throw away for some of these folks.

Earring sucked in his cheek unhappily, and continued. "So the Council will investigate—with whatever tools they think appropriate. They will investigate as thoroughly as they can. They will continue the Inquiry for as long as it takes, until they can determine once and for all if the prisoners have truly come from Oerth. If the strangers do have magick abilities, then that will probably serve as proof that the Oerth-people have maizlish intentions...."

"What will they do to the scouts?"

Earring shrugged. "We don't know. The Linnean Church has acted badly in the past. They may do so again. Historical precedent carries enormous weight. So does fear. But maybe not in this case. Despite the superstitions of the Linneans, we like to believe that reason will prevail. These people have good souls. I know them. Not all of them go crazy with madness at every wild rumor. Given enough time, their natural skepticism of the outrageous may outweigh their fear of strangers."

"And the bad news—?" called someone from behind us. I didn't recognize the voice.

Earring scratched at his nose, as if he were considering his next thought with distaste. "At the moment, the scouts remain in custody. As long as that confinement continues, they'll stay safe. But we don't know how much time we have. And if the situation turns dangerous, we cannot protect them, because we cannot extract them from the middle of the city. It would take an armed regiment, and the Gate Authority won't allow that. Even a smaller effort carries risks. The Agency remains adamant that we not perturb the Linnean culture. A disturbance would likely produce unpredictable consequences; so we have to keep ourselves effectively invisible. The Charter—and our own oaths—limit our ability to proceed.

"Understand," Earring continued. "If the High Council determines any *tangibility* of magick in the scouts, it will represent a major shift in their theology from a faith-based system to an empirical one. It would dramatically change the worldview of the entire society, and not for the better. Dogma generates toxicity. We've seen it in our own history. This kind of incident will trigger ripples of shock that can reverberate throughout a society for decades—or even centuries. No question, but the people of Linnea will have violent reactions as they attempt to assimilate this new information about their world. They will not accept it easily.

"In its own way, the High Council knows this. Every political institution has survival as its first priority. The churchmen will realize the potential for cultural disruption here and the corresponding necessity of preserving their authority. So the possibility exists for a resolution within the Linnean context. Perhaps the Inquiry will acquit our scouts—"

"And the bad news?" the voice behind me called again.

"That doesn't appear likely. Our scouts do not have registered identities. Their papers will pass close examination, but any serious investigation of their invented histories will turn up little supporting evidence. And that may prove damning. If the Council determines that our scouts have indeed come from Oerth, then they have to declare them nonhuman—outside of the protection of Linnean law; not good for our scouts. But that leaves them with the dilemma of a *tangible* world of magick on the other side of the mountain. To avoid that, they could rule our scouts human. But then they'd still have to have to determine the identities of our scouts and if they intend to commit 'evil mischief.' Without records, they'll have to assume that the scouts came to Callo City as outlaws.

And if they discover that they have no past in their world, that would certainly prove it. With either of these outcomes, the scouts can expect dire consequences."

"What do you mean by 'dire consequences'?" someone shouted. The room was getting unruly.

"If the Council decides that our scouts represent a threat to the souls of Linneans they will, in all likelihood, authorize a public execution. Despite their traditional sanctions against such horrors, they have in the past made exceptions for cases of extreme significance. If we can believe the reports, this appears such a case, and the risk of execution does exist."

Earring ignored the rising chorus of shouts. Despite the fact that he wore no apparent microphone, his voice carried over everything. "Understand this: if we act in the defense of our scouts, we call even more attention to ourselves. And that puts even more people at risk—everyone we have on the other side! *Anything* we do on behalf of Jaxin and the others will affect them. *Every* stranger will find himself under increased suspicion."

And that's when Administor Rance interrupted. She came up to stand beside Earring, waving futilely for silence. When at last the room had quieted enough for her to speak, she said simply, "I have to inform you that under the present state of our charter with the Gate Authority, we cannot do anything but observe."

That brought nearly everyone in the room to his or her feet, shouting and clamoring for attention.

Administor Rance held her hands up wide. The gesture said, "Please wait. I have more." It took a moment, but eventually the room did quiet down. "We did not summon you here to incite you to riot. We called you here tonight only to inform you of the gravity of the situation, so that you could understand the world that you have trained for. We cannot allow any talk of military action, lest we endanger our charter status. You may choose to accept this ... or not.

"You will find me in my office all day tomorrow. If you wish to resign from this program, you may do so without penalty." She rang her bell. "I now adjourn this session."

And then she exited from the stage and the auditorium just like she always did; but this time I thought I saw her wiping her eye just before she passed out the side door.

THE MEETING THAT DIDN'T HAPPEN

AFTER A MOMENT OF CONFUSION, people started to leave. I got up too; so did Mom-Woo, but Da-Lorrin put his hand on her arm and said, "Wait." She sat back down again.

"Huh—?" I started to ask, but Lorrin leaned across and said, "Shh. Sit down, Kaer." So I did. Obviously, something was up.

We weren't the only ones staying in our seats. At least half a dozen other families waited patiently while everyone else filed out. I noticed that the Kellys weren't among them; they were already heading for the tractor-bus. Most of the families who stayed were long-time trainees, but not all. The ones I knew were all folks who had high work-scores and were considered good candidates for crossover.

The Man with the Silver Earring waited patiently on the stage, watching people exit. Several folks approached him and tried to engage him in conversation, but he just shook his head. It looked like he was saying, "Administor Rance has given you the official position. I support her totally." He had to say that quite a few times, but finally the last of the crowd filtered out.

He waited until the doors were closed—and locked. I looked back and saw that there was a scout by each door. Earring glanced quickly around the room, as if counting us off on an invisible list. Satisfied, he said, "Please move forward and fill up the front rows." His voice sounded different now.

When we had all taken our new seats, he continued. "Anything that

188

gets said in this room must stay in this room. *Officially*, this meeting didn't happen. Does everybody understand that? Anyone not willing to abide by these conditions?" He glanced around. "No? Good."

He took a deep breath. For a moment, he seemed almost human. "Despite the restrictions of the Charter," he said, "we do intend to mount a rescue operation. We've applied for an exemption and we expect to have it signed by morning. So we will proceed with our preparations on the expectation of authorization. But whether or not we get that exemption, we *will* proceed. Legally or not.

"We have armed scouts crossing over tomorrow morning. We've sent three choppers through the gate, fully loaded with nonlethal weaponry. We have a team of twelve prepared to make an assault on the prison where the Linneans hold our scouts. We have little hope for a peaceful outcome. We *expect* to act—and we will prepare as fully as we can.

"Our observers on the scene report that the Linneans have posted at least twenty guards, all armed with crossbows. They look like experienced military men, so it doesn't look good for a frontal assault. And besides, the Charter mandates that we take no lives...unless absolutely necessary. We would all prefer that such 'necessity' does not arise. So we have to consider all of our options. Whatever we do on the other side, we expect enormous repercussions. Both here *and* there."

"You'll need more than twelve scouts," said Da-Lorrin, in his sergeant's voice. "Where can I volunteer?" Immediately, five other men stood up too.

Earring waved them back down. "If we cannot do it with twelve, we cannot do it with twelve hundred—"

"Some of us have military experience," said Lorrin. "Have your scouts ever seen actual combat?"

"Some. Not all."

"I repeat my request," said Lorrin. "You need me. Us," he corrected.

"We appreciate the offer, but—"

"If you didn't want us to volunteer, then *why* this meeting?"

"We do need volunteers, but not for military action. We think the scouts should handle that part, but we need on-site monitors and support teams."

Lorrin shook his head. I knew that shake. That was the "this is a *very* bad idea" head-shake. He said, "You've already acknowledged that someone from a *disappeared* family probably betrayed Jaxin and the others."

Earring nodded. I guess he'd seen that head-shake before, if not from

Lorrin, then probably from his own da. He chose his next words carefully. "Yes. Unfortunately, we do have reason to suspect that."

"Then you don't dare send anyone else into Callo City that the disappeared families would recognize," said Lorrin. His words had an immediate effect on all the scouts.

"That one worries us a lot," Earring admitted. He exchanged a serious look with Smiller and Byrne. "If such a situation exists on Linnea, it means that none of our present scouts can continue working and observing anywhere they might risk identification. It would cripple the program." And then he added, "Enormously."

"Then I do have a point, don't I?" said Da-Lorrin, smiling wryly.

Earring nodded sadly. It was the first time I'd ever seen him look anything less than ferocious. "Let me say it bluntly. We have to get our people out with a minimum of attention—and as little cultural upset as possible. Right now, our best plan involves a team of stealth operatives hitting all the guards simultaneously with self-vaporizing anesthetic darts. With tear gas as a backup. We know we can do it. We've scanned the prison, we know the layout, we know the routines of the guards. We've run simulations of six different assaults. We have an excellent chance of success. To the Linneans, our people will have simply disappeared from a locked cell."

"And that will add to the belief that Oerth-people have mysterious powers, won't it...?"

"Our other on-site teams will start rumors that a sympathizer freed them, that someone saw them riding out of town. We'll take their horses at the same time."

"Won't that put the guards under suspicion?" asked a farmer named Brill. "Won't that endanger otherwise innocent people?"

"Probably," said Earring. "But I doubt that you could call this squad of military guards *innocent*. They have a nasty reputation, well-deserved. I don't have a lot of sympathy for their needs right now. But the question does merit consideration. All of our questions do. We have to consider all our options and their consequences before we act."

He glanced at the clock. "I think we've said enough for now. Midnight approaches; so does winter. You all have work to do. Those of you who want to volunteer, give your names to Smiller—then go home and talk this over among yourselves. In your own homes, nowhere else. Remember, no one goes unless his or her family agrees. Oh, and don't worry about the hidden monitors; tonight's snowfall will probably knock some of them out for a few hours. Weather often has funny effects like that.

You all know the situation, so you shouldn't have any disagreements about the facts. Just decide if you can afford to take the risk. If you can, make your good-byes tonight. We'll pick you up in the morning. Oh, and one more thing," he said. "Thank you."

THE DECISION

THE TRACTOR-BUS WAS WAITING FOR US, its engine already running. I wondered what the driver had told the Kellys about why we hadn't gone back with them, but I didn't worry about it too much. We had a more important subject to discuss.

But once we got home and started passing out tea mugs, there really wasn't much to say about it one way or the other. Jaxin had demonstrated enormous kindness to all of us. While we had a sense of protective loyalty toward Linnea, we had an even greater sense of comradeship with the scouts who trained us. We didn't know the other scouts, but whatever it took to rescue Jaxin, the whole family supported it; so we went to bed quickly, leaving Mom-Woo and Lorrin alone in their little corner of the house. They probably had a lot to talk about and not a lot of time.

The next morning, Smiller rode out on Mountain to pick up Lorrin. We were already shivering in the cold air when she came thundering over the hill, stirring up clouds of fresh powdery snow in her wake.

Almost her first words, she said, "The Gate Authority turned down our request to mount a rescue operation."

"What does that mean—?" Lorrin started to ask.

"It means we'll have to send in a team of *observers* instead," said Smiller. She tossed down the rope ladder. "Come on, let's go." *Observers*. We knew what that meant. They would be operating outside the restrictions of the Charter. Whatever happened on Linnea, there would be hell to pay back here on Earth. But that would be later, and right now nobody was worrying about *later*.

Lorrin tossed up his bag, then turned back to us for farewells. He looked grim when he told us not to worry, but how could we *not* worry? He hugged each of us in turn—he ruffled my hair and told me to take care of Aunt Morra and Uncle Bhetto—then he climbed up the ladder into the basket on Mountain's right side, and they headed off in the direction of the Brill farm. We didn't know when we would see him again...and the possibility that we might *never* see him again suddenly scared me. For the first time, I think, mortality was a real thing to me.

But almost immediately, Mom-Woo began pushing us back to work. She pulled her boffili robe tighter around herself and said, "Well, don't everybody stand around waiting for him to return. We still have a lot of work to do." She gave me a push in the direction of the house and said, "Come on, Kaer. Let's clean up the breakfast dishes."

Later that day the snow started coming down again, this time so thick and fast it scared us. We worried that the dome's snow-making machinery had broken or something. We all took turns climbing the ladder to peek outside, until finally Mom-Lu complained that we were letting all the heat out. When Irm came back down the ladder with nearly an inch of white frosting on top of his cap, Mom-Woo said, "All right, everybody. We'll have no more peeking at the snow for now. Come on, Rinky, help me get lunch on the table."

By the third day, the snow was two meters thick. Our water tank was full, and so was the cold-room, where we kept our food. The big pile of fuel bricks and boffili chips that we'd left upstairs had turned into a giant snow cone. We took some leftover boards from the wagon we'd "dismantled" and practiced sledding with the little-uns.

But the snow kept coming down, even thicker than that, and after a while, it was all we could do just to clear it away from the doors. We had a lot of time to ourselves then. Aunt Morra helped all the kids with our lessons, while the moms concentrated on their sewing. In the evening, we sang and told stories and acted out plays—just like Jaxin had told us we would. And even though it was cramped, we had fun.

It would have been more fun with Lorrin—we all missed him so— but Mom-Woo just said, "He'll come back, I know it." And then she'd resume stirring something at the stove, or she'd pick up her knitting or whatever else she had been doing.

We had to work harder without Lorrin's strength, but nobody complained. We couldn't exactly ask for news, but every two or three days one of the scouts would call or stop by to check on us, and in the course of her visit, she'd remark, "Lorrin sends his love. They've crossed over." Or: "They've arrived at camp, only twenty klicks from Callo City. Lorrin says he misses you."

We weren't totally cut off from everybody else. In the evening, we had a half hour of news from the Administration. It was like going to Meeting, only we didn't have to walk two klicks to get there.

Administor Rance said told us that we would have to get used to not having the latest information piped into our homes, that we had to learn how to live in real isolation, and we all knew she was right. Even so, the evening broadcast was the high point of our day, and nobody ever missed it. We'd gather around the screen almost hungrily. On Linnea, we wouldn't have even this much, unless we were willing to dig a secret room like the Kellys.

After the news ended and the darkness returned, Mom-Woo would light candles, Mom-Lu would pour tea, and we'd talk about what we'd heard, speculating about what each thing meant to us.

One thing had been bothering me since the night winter was postponed. "I don't understand it," I said. "How can anyone be so stupid that they would tell the Linneans about Earth? Didn't they get trained properly? Don't they know that they're putting other people at risk? Why would anyone do something like that?"

Gampa came over and sat down next to me, putting his arm around my shoulder. "Kaer, you have asked a very sad question. You probably won't like the answer." I leaned into his shoulder, letting his hug protect me. "Some people . . ." Gampa said slowly, "Some people do not believe they have to keep their word. They say whatever they think others want to hear while they create personal loopholes for themselves. They tell themselves that rules exist for other people, but not for them. They have their own selfish agendas, which they don't share with others, so they use other people to get what they want. They pretend to go along with the program while they further their private plans."

"But what kind of plans? Why would they betray the Agency?"

Gampa shrugged. "Think about it, little peanut. Linnea resembles our own world, three hundred years ago. Imagine if you could travel back in time, you could invent the steam engine, railroads, electricity, the telephone, movies, automobiles, airplanes, all of the great industries that changed the world. If you could do that, you could *own* the world. Perhaps some of the people who crossed over to Linnea may have succumbed to that temptation. Yes, I know, we all want to think the best

of everyone who makes it through the training. But those three families
that disappeared...I wonder if maybe they had planned to do that all
along."

I thought about that. It made me sad and angry to think of someone
going through training, lying and pretending just so they could get to
Linnea, knowing all along that they intended to abuse the trust of so
many others. I couldn't think of the right words in Linnean to describe
such actions; we hadn't learned many Linnean cusswords, but the few
I did know were pretty bad. Anyone who would betray two worlds at a
time had to be double-maizlish.

"But, Gampa, why would they tell the Linneans about Oerth? Earth?
What do they gain by that?"

"I have a theory," said Auncle Irm, filling his mug and joining us.
"The traitors—yes, I would call them traitors—want the gate closed.
If they can turn the Linneans against Oerth, the administors will have
to stop sending families, will have to pull back the scouts. That would
explain why they had to disappear—so the scouts couldn't track them
down and extract them. Or maybe even...kill them. Considering the
stakes in this game, the traitors will have to play for keeps. And so will
the scouts." I must have looked horrified, because he added, "Kaer, if
you want to own a world, you have to get rid of the competition. I fear
that Linnea has become the site of a secret war. And I fear that the people
who cross over will find themselves on the front lines of the battle."

EVEN MORE SNOW

IT WAS STILL WINTER. There were still storms. The snow kept falling. Somewhere up north, a couple of lakes must have been drained. I gave it only a passing thought. In our minds, we were already on Linnea.

And we finally figured out how to keep warm. It was a matter of adjustment—us as well as the burrow. We hung robes on the walls. We hung woven mats of dried grass. We hung the extra canvas from the wagon. Every bit helped to keep the heat from seeping out through the bricks. This hadn't been in any of the trainings; we had to figure it out ourselves. And later on, we realized why it hadn't been in any of the trainings—because we were *supposed* to figure it out ourselves. Real Linneans are resourceful.

With the double insulation of our walls, the combined body heat of all twenty of us in the same room was enough to raise the temperature another ten degrees. And by dinnertime, the cook-fire had added ten more degrees of warmth, so if anything, we were sometimes too warm in the house and we had to open up both of the ventilation shafts all the way just to cool down. It took us a few days, but we finally worked out a system so we were mosty comfortable.

We had two ventilation shafts at opposite ends of the house. Above us, one terminated just above ground level; the other went up a two-meter chimney. The pressure differential as the wind blew over the two shafts created a steady flow of air through our underground house. We also had a third chimney directly over the cooking bay, and a lot of warm air went up that shaft, melting the snow up topside so it would flow down into our water tank.

Of course, with all the snow coming down, we had no shortage of water. The tank filled up quickly and stayed filled. Because the tank was more than two meters underground, the water in it didn't freeze; it was always cold and refreshing—except at bath time. Mom-Woo didn't want to waste valuable fuel boiling too much water for baths, so we had to learn how to bathe in cold water. That was always good for an evening of shrieking. But nobody complained about bundling up into a nice warm bed afterwards.

Every so often, just for the fun of it, someone went up the ladder, pushed opened the hatch, and scooped out a few buckets of fresh snow to look around and see how high it had gotten. There were a couple of days when we had no idea how much white had piled up topside. On the evening news Administor Rance said we had gotten four meters of snow—simulating a light Linnean winter. Our ventilator chimneys could be raised above the snow level, so they both stayed clear, but the periscope Klin rigged showed only white.

One of our projects was something we hadn't had time to do before the snow started; but now we did. We built a real bathtub. We used some of the razor grass fuel bricks to boil down some tarpay, and we made a huge brick tub against one wall with a firepit under it, like a stove. Now we could take hot baths, two or three at a time—or as Gampa said, we could also use it to make a *lot* of soup.

Mom-Woo wouldn't let us have much fuel for the fire. But at least now we were able to keep clean—and that was very important for a large family cramped together in a small house. Not all the bed shelves had been installed yet; we had run out of time before Lorrin left and winter started, so Rinky and I decided to use the tub as our bed so we wouldn't have to sleep on the floor anymore. But it echoed when we giggled.

During the days, the moms made everyone practice their lessons, we all had our sewing to do, and we took turns cooking. We experimented with different recipes to see what we could do with Linnean food; but we also had to practice making the traditional meals too.

And we had to exercise too. Mom-Trey insisted on that. Not just our fitness and stretching exercises, but also our aerobics and our Tae Kwon Do. Mom-Trey wouldn't let us quit until we had worked up a serious sweat. Everyone had to participate, no exceptions. Gamma and Gampa grunted a lot and the little-uns giggled too much, but everybody did their numbers every day.

The news from the other side of the gate trickled off. We knew that six choppers had crossed over, and three dozen scouts and volunteers. On the evening news, Administor Rance told us that the High Council had accepted Callo City's petition for an Inquiry, but instead of the Council coming to Callo City, the prisoners were ordered east. That didn't sound good. She didn't say anything at all about our *observers*. And that worried us even more. The not-knowing hurt the worst.

Meanwhile, the snow kept coming down.

We'd reached the point where there was little more to say, so we said nothing and did our work in silence, each retreating into our own winter-soul. We had our work to keep us busy, and sometimes in the evening we played games, but it seemed as if our lives were slowing down to zero—a little slower every day, until one day we wouldn't be moving at all.

Most of us hadn't been outside in over a week—and even though there was nothing to see upstairs except snow in all directions, it was still a chance to get away from the sometimes-oppressive closeness of the house. I wished for a window, someplace where I could just stand and look out at the world. Even that would have made a difference.

Auncle Irm said it best one night. He was bitter and frustrated and complaining about being locked in a hand-built sensory deprivation hole. He said, "It doesn't matter how large a hole you dig, or how deep, if all you want to do is jump in and pull the dirt over you. We've dug our own grave here and all we can do is sit and wait to die."

Under ordinary circumstances, that would have started a fearful argument. But instead, Mom-Woo apparently ignored his outburst and moved quietly and calmly around the room, hustling all the children off to bed. "You too, Kaer, Rinky."

We complained of course, but it didn't do any good; it never did. So Rinky and I went and made our bed up in the tub. We pulled the curtains closed and tried to hear what the parents were talking about, but it was all an indistinct mumble. We whispered together for a little bit, like we always did, and then eventually, we fell asleep.

The next day, it snowed some more. And the day after that too.

AUNCLE IRM

AFTER THAT, THINGS IN THE BURROW WERE TENSE. All the adults seemed to know something, but nobody was saying anything, so we just sort of moved through the next few days like zombies. We were deep into our winter-souls. It wasn't just the world that was freezing—it was our hearts. We were hardening inside ourselves.

The moms weren't talking, Auncle Irm and Aunt Morra and Uncle Bhetto had gone bitter and snappish, the little-uns were restless and cranky—and I felt like a caged rat. I went back and forth from room to room, up the ladder and down again, back and forth. I felt cramped and angry. My stomach hurt. I missed my da. I wanted to cry. I even kicked the wall, but that made my foot hurt, so I said some maizlish words. Finally, Auncle Irm looked over at me and said, "For the Old Woman's sake, Kaer—stop it! Park yourself in one place or I'll shove you into the potato bin."

I made a face, I stuck out my tongue. "Thbfffpt."

Auncle Irm didn't hesitate. Before I could turn and run—there was no place to run to anyway—he scooped me up into the air, and a moment later I came plopping down on Auncle Irm's lap wrapped in a basket hug. There was no escape.

"No," said Irm. "No. You will learn to manage yourself. No matter what. Whatever it takes." And then added. "Just like the rest of us."

"Let me go," I said. "I don't want to stay here anymore." I didn't know if I meant Irm's lap, the burrow, the dome or the entire program. I just

199

didn't want to be *here*. "I'm hungry, I'm cold, I hurt all over. I want to go home." By now, everybody was looking at me. All three of the moms, Morra and Bhetto, Gamma and Gampa, Rinky, the little-uns, everyone. "Why are we doing this? Why? This isn't any fun anymore. I want to go home."

"We are home," said Irm.

"No, we're not. Home is—home is—" I started crying uncontrollably.

Irm just held onto me, rocking me gently in those great enfolding arms. "Home is wherever we are, Kaer. You know that."

I shook my head. I didn't want to be consoled.

"Shh, sweetheart, shh. Everything will turn out all right."

"No, it won't," I sobbed. "Da isn't here."

"Will crying bring him back?"

I didn't want to answer that.

Irm repeated the question. "Will crying bring him back?"

"No," I sniffled.

"What? I didn't hear you."

"No."

"Thank you. Will having a tantrum make anything better?"

Didn't reply to that one either.

"Answer the question, Kaer. Will having a tantrum make anything better?"

I shook my head. "No."

"Then why are you doing it?"

In that moment, I really hated Auncle Irm—for taking away all my reasons.

"Why are you doing it, Kaer?"

I didn't know.

"If it doesn't make a difference, then why not do the happy dance instead?"

That one I knew the answer to. "Because the happy dance doesn't make any difference either."

"So what? If neither makes a difference, then it doesn't matter. Which one is more fun? Having a tantrum or doing the happy dance?"

I really wanted to answer tantrum, but there was no arguing with Auncle Irm's sideways logic.

"So why not do the happy dance with me?" Irm lowered me to the floor, turned me around so we were facing each other. "Happy, happy, joy, joy!" Irm's great belly shook like pudding. Resentfully, I copied the moves, and despite myself, I started giggling. Shona and Nona and Mikey came running over and started dancing with us. And then Rinky and Klin. And then everybody was happy-dancing, for no reason at all. And then we were all laughing, for no reason at all. And for a moment, I actually understood. There wasn't anything else we could do; we might as well do this.

Afterwards, still laughing, still smiling, I collapsed back into Auncle Irm's ample lap. "Thank you. That was fun. I love you, Auncle Irm."

"I love you too, Kaer."

And then, after another little bit, I asked, "Why were you so unhappy the other day?"

Irm chuckled deeply. "For the same reason as you. I forgot to do the happy dance. Thank you for showing me what I look like when I forget."

And then, after a longer bit, I asked, "How long do you think Da will be gone?"

"Not too long, I hope. Maybe a Nineday, maybe longer. It all depends."

"I wish we could have gone with."

"That might have been—" Irm didn't finish the sentence.

"—Dangerous?"

Irm didn't answer.

"I thought you said it wouldn't be—"

"Well, it shouldn't be—"

"But it is?"

"Probably."

"I don't care. I still wish we could have gone with."

"And what would you have done?"

"The happy dance."

Irm laughed. "No. I mean, on the mission."

"Whatever I could. That's the Linnean way. Families stay together. We should have all gone."

Irm said, "Kaer, listen to me. Someday, we will separate. Someday half of this family will cross over and half of this family will stay here."

"You could come with—"

"Kaer, listen to me. I'll tell you why I was upset. It was because I'm old enough to have learned a very sad thing—that life is about saying good-bye to the people you love, over and over and over again. Someday you'll have to say good-bye to Gamma and Gampa. Someday you'll have to say good-bye to me and Morra and Bhetto. Someday, you'll even have to say good-bye to the moms and to Da."

"I don't want to say good-bye."

"Nobody ever does. But that's the way life works. So what do you think we can do about it?"

"I don't know—"

"Yes, you do. You're a very smart child."

"While we're still together . . ." Was I guessing? "—we try to make our time together as special as possible?"

"That's right," said Irm. "Absolutely right. We give each other as many good memories as possible so we can live on in each other's hearts. And that's why I was upset. Because I haven't always remembered to do that. And I was feeling bad that Da-Lorrin might have gone away without knowing how much I really love him—"

"He knows," I said.

"I hope so," said Irm.

"You'll tell him yourself when he gets back."

"Yes, I will."

"I hope it's soon."

"Me too."

And then we just sat there for a while, rocking and not talking.

THE RETURN

TWO DAYS LATER, I GOT MY WISH.

The snow stopped as abruptly as if Administor Rance had flipped a switch. Maybe she had.

Then, just as suddenly, the video sprang to life and a scout we didn't know told us to dig our way to the surface, as fast as we could. She looked grim, and Mom-Woo immediately cried. "Oh, no. Something has happened to Lorrin. Hasn't it?"

The scout replied quickly, "Nothing has happened. I assure you. But we need you on the surface. Lorrin will meet you. Please get yourselves ready." And then she blinked out.

But this worried Mom-Woo even more. If nothing had happened, why was Lorrin coming back? Mom-Lu and Mom-Trey and Aunt Morra had already started pulling out boffili robes. "We won't find out anything just standing around worrying. Come on, let's get bundled up and let's get upstairs and find out. Come on, all of you—get ready for Lorrin."

We climbed up the ladder one after the other, little avalanches of snow tumbling down around each of us. We climbed up out of the ground, up through a tunnel of cold blue snow, and then up into the underside of the great-wagon. It was parked right over the house. Big Jes and Klin had finished the ladder Lorrin had started. It went from the bottom level of our burrow-house all the way up to the underside of the wagon. At least two or three times a day, they went upstairs to check on the wagon and shovel the snowdrifts off the ladder and the top deck and

203

whatever else they thought might need it. At least, that's what they said, but I figured it was also because they wanted some time to themselves, and the daisy-wagon was a good place for privacy.

All of us would have lived in the daisy-wagon if we hadn't finished the house in time, but it would have been a lot colder and a lot more cramped. With the canvas sides rolled up, we could use the wagon as a high wooden observation platform, and on Linnea that would be exactly what we'd do. The wagon would be our summerhouse. In the winter, however, it was just dark and cold and empty.

We climbed up through the great-wagon, without stopping, up to the second floor, and then from there up to the top deck, where we stamped our feet and shivered. The glare on top was dazzling, and when I stepped out into it, I was momentarily blinded. The sunlight blazed off the snow like a frozen detonation.

And silence. Except for the sounds of our own breath and the crunch of snow underfoot, the world had gone as still as a tomb. In its own bright way, it was even more oppressive than the underground solitude we'd been suffering. All we could see was white silence in every direction.

In dry weather, the daisy-wagon would tower over the landscape like a lighthouse almost five stories tall, giving us a long view over the hills—but now the snow was so deep that it completely covered the wheels of the wagon. In some places, it piled up almost all the way to the top deck. It was dry and powdery and if you fell into it, you'd probably fall all the way to the bottom. But Big Jes wouldn't let Rinky try it.

Aunt Morra shaded her eyes and squinted off toward Callo City. She worried aloud. "How are they going to get a wagon through all this?"

Something made me look at her, and then past her shoulder—toward the part of the dome called "the wilderness." Nobody was allowed to go there without permission, because it included a lot of test areas for new arrivals, plants and animals. It wasn't officially off-limits, just sort of. That was where most of the boffili and the emmos roamed free, and even the kacks now that the Administration knew the stun-implants worked.

"Not a wagon," I shouted. "Look—" I grabbed her arm and turned her around to see. There was a blazing orange light in the sky, flying low enough across the snow to stir up sparkling clouds of it in a swirling wake, and all the time wailing like a chorus of banshees.

As it came in closer . . . we had to blink and wipe our eyes. It wasn't an aircraft at all. It flew like one, but—it wasn't like any aircraft we'd ever

seen before. It looked like a fiery chariot and it sounded like a sky of demons. And it blazed with color, all red and orange and yellow. The lights
glared off of it, and bright beams swiveled and searched in all directions.
Whatever it was, the air glittered around it; the snow beneath it glowed
with golden reflections. For a moment, I wondered if maybe somehow
a eufora had gotten through the gate—

"What in the name of the Mother's loving soul—?" That was Big Jes.

And then I blinked and saw that it was a chopper after all, but one
that had been painted with glow-brite paint and studded with thousands of bright pinpoint Christmas lights, flashing animated patterns.
Even the protective rings around the blades had been illuminated to
look like a halo. And there were outboard spotlights all over it. It was
all flames and dazzle. And they were playing some kind of weird howling music that seemed to come from everywhere at once, until they got
closer and they switched it off.

"*Swing low, sweet chariot...comin' for to carry me home....*" sang Klin.

The chopper clattered down, blowing snow in all directions. The
snow hadn't hardened enough to provide a firm support, so the pilot
hovered and dropped a huge flotation platform which inflated as it fell.
They used those things for ocean landings sometimes; I hadn't realized
it would work on powdery snow as well, but apparently it did. It looked
as wide as a field, but it was hard to tell in this all-white world where
there weren't any visual references.

When the platform had stabilized itself, the chopper settled carefully;
but the pilot kept his rotors turning. A door and a ramp popped open
and several white-suited figures unrolled an inflatable ramp across the
snow to the daisy-wagon. They scrambled clumsily toward us. At first,
we didn't recognize any of them, but then something about the second
one in line, the way he moved, Mom-Woo screamed, "Lorrin!" And we
all started waving madly.

Big Jes and Klin dropped a rope ladder down to the inflatable road
and Da came scrambling up, followed quickly by Smiller and Molina
and two others I didn't know. Da hugged each of the moms tightly, taking as much time as he could, whispering privately to them; Mom-Lu
started shaking her head, Mom-Trey started arguing—but Da was insistent. "If we don't, someone else will have to. Who do you trust to do
it right?" Mom-Woo nodded first, whispering to the others until they
finally added their reluctant assent. Meanwhile, one of the two scouts
I didn't recognize kept asking Smiller, "Which one?" until she hushed
him firmly.

"We can't stay long," Da finally said to Woo. "We have to get back to the other side." And then he turned to me, hugging me quickly, pushing back the boffili hood off my head and studying me as if he'd never seen me before. "Yes, even more than I thought."

"Even more what—?"

"Kaer, will you come back to Linnea with us? Will you help us rescue Jaxin?"

"Huh?" I heard the words, but I didn't understand the meaning. Not immediately.

"I can't explain it quickly or easily. I can't explain it here, because we need to keep the plan a secret. But we *might* need you to help with a very important part of the rescue."

"To do what?" Everyone crowded close, demanding answers to a thousand simultaneous questions. "Tell us what happened. Where did you go? Did you rescue the scouts? Why do you have to go back?" And all the little-uns were clamoring around us too.

Da waved them off. He focused on me. "Maybe we won't need you, Kaer, but we *might* need you, so we have to take you over with us to-night, just in case. Because if we do need you, we won't have time to send for you later. If not you—someone else. Another child. We need a child your size, your age, with the right kind of look, for it to work. I said that I thought you could do the job better than anyone else. You don't have to if you don't want to; I know that we've come back very suddenly, and I won't blame you if this scares you, but I think you can handle this, and I think we can trust you to do it right. Will you come back with us? Now?"

I didn't have to think about it. "Da, I'll go anywhere for you. You know that—"

"Yes, but I need to hear you say it, so I know that you know it too. I couldn't just come and take you." And with that he turned to the moms. "If we do our job right, we'll have almost no risk at all to anyone. I can't tell you the details, but I promise you Kaer and I will come back unharmed."

Mom-Woo said it for everybody. "Lorrin, you can't simply drop in here out of the sky like some crazy hairy maizlish thing and swoop off with Kaer without telling us the plan—"

"But I have to," said Da, "because I have to. I can't explain. We have to go now. If you have ever trusted me, Woo, will you trust me now?"

Mom-Woo bit her lip. "Of course, I trust you, Lorrin." She grabbed him by the shoulders and held him tightly, as if she wanted to shake an explanation out of him. "But—*oh, the hell with it*," she snapped in English. "I do trust you. And Kaer too. Just tell me that—"

"Yes, Woo. We have no other way to do this. But I won't take Kaer if you say no."

My mother looked deep into my father's eyes. "I would never say no to you, Lorr. I know you wouldn't ask this if you didn't absolutely need to. I trust you. Take care of our child."

Lorrin glanced around to Mom-Lu, Mom-Trey, Big Jes, Klin, Parra, Cindy, Irm, Bhetto, Morra, Rinky and all the others. "Do you all agree?" Nods all around. And Da grinned. "Thank you!" He went from one to the other, hugging quickly and intensely. Irm whispered something into Da's ear and the two of them looked into each other's eyes, smiling, and then hugged again.

Meanwhile the moms surrounded me for hasty good-byes. Hugs and kisses. Everything. Even Aunt Morra and Uncle Bhetto too. And especially Auncle Irm, turning away from Da. Big Jes gave me a punch on the shoulder and Klin snuck a quick kiss—

Then Smiller was saying to everyone, ". . . You cannot tell anyone that we came back this morning, or how we came back. Don't even speculate among yourselves. Remember, you don't know who listens to your table chatter. Please. You could put us at risk. Lorrin will explain when he gets back. No more than a Nineday. I promise. Lorrin, Kaer? Let's go now!"

Inside, the chopper was just as cold as outside, but the seats were heated and more comfortable than anything I'd sat in since we'd come to Linnea Dome. Lorrin moved me to a place by the window and sat down next to me.

Almost immediately, someone I didn't know sat down opposite and began unpacking a military field medi-kit.

"Are you a doctor?"

"Shh," he said. He started sticking little tabs across my forehead. "Open your robe, please."

I looked to Lorrin. He nodded. "We don't have much time, Kaer."

I opened my robe. I wasn't wearing much underneath. I'd stopped wearing underwear a long time ago, but the doctor didn't even blink. He just pasted a few more tabs across my chest. Then, while the machine calibrated itself and listened to my inner body functions, he looked down my mouth, up my nose and into my ears. If he saw anything, he didn't even grunt. He glanced at the readouts of his field kit, then started pulling the tabs off my chest and forehead. "All right," he said. "Surgeon says go."

He rummaged around in his kit some more and pulled out a syringe and a vial of pills. He pressed the syringe against my arm and it hissed something through my skin. Then he handed me a pill to swallow. "Take it now, please. You can close your robe." Without saying anything more, he got up and headed forward to confer quietly with Smiller.

"Buckle up now," Da said. As soon as I was buckled in, we jerked roughly up into the air. The chopper reeled in its portable landing pad and we were off.

The trip was only a few minutes long, and we were heading straight across the wilderness part of the dome. Maybe we'd see some kacks. There was a pink glow racing across the snow beneath us. Everything was so unreal and happening so suddenly, I couldn't believe it. Lorrin took my hand in his; I guess he'd missed us all, and this was probably just as hard on him as it was on me. But we were up in the air now and I just wanted to look out the window and enjoy finally getting out of the house—except I didn't get the chance.

Da put his arm around me and pulled me close. "It pleases me that you said yes, Kaer."

I looked to him. "What do I have to do?"

Instead of answering, he asked, "When you looked across the snow and saw this aircraft, what did you see?"

"I saw a chopper—" And then I realized what he was asking. "Oh, I know what you mean. I thought I saw a—a eufora spirit. Even when you got closer and I knew it for a chopper, it still looked like one of the eufora. Whatever the eufora look like," I amended quickly. "I mean, if I didn't know what a eufora looked like and I saw this chopper, then I'd say that I'd seen one."

Lorrin smiled. "Then it works. We had some uncertainty about that. So we tested it on you. What did everyone else see? Did the rest of the family see a spirit too?"

"I think so." I repeated what Big Jes and Little Klin had said. "You made quite an impression."

"Good. We want to do that. But you should see the vehicle at night," he added. "It has an even more astonishing appearance, because you can't see the machinery, only the light."

"But why? What do you need it for?"

He put his arm around me and hugged me close. "I hate to say this, but we might need to put the fear of God into the Linneans."

CROSSOVER

On the far side of the wilderness, 180 degrees away from Callo City, there's another installation in the dome. Much bigger, and with almost no attention to Linnean detail. This is the real Administration of the dome. And the gateway. Most of the trainees in the dome don't know where the gateway really is, and the Administration likes to keep it that way. All things considered, that was probably a wise decision.

The Administration buildings were on higher ground, and while they had the same high foundations and steep roofs and covered arcades of Callo City, they were almost totally free of snow. After what we'd been living through, I had to blink in surprise. The buildings were clearly Earth buildings, made of shiny polycrete and glass, and although they were shaped against the weather like Linnean structures, here in the dome their appearance seemed *otherworldly*. I guess I was thinking more like a Linnean than I'd realized.

As soon as we landed, a team of mechanics rushed the aircraft. Even before the door was popped, they were doing things underneath—servicing it, I guess; I heard clanking and banging. From my window, I saw a truck filled with supply containers pulling up behind. But before I could see anything else, Da said, "Come on, Kaer. We don't have time for that." We hurried down the ramp after Smiller and the doctor and rushed for the transit building. I managed one quick glance backward. Behind us, the mechanics had finished securing the chopper; they were rolling it up onto a truck platform.

As soon as we were inside the building, we were rushed to the decontamination section. We pushed through three revolving door airlocks into a steaming room where we were surrounded by technicians in isolation suits. We had to strip off all of our clothes—in my case only my robe and my boots. Da said to me, "Kaer, why don't you wear underwear?"

"It itches," I said.

He laughed and said, "Good reason."

The technicians in isolation suits put our clothes into large wire baskets to send them through the irradiation tunnel. We had to decontaminate the hard way. As we all stood around naked, me wondering what to do next, Da handed me a plastic bag with a label that said "Internal Decontamination Kit." Inside was a toothbrush, toothpaste, mouthwash and a plastic squeeze bottle filled a green foamy liquid; it had a long, slender nozzle on top.

"Brush your teeth for five minutes, top and bottom, front and back, then swirl with the mouthwash for two minutes."

I nodded. "I know how to brush my teeth."

"No, Kaer—brush your teeth as if Mom-Woo will inspect."

I got his meaning. "Yes, Da." I took the plastic bottle out of the bag and sniffed it. "What does this hold? Something else to drink—?" I started to take the top off.

Laughing, Da stopped me. "No, Kaer. The other end."

"Huh?"

He explained. "Everybody has to have an antibiotic enema. Everybody."

I looked at the bottle. I looked back to Da. "You mean I have to stick this up my—?"

He nodded. "And squirt." He pointed me toward a booth with a toilet in it. "Three times, Kaer."

An enema doesn't really hurt—well, not too much—but it's embarrassing and unpleasant, and it's probably the worst part of crossing over to the other side. Even though the purpose of it was to clean out my insides so I wouldn't accidentally carry any weird bacteria over to Linnea, I didn't feel all that clean afterwards. Mosty, I felt squooshy.

Then, all of us were ushered into the foam-and-scrub room, where great sheets of peppermint-smelling foam dripped from the ceiling, covering us like whipped cream. We looked like snowmen. It would have been funny, if we weren't in such a hurry. Da handed me a pumice scrubbing stone and told me to sandpaper the foam into my skin everywhere I could reach, as hard as I could.

The places we couldn't reach, we had to sandpaper each other. And it *hurt*. We had to scrub the foam into our hair, our skin, everywhere. Inside, under, around, between—all those places that polite people pretend they don't have.

"This stuff *stings*—!" I said.

"The *germs* bite when they die," said Da. Actually, he didn't say "germs." The Linneans have no word for germ, so he used "maiz-likka" instead. But I knew that he meant germs. He added, "It helps if you cry out, 'Die, maizlish, die!'" He handed me his pumice stone and turned his back. "Scrub my back, Kaer."

After we finished in the foam-and-scrub room, we entered the hose-down chamber, where jets of disinfectant of a different kind shot out at us from the walls, the ceiling, even from the floor. The last of the foam washed away quickly, while we turned around and around in the needle sprays. I kept my eyes closed tightly, just in case it stung. It didn't, but just in case.

"Hold your arms out, Kaer," Da said.

After the disinfectant, which took five long minutes, we were sprayed down with warm water. Then the water jets went off and heat lamps switched on, and we were hit with blasts of hot air. In less than a minute, we were completely dry. I felt tingly all over.

In the next room, we had to line up and go through what Da laughingly called "the security check" because it looked like the row of scanners you have to pass through at the airport. Only these were full-spectrum body-scanners, with much greater resolution. There were a bunch of technicians behind a glass wall, apparently studying display panels and readouts and monitors. I don't know what they were looking for, but they didn't find anything in any of us. Or at least they didn't say if they did. One of them gave us a thumbs-up signal, and Smiller called out, "Surgeon says go."

I didn't mind being naked in front of all the scouts, or even Da. Everybody had to get naked. And it was interesting to see what some of them looked like without any clothes. But I was just as glad to get dressed again because I didn't like being naked in front of all the technicians and the helpers in isolation suits. They looked like space-aliens or eufora or even maiz-likka, and it made me feel like a specimen.

Once through security, they let us get dressed again. In the next room, there were baggy brown jumpsuits for all of us, with camouflage patterns all over them. They even had one my size. The material was rugged, but so soft and comfortable in comparison to Linnean clothes it felt like pure luxury. The jumpsuit looked and felt sort of like an exercise suit; it had baggy pockets too, already stuffed with ration packs and other things I'd have to investigate later. There wasn't time now. And fresh underwear too—*real* underwear—the Earth kind! Da said that we'd get our Linnean clothes back after we crossed over. I told him the jumpsuit pleased me *just fine.*

There were clean hair brushes and combs for us to use, but we didn't get much time to use them. "Bring the combs and brushes, Kaer," Da said, scooping up two or three. "You'll do your hair on the other side. Come on, let's go." He pushed me in the direction of Smiller and the others, a little harder than he intended to, because he added, "I apologize for hurrying you, sweetheart. Remember, we do this for Jaxin and the others."

"I know, Da. I have no complaints. Whatever I can do to help, just say so."

"Thank you, Kaer. That means a lot to hear you say that."

We went through a couple more revolving door airlocks and finally came out into a huge tube, at least fifteen meters high, with rings of glowing light outlining every section. There were huge pressure doors at each end, and a conveyor bridge wide enough for two trucks to pass was suspended through the length of the tube, with guard rails at the sides, so nothing could touch the walls. There were industrial noises all around us. Underneath us, on the bottom level of the conveyor bridge, I could feel the vibrations of things rushing back past us. This was the transit tunnel. I felt a sudden rush of feelings, all mixed up—anticipation, fear, wonder, panic, dread, excitement.

Da started to say something, but I cut him off. I said, "I know. I recognize it from the pictures."

We walked down the center of the bridge toward the far pressure door. I assumed that was the entrance to the actual gate chamber. But when we got there, it didn't open for us. Instead, we stepped off the bridge and out through a side-chamber.

I hesitated. "Why do we have to stop here?" I asked. "When do we cross over?"

"We just did," said Da.

I looked back the length of the transit tunnel. "We just went through the gate—?"

Da laughed. "Yes, Kaer. We just went through the gate."

"But I didn't *feel* anything! Not even a shift in gravity!"

That made him laugh even more. He ruffled my hair. "Come on, my little eufora. We still have a long way to go."

"Yes, Da!"

FROM DAVID GERROLD'S
UPCOMING SEQUEL,

CHILD OF GRASS

AIRBORNE

We were still inside. The corridors on this side of the gate looked just like the corridors on the other side. I shook my head as I followed Da-Lorrin through some more revolving door airlocks. "What a disappointment. I always thought the gate would look like a big window, that we would see the Linnean landscape on the other side, and just step through into it."

"I tried to tell you."

"Oh yeah. You did. Boy, do I feel stupid." And then I thought of something. "But *why* didn't I feel the gravity change?"

"Earth has four-and-a-half-percent higher gravity than this planet. You won't feel that small a difference. And the ramp has an arch to it. You'll feel more effect walking slightly up and slightly down."

I thought about what he said. We were still hurrying. We came out into a brightly lit hangar with humongous pressure doors sealing it. The whole place smelled of industrial cleanser.

The heavenly-chariot chopper was here too, still on the same truck bed. Several mechanics were just rolling it down toward the hangar doors. Smiller and the doctor and the other scouts were gathered there, waiting in an impatient group. The pilot and copilot were conferring over a clipboard, probably their flight plan or checklist. For the first time, I had a moment to catch my breath.

And then something else occurred to me. Da had said this planet.

He hadn't said Linnea. And Earth had *nine*-percent higher gravity than Linnea!

"Da?"

"Yes?"

"This planet—?" I asked him. "It has a name?"

"I wondered how long it would take you to figure it out." He grinned. "I told them you would. Can you keep a secret?"

"Da...?" I gave him *the look*. It was actually Mom-Woo's look, but I'd been practicing it.

"They didn't build the gate to Linnea on Earth. They couldn't. The physics won't allow it. So they opened a gate to an intermediate world, and from there, they opened a gate to Linnea."

"So why didn't we just come out of one gate and into the next?"

"Because of the physics, little pumpkin. We have to fly ten thousand kilometers south to get to it."

"Huh?"

"Earth rotates. That means that an object at the equator will have more speed than an object at a higher latitude. So you can only open a gate to a latitude where the speed is the same. Because the planets all have different sizes and different rotational speeds, you have to build the gates to compensate. You open the gate on the slower world close to the equator and the gate on the faster world as far north or south as you have to go to match rotational velocity. You can't every match everything perfectly, of course—you always get some leakage—so you build a margin for leakage into the system. The extra energy is channeled back to power the gate engines; so that makes the gates self-sustaining. You only need to power up the gate once—to open it. But if you can't find a match for the two worlds' rotational speeds, you can't open a gate. If you tried, you'd get too much energy blasting back through the system, and the gate would rip itself apart instantly. That happened once. And after that, they decided to build gates across as many intermediate worlds as necessary, so that they would only have to work with controllable power surges. Even so, if a gate blew up, it would make a hole the size of that big meteor crater in Arizona."

He stopped then, because it was time to go. Da gave me a gentle nudge, and we followed the others up the ramp and into the chopper. We took the same seats as before. The engines began stropping almost immediately. This pilot was impatient to get going. Smiller sealed the doors and took her seat quickly.

Da reached into the pocket of his baggy jumpsuit and pulled out something in a cloth bag, a pair of dark plastic goggles. "Put yours on too, Kaer." I felt around in the pocket he indicated and found my own goggles. I had to adjust the strap to get them to fit. "Why do we need these?" I asked.

He nodded at the window. "You'll see, as soon as they open the hangar doors."

I looked out. The last of the mechanics was waving at the pilot, giving him a thumbs-up signal. Then he turned and ran to a pressure door in the wall behind the chopper, pulling it shut after him. I could see the wheel on this side turning as he sealed it. So they were sealing off the gate?

I craned my head forward. The big doors at the front of the hangar were sliding open now. Despite their huge size, they moved apart quickly, revealing a widening bar of light so bright I couldn't look at it. Outside the doors, the world was blazing shards of blue and white—a color called *actinic*. It hurt my eyes to look at it. The wider the doors slid open, the more it hurt. Finally, I popped the goggles on. That helped some, but it was still hard to see. Crimson after-images floated in the air in front of me.

"This planet circles a blue-white star," said Lorrin. As if that explained everything.

"I thought they only opened gates to Earthlike worlds." I wiped my watering eyes on my sleeve.

"The intermediate worlds don't have to be quite as Earthlike as the destinations," Da said. "Sometimes, you have to take what you can get."

The chopper was already rolling forward into the brightness. Some of the other passengers pulled dark filters down over their windows to block the horrific wash of brightness coming through. Lorrin pulled down a shade over our window and that helped a lot. When all the windows were filtered, people began pulling off their goggles. So did I. The cabin was warmer than before. I didn't feel quite so shivery anymore.

"They've pressurized the plane," said Da. "We can't breathe the air on this world; it doesn't have any life yet—maybe someday it will—but right now the atmosphere has the wrong mix of gases. Almost no free oxygen."

"Will they terraform it?"

"Yes, they say they want to. If they ever find enough kinds of plants that can survive a forty-hour day of acid-light, they probably will. But who would want to live here under that sun? Right now, except for the transit stations, we only have miners here—mosty mining the gases in the atmosphere. Every time that hangar door gets opened, they lose a roomful of air. So they have to import more air from Earth; but they pay for it by exporting different gases back."

The chopper bumped up into the air then, and I looked out the window to see the transit station dropping away. It was surrounded by jagged black rock. Through the filter, it was hard to see all the details; but as we rose, I saw other buildings too. Soon, it became apparent that the transit station was the smallest installation here. Beyond it, there were shimmering industrial structures, gantries and towers and tanks, all standing naked and harsh in the cold blue light, and a lot of other stuff I didn't recognize. It surprised me that there was no snow on the ground, but after I thought about it, why should there be? It isn't winter everywhere at the same time.

Da said, "All the buildings, everything you see—the people who built it had to wear airtight construction suits. A little bit like scuba gear. They could only work two hours at a time."

As we lifted, I saw three huge tractors carving away at a nearby hillside. I pointed them out to Da.

He nodded. "They've found so many different metals here—copper, iron, nickel, rare earths, gold, platinum, silver, all kinds of things we need for industry—that they have to build more facilities to process the ore. Eventually, they'll ship only pure ingots back to Earth."

"They must make a lot of money."

"Not yet, but they will. First they have to earn back the cost of opening the gate. That will take thirty or forty years. At least."

Once we were up and away from the gate, the ground was pretty bleak, all black and white with sharp blue edges. Not much in the way of scenery. Mosty rocks and more rocks—and a lot more rocks beyond them. The pilot swiveled the jets rearward, and a sudden surge of heavy acceleration pressed me back into my seat. Da patted my hand and said we'd be traveling over fifteen hundred klicks per hour. We had a long way to go.

Another thought occurred to me then. "If this atmosphere has no oxygen, why do the jets work?"

"The atmosphere has methane. We carry liquid oxygen. We still get combustion. We'll switch the mixture back when we get to Linnea."

"Oh." I pressed my nose to the window again. Knife-edge escarpments cut upward from the ground. Jagged, un-eroded hills looked like broken blocks of concrete. Where there were plains, the ground was barren and strewn with boulders the size of houses. Some places it was cut with gullies so bad it looked like a wrinkled bedsheet. It all swept past beneath us, each dreadful landscape giving way quickly to the next in a sliding mural of black and blue desolation. At least it wasn't winter here. But it was still ugly, and I said so.

Da nodded. "It takes life to make a planet beautiful. At least, I think so." He patted my arm. "I think you'll find Linnea beautiful. Wait until you see the dandelion trees. They tower into the sky in great forests, and from a distance, they turn the whole landscape silvery."

"How long will it take? How far do we have to go?"

"Five hours. We have to go all the way south to the equator. And up a mountain. It might get a little bumpy. As soon as we land, they'll put the chopper through the gate to Linnea. We'll service and refuel on the other side. That shouldn't take too long. And then we have another long flight ahead of us to get to North Mountain One. We'll meet the rest of the team there and all head east together."

As if on cue, Smiller joined us then, bringing us mugs of hot tea. She sat down opposite me, putting her own mug in the holder in the arm of her seat. For a moment, she didn't say anything at all; she just studied me carefully, tilting her head and squinting. "Did Lorrin tell you anything yet?"

"I was waiting for you to explain," said Da.

Smiller grunted an acknowledgment. "Probably the best thing. I can understand your reticence." Then she turned back to me. "Then you must have a lot of questions, Kaer?"

"Only one."

Smiller waited for me to ask it.

I said, "I've already figured out that you want me to play the part of an angel. But after everything you and everyone else have said about not wanting to contaminate the Linnean culture...why do you want to do this?"

Lorrin laughed and said to Smiller, "I told you Kaer would ask."

REINVENTING THE WORLD

SMILLER SAID, "KAER, how many years have you?"

"I have twelve. Almost twelve and a half."

"Some people might think that too young. I don't. The Linneans do not distinguish childhood the way we do on Earth. You take on adult responsibilities when you can handle them, and that makes you an adult. I need you to take on an adult responsibility now. Can you do that?"

"Da thinks I can."

"Do you think you can? Don't answer too quickly." She stared into my eyes, studying my face, waiting for my reply.

I said, "Yes, I think I can—but even if I had doubts, it wouldn't matter, because you've already chosen me and you have no one else to do the job, do you? So I'll do it, whether I think I can or not."

Smiller blinked, surprised. And then she grinned. "You'll do fine, Kaer. I could not have asked for a better answer." She shook her head with rueful amusement. "I did ask for that, didn't I?" And then, her smile fading, she looked into my eyes again. "I have a lot to tell you. Much of it will upset you. But the sooner you can get past your upset—"

"You can't rescue the scouts, can you?"

"It looks difficult," she admitted. "The situation has gotten much more complex in the past few days. The High Council won't travel to Callo City. They fear the political risk—don't ask. When politics and religion mix, nothing makes sense. Let's just say that they don't want to

219

leave the safety of their city on the hill and put themselves at physical risk on the lowlands.

"Instead, they've sent a panel of Magistrates to Callo City to examine the prisoners. If the Magistrates find cause, and we expect they will, then they'll probably order the captured scouts transported east to Mordren Enclave, where the High Council will hold a formal Inquiry." She paused. "What do you know of the Enclave?"

"Not much," I admitted. "Some kind of fortress, I think."

"Aye, some kind of fortress. When the Linneans first began colonizing this continent three centuries ago, they had a series of long bloody wars over who would control what. Eventually, the settlers seized control of their own cities—but then the cities started fighting among themselves. Peace came hard to these people and it continues only as the product of an uneasy balance of power. The cities need each other for trade more than they need to conquer each other. But they still distrust each other. Faith in Mother Linnea remains the only unifying authority among all the cities, so whenever a conflict arises, the Church has the only authority and the only machinery for any kind of a resolution. Do you follow this, so far?"

"We studied this at home. I mean, in the dome."

"I know, but I need to make sure you understand. You see, when the Church decided to build a High Temple in the new land, they needed to choose a city-state so powerful that no other city-state could conquer it. A number of cities competed for that honor, because they all knew that whatever city the Church chose for its continental administration, that city would become the capital city of all the states. It would have enormous power over the others. The Church eventually chose to build its own city, on a site of its own choosing. Mordren Mesa. It towers nearly a kilometer over the land, and only three narrow winding trails lead up to the top. They have long since widened the trails, of course, but the avenues give them total control over the access to the city. No one gets in or out without appropriate papers.

"On top of the mesa, they grow most of their own crops, they raise boffili and emmos, they have a vast reservoir in which they store water against the summer droughts. They live very well up there. The city has gleaming walls of shining pink marble, minarets and towers. Beautiful trees line broad avenues. And if you could walk through its streets, you would think it a marvelous place to live. But it serves as both a fortress and a prison. And if they take our scouts there, we will likely never see them again." Smiller paused there, to give me a chance to understand.

"Will they torture them?"

"Very likely, yes."

"Then we have to rescue them, don't we?"

"Yes. Everybody feels that way." She smiled gently. "You know Jorge?"

"Yes," I nodded. "I call him Earring."

"That will make him laugh, when he hears. He went into Callo City last week to prepare a plan. But almost immediately, he had to go into hiding. The Soldiers of the Church have sealed the entire town. The rescue operation that we wanted to do won't work anymore. We can't get our people in close enough."

"But I thought—?" I stopped. It didn't matter what I thought.

"So did we. We all thought that our anesthetic darts and our tear gas and our night-vision goggles would work because they gave us such a significant advantage. We still think we might have a chance using them. But our people can't move. Almost all of them have had to go into hiding. We don't even know if our safe houses remain safe. The Soldiers have begun searching."

"Searching—? For us?"

Smiller looked grim. "Yes, they search for more Oerth-people." She explained, "We have found out that a family we thought killed by hostiles did not die at all. The Hale-Stone family. James, Andrew, Jack, Brent, Stephen, Brad, Morgan, Alia, Patty, Donna and Philip. I don't remember the rest of them; they had a very large marriage, all of them very grim about everything. Very serious and severe. All except for Phillip. He had some kind of brain defect; he babbled and raved and ranted like a lunatic—so of course, that made him seem like the most intelligent one in the bunch. And probably the most likable. How they got approved remains a mystery. But the Linneans think that crazy people speak with the Mother's voice, so maybe the Administration considered crazy Philip an asset to the Hale-Stones once they crossed over.

"Jorge remembers them as the biggest problem he ever saw in training. But they had a lot of political backing to get them into the program, and apparently the Dome Administration had to send them through the gate to ensure the support of some of the members in the recalcitrant voting bloc in Congress." She spat sideways, an eloquent opinion.

"I'll tell you, Kaer, I didn't like them. I didn't mind hearing that they'd died—and it annoys me to no end that they didn't. Two of our scouts spotted Stephen, Jack and Andrew in Callo City, posing as prosperous merchants. They saw them spreading around a lot of money—all kinds of pelts, gold and silver, and who knows what else—so now they have the best friends that money can buy. And now we know where the stories of fabled Oerth have come from. They've become active in the leadership of Callo City. They did what we trained them to do, but they didn't do it for us."

In all seriousness, I asked, "Will I get points taken off if I say what I think of such people?"

Smiller laughed. "Nah, you'll probably get a round of applause. But we still have a problem. The Charter limits our actions. But not theirs anymore. And they know it. So they can say and do things that we can't."

I said what I thought.

Smiller nodded her agreement. "Yes. One of those bas—individuals—identified Jaxin and the other scouts. Stephen S. Hale-Stone. The 'S' must stand for snake. Do you know what they've done? They've put our scouts on public display. In cages. Suspended above the public plaza in the center of the town!

"Even worse, they've stripped our scouts naked. The Hale-Stones must have suggested that. So we have no monitors on them anymore. No transceivers, nothing. We have no communication from them at all, and no way to get someone in close enough. A religious hysteria has swept Callo City. Pilgrims have traveled from all over the region to see the Oerth-men. Preachers hold daily services. They hold prayer vigils all night long. Crowds surround the cages and mock the prisoners. They throw trash and garbage and offal at them.

"The only good news in any of this, the swarming crowds have given some useful cover to the last few observers we have who can still move safely through the streets. We have five or six who remain unknown to the Hale-Stones. Your da's suggestion to use colonists instead of scouts has proven very wise. Here—" She fumbled in her pack and pulled out some ragged sheets of paper. "Look at these. They've circulated handbills and posters identifying almost all of our senior scouts. At least they've done us a small favor here; they've let us know who to warn or recall."

They were drawings of people I knew. Scouts. Below their pictures, Linnean writing spelled out their names. Across the top, each one said in big letters: *"Beware of Oerth-folk!"*

I paged through them, astonished. "I see you. And Earring—Jorge. I recognize this one, but I don't know her name. This looks like Byrne. Novotny. I don't know this one or this one." I looked up. "These likenesses, all so accurate—they must have used a camera. How could they do this?"

"Obviously, they planned this for a long time," said Smiller.

"I guess so." I felt sick inside. As if somebody had taken a bulldozer to the home we'd worked so hard to build.

"The Magisterial Panel will convene in four days—the day after they arrive. We expect a very short hearing."

"And then what—?"

"Jorge says that four armored railcars arrived this morning. The Callo City authorities wouldn't prepare for such a trip if they didn't expect to make it. Politics plays a big part here. With such hysteria in the city, the Magistrates can't afford to dismiss the investigation. Better for them that they should pass the responsibility upward to their masters. If the situation blows up, let it blow up in someone else's face.

"So just about everyone believes that the Magistrates will order the prisoners sent east to Mordren Enclave. They've already announced how they'll do it. They'll send a caravan of rail-wagons east, with armed guards surrounding each one."

"Armed guards—?"

"They *expect* a rescue attempt," said Smiller. "The Hale-Stones have warned them that the Oerth-people always try to rescue their own. So the Soldiers of the Church have armed themselves as if for a war. I want you to think about something. We had a good plan to rescue our people from the jail. We moved a team through the gate, but before we could get on-site, the Linneans moved the hostages to the town square.

"So we came up with another plan. Let them transport the prisoners, and we catch them on the prairie. Destroy the tracks, stop the rail-wagons, put everyone to sleep and break the cars open. We start moving more equipment through the gate. All of a sudden, the Linneans announce they'll send guards with the train. How do they know so much?"

"The Hale-Stones tell them?" I offered.

"How do the Hale-Stones find out?"

I realized she was waiting for me to reply. I guessed. "Their equipment for making miracles. The person who smuggled it through the gate probably sees all the other equipment that comes through the gate. He signals them, I'll bet."

Smiller looked to Da, pleased. "You have a very smart child, Lorr."

Da grinned. Smiller turned back to me gravely. "So you see the problem?"

"Yes'm. All too clearly. They've locked us out of our own planet. I mean, they've locked us out of the Linneans' planet. And we can't protect the Linneans from the Hale-Stones without creating even more uproar, can we?"

"You got it."

Da spoke up then. "Might as well tell the rest of it now, Smil."

"It gets worse?" I asked.

"Yes," he said sadly. "Do you remember Buzzard Kelly's Bible?"

I nodded. "Everyone does. Administor Rance nearly threw the Kellys out of the program."

Smiller sniffed. "Like the Hale-Stones, the Dobersons and the Kellys both came to us as a Congressional scholarship. Fortunately, the Dobersons disqualified themselves very quickly; but we have suspected the Kellys of the same sympathies for some time. How did they get the chocolate into the dome? And the Bible? They must have had some help, obviously. Someone has compromised dome security somehow. Yes, Administor Rance *wanted* to expel the Kellys. And she would have, but right now it serves us to keep them in the dome and watch them carefully and see if we can find out who they work with."

"Someone we know?" I looked to Da worriedly.

Smiller shook her head. "I don't want to say. What if I say the wrong name? What if we have more than one spy? I don't want to start any gossip about something so serious. But I'll tell you this—we never thought we'd have this kind of a problem. We never thought anyone would betray the program and leak our secrets directly to the Linneans. The Hale-Stones have caught us totally off balance.

"But, Kaer, now do you understand why we have such secrecy around this effort? We don't know who we can trust anymore."